Three Words
If You Love Someone, Tell Them

Izzy Robertson

This is a First Edition of the paperback
Three Words: If you love someone, tell them
Copyright © February 2017 Izzy Robertson
ISBN: 978-1-910094-22-8
eBook ISBN: 978-1-910094-43-3
Published February 2017
By Magic Oxygen
www.MagicOxygen.co.uk
editor@MagicOxygen.co.uk

Izzy Robertson has asserted her right under the Copyright, Designs and Patents Act 1988 to be identified as the author of this work.

A catalogue record for this book is available from
the British Library.

All characters appearing in this work are fictitious. Any resemblance to real persons, living or dead, is purely coincidental.

All rights reserved. This publication is not included under licences issued by the Copyright Agency. No part of this publication may be used other than for the purpose for which it is intended nor may any part be reproduced or transmitted, in any form or by any means, electronically or mechanically, including photocopying, recording or any storage or retrieval system without prior written permission from the publisher.

Requests for permission should be addressed to:-
The Editor, Magic Oxygen
editor@MagicOxygen.co.uk

Printed by Lightning Source UK Ltd; committed to improving environmental performance by driving down emissions and reducing, reusing and recycling waste.

View their eco-policy at www.LightningSource.com

Set in 11.5pt Times New Roman

Titles set in Unzialish

DEDICATION

My parents Ann and Roy Bain – thank you
for bringing me up on fairy tales

Jenny Dixon – a mermaid

THANK YOU

Brian, Jed and Zack Robertson: for always being there

Tracey and Simon West: yet again you've given my words life

Sylentium: Jed Robertson, Zack Robertson, George Hunt, Jake Stow, Harry Eastwood: for musical inspiration and for making my ears ring!

Ann and Roy Bain, Jenny Dixon, Nayna Kumari and Jasmine Roberts: for reading and commenting and helping me get this book into shape.

Also By Izzy Robertson

Dreaming The Moon
When Joe Met Alice
Catching Up With The Past

Coming Soon

Dead Man's Rill

Prologue
Present Day

Serena set the last box on the kitchen table and wandered heavy hearted through the cottage. She was grateful to be there, back by the sea, especially after London, but the circumstances still made her want to weep. Awaiting the finalisation of a divorce had never been in her plans, but given what she had done, given up, to be with Steve in the first place and what the consequences were likely to be now that he had abandoned her didn't bear thinking about.

She opened a couple of boxes, thinking to unpack, but realised quickly that she couldn't face it. Slipping on a sweater against the cool sea breeze, she locked the door and headed down to the beach.

The sun was still warm, the late September glow softening the edges of buildings and glittering off the restless sea. Serena walked along the front and down onto the beach, making her way over to the rocks where it had all begun. She climbed up and sat looking out to the horizon, letting herself remember.

Seth laced his trainers and left his flat, anger roiling through him. Anger at himself mostly. Jessica had left again, but he had known that she would. She always did. And he had let himself get pulled back in, despite his vows to himself that he wouldn't. Too many times now. He didn't understand why it still hurt when he knew she didn't really care. He wasn't even sure he felt anything for her any more. Not love anyway. But then, love was the strangest thing. People did all sorts of things in the name of love, he more than anyone knew that.

Confusion was a hurricane in his head, had been for five days since she'd left. So he did the only thing he could to escape it for a while. Jammed his headphones in his ears, turned the music up loud and ran.

Chapter 1
July, Three Years Before

Serena swam through the silvered aquamarine shadows of the deep, drawn helplessly toward the coast and the humans. Despite the cold disdain with which the rest of the mer regarded them, there was something about them that she couldn't fight, a fascination for their strange two legged ways and a longing for the things they shared that the mer had no time or patience for.

Love. Passion. Friendship.

The mer regarded these as weaknesses, unnecessary distractions from their role as protectors and judiciary of the deep. Mer families were bound by duty and affection, not love as the humans knew it. But Serena wasn't convinced. She had seen a strength, a deep loyalty in the bonds that formed between people. She watched them on the beach and the rocks, throwing balls and Frisbees to one another, shouting and laughing, paddling in the shallows together or swimming out with boards and whooping as the waves swept them in a rush back to land.

Most of all she watched the couples, old and young, walking hand in hand or with their arms wound round one another. There was something in the way that they looked at each other that she envied, something that she didn't have, that she needed to make her whole. Much as her sisters scoffed at her intrigue, telling her she was as bad as the humans and the way they romanticised the mer in their stories, she couldn't help feeling that there was something she was missing.

She was twenty-one when she saw him and her life changed forever. He was sitting on the rocks gazing out over the sea. Dark haired and fine featured, his brown eyes seemed to look right at her, into her, even though she knew that was impossible. She felt the tug then, deep inside her heart. It was no mere distraction but a visceral, palpable sensation.

She drew closer and watched him until he rose to leave.

Each day after that, she swam in near the shore to watch for him. Even though it was risky, even though it was forbidden. He and his friends were at the beach every day, playing ball games, throwing themselves into the water with their boards or teasing the girls who wandered past. He always seemed slightly separate, almost imperceptibly so but she noticed it because it was how she felt with her kind. As if somehow she didn't quite fit.

Often he lingered after the others left and the beach emptied, swimming or boarding or sometimes just watching the sea. She moved closer then, close enough that she could feel his energy. It was so different from that of her people. Mer energy was cool and controlled and indifferent; human energy was warm and unpredictable and fizzed like the fireworks they let off now and then on the shore.

Sometimes, at those moments, he would stop and tread water, looking around him. It was almost as if he could feel her there too. And each time she saw him the tugging in her heart became more intense, a slow crescendo of emotion that built like a tsunami far out to sea.

One afternoon, as she was floating through the water, watching him catch the last few waves before the weather finally chased him back onto the land, the question was answered for her. The sea was deserted but for the two of them, and rough. The beach was almost empty too, the sharp wind and bladelike raindrops keeping all but the fearless and foolish indoors. He had swum out further than usual, beyond the rocky promontory, and was prone on his board preparing for the next wave. He turned his head and looked straight at her. Their eyes locked and she was lost.

"Hey," he called. "Are you OK? You're a long way out."

Her voice escaped her, so she nodded, unable to move. She knew she should turn tail and swim away but she was frozen. Then he began to swim towards her.

"What's your name?" he asked.

She shook her head and began to back away.

"Wait, don't go any deeper, it's not safe. There are no lifeguards on and the tide is going…" His voice was lost in a sudden swell and the ensuing wave caught him off balance. He tipped off the board, catching the side as he went. The edge of the wave made it buck and it came down hard on the top of his head. Serena saw him go limp and sink beneath the surface.

"Oh no," she thought.

With a flick of her tail, she was under the waves and over to him in seconds. She managed to drag him to the surface and get his face out of the water. Catching hold of the board with her other hand she wrestled it under his shoulders to support his head. Then she kicked rapidly toward the beach and managed to get him far enough onto the sand that he wasn't in any further danger. The tide was on its way out.

When she looked at him however, she realised there was a problem. His chest was still, no rise and fall that indicated what the humans called breathing. Serena had seen the lifeguards perform mouth to mouth on occasion but she didn't have any breath to offer him. She did the only thing she could think of. She opened his mouth and sang her magic into him.

To begin with, nothing seemed to happen. Then, finally, he gave a cough and drew in a breath, and the pallor that had been building in his face began to fall away. Slowly he opened his eyes and saw her leaning over him.

"Hi," he said.

She smiled and sent out a heart call for help to the nearest people his energy linked with. He tried to sit up but fell back again, clutching his head.

"What happened?"

"You came off your board," she whispered. "Don't try to move. Help is coming."

"I saw you in the water," he said. His eyes were beginning to lose focus. "Did you rescue me? Who are you?"

She saw two of his friends at the far end of the beach, looking around until they spotted the board. They began to run over.

"Serena," she murmured in his ear as he lost consciousness again. Then she slipped quietly back into the sea and swam away.

She returned nervously the next day, keeping her distance but relieved to see him there. He just sat, looking. Constantly searching. For something. Someone. Her. She could feel it. She felt the same.

On the evening of the second day, when he was still sitting on the rocks long after his friends had left, staring across the water, she knew that she had to follow her heart, whatever her sisters or others said. She was linked to him now – a life without him would be impossible.

Serena swam home slowly, realising what she had to do. She knew the risks involved but what she felt for this man was undeniable, what she had seen when he had looked at her was true. Her sisters would try to persuade her against it but it was no longer a choice for her. It was a necessity.

That night, she gathered her family together and told them of her calling to him. And her plan.

"You are not serious?" her oldest sister said.

"Of course she is not," said her mother.

"It's certain death. I forbid it," her father boomed.

"I'm sorry, Father," Serena said. "But I must."

Tia, her closest sister, understood her best. "She will go. It won't matter what we say. It's beyond choice now."

"No. You are being foolish, child. You know the cost."

"Yes," her mother agreed. "It is a fool's errand and one you will not survive."

But Tia disagreed. "Look at her, please. Look truly. She will not survive if she stays. Her heart has always been too warm and it will surely break if she does not follow it."

"She can recover if she so chooses," her oldest sister scoffed, but while her younger sisters continued to mock, her parents observed her carefully, as if with new eyes.

"I see it," said her mother.

"You always had ways strange to us," said her father. "I do not pretend to understand, but I see the truth of your sister's wisdom. We do not wish it, but if there is a chance for you to find fulfilment in a different life then perhaps you should take it."

"Thank you," Serena whispered. Tia took her hand and squeezed it.

"Your father is right," her mother said. "You may go with our blessing."

Her sisters crowded round her then to ask questions and try to comprehend her decision.

Later, as Serena prepared for the journey she was to make, Tia came to her.

"I will go with you to the Sea Witch's cavern," she said. Serena looked at her in gratitude.

"You don't have to," she said.

"I know; but I will."

They left as the moon sank into the deep, swimming strongly to the west and the cave of the Sea Witch. The rock towers and turrets, dark in the indigo, were beribboned with soft strands of kelp and jewelled by corals, anemones and all manner of shelled creatures. The swaying curtain of weed that covered the entrance to the cave parted of its own accord and they heard a soft invitation to enter.

The Sea Witch was sitting in an ornately carved stone chair beside a small stone table. The cave was circular, glittering in soft light. Two apertures led off to hidden caves behind and rocky seats ran around the walls. In the centre was a cauldron on a stone plinth.

"Welcome," the Witch said. Her long white hair was piled on top of her head, and her skin was soft and flawless. Her eyes were a bright, bright blue; laughing eyes that held love and the wisdom of millennia.

The sisters inclined their heads in deference, silenced and awed by the power that emanated from the being before them.

"Do not be afraid," she said, looking at Serena. "I know why you have come. Your heart is calling you to a different life, is it not?"

Serena looked up at the Sea Witch and her fear began to ease.

"It is," she said. "It's a call I can't deny. Please, can you help me?"

"I can help you child, but this is not to be undertaken lightly. It requires a deep and ancient magic. Once the change is made it is irreversible and governed by rules that cannot be defied."

"I know," Serena said, squeezing her sister's hand. "But I've felt for so long that I am not whole, and this is beckoning me toward completion."

"I understand." The Sea Witch rose and approached them. "I see you are troubled and that you have thought about this possibility for a long time. But I am honour bound to explain the laws that govern the transformation and the consequences that may arise from it. Please, sit."

Once they had settled on the rocky benches, the Witch began.

"From time before memory there have been those who have been pulled to life on the other side of the surface. The transformation from mer to human is rare, from human to mer rarer still and it is made using an exchange of energy. The mer have magic, the humans have souls; the transformation of these allows one to become the other. The original energy is released and is replaced with the new. These energies are stored in the great vortices, separate but connected; one contains a combination of mer magic, while the other is an amalgam of human souls. Your magic will return to the void and in return it will gift you a soul. The change is permanent and irreversible. The essence, the memory of your original self is retained, but all the knowledge that is required to live in the other world will be just as real.

The rules for exchange in the two directions differ, for although the mer usually know of an exchange, the humans do not. We are aware of their existence, but most of them regard us as a myth and it is better this way. You are forbidden from telling anyone of your origins unless they ask you directly and honestly. They must not speak of it or both you and they will be lost to the sea. The one you love must love you truly with his heart and say it in words within a year and a day of transformation. Human marriage makes this permanent. Your love may not be coerced or tricked into stating his love for you and if the love between you fails on one side or the other, or if you are divorced, you will have a year and a day to find new love.

When you make the change, you leave the mer kingdom forever, for although you may be able to see your kin out in the waves you will not be able to speak with them. Also, although I do not like to say it, you must know that exchange in this direction does often fail and there is no way back."

There was a moment of silence before Tia asked what Serena couldn't bring herself to.

"What happens if it fails?"

The Sea Witch sighed. "Then you will become foam and your soul will be forfeited to the vortex."

Serena felt her sister shiver beside her. The thought made her feel cold as well, but she remained determined.

"It's not a choice for me. I understand and accept the risk," she said. "I have to do this."

"Very well." The Sea Witch crossed to the great cauldron in the centre, running her fingers gently round the edge and beckoning Serena over to her. "We must create a potion of exchange. The first draft you drink will absorb your magic. When I open the vortices, you will gift your magic to the void so it can read you. The energy for transformation will be contained within a second draft which you will drink when you reach the land. As we distil the mixture, keep your truth and your desire open."

Serena nodded. "What must I do?"

"Stand there as I make the potion. I will require some things from you."

The Witch began to sing in the old language of the mer. Serena and Tia could feel the power rising although they did not understand the words. As the Witch added ingredients to the cauldron it began to bubble and intermittently she stirred it with a long silver blade. From Serena she took a lock of hair and a drop of blood and allowed them to fall into the mixture. The liquid foamed and boiled, coalescing into a deep bright blue. Gradually the tumult in the cauldron calmed and the surface became still.

"It is ready," the Sea Witch said. She took a silver ladle and poured some into a tiny bottle which she gave to Serena. "Are you certain that this is the right thing for you? Once you drink, there is no going back."

Serena nodded.

"I'm sure."

"So be it." The Sea Witch filled another identical small bottle with the potion, then led Serena over to the only area of cave wall that was not fronted by a bench. The floor there was covered by a wooden trapdoor, split in two and overlaid by an exquisitely wrought silver grille which the Witch lifted and rested on two ornate hooks obviously placed there for that purpose. She positioned Serena in front of the left hand half of the trapdoor.

"Drink the potion and as you do so, focus on your truest purpose and need. I will open the vortex and when you are ready, offer up your magic for exchange. Take a moment to calm yourself and open your heart before you drink."

Serena remained still and closed her eyes, trying to subdue her fear. As she allowed her heart and mind free rein she could picture him; the fire in his eyes when he had asked for her name, the restless gaze as he searched for her. But she could also see the couples that she had so envied as they walked entwined, and the friends who hugged each other, shook each other by the hand or slapped each other on the back with obvious affection.

"That's what I want," she realised. "Not just love but warmth and affection and kindness. And to give it as well as to receive it."

As her eyes snapped open with the sudden clarity of her desire she saw that the Sea Witch was opening the vortex with an ancient chant. Serena couldn't hear anything except her heart and her thoughts but she knew it was time to drink. She sent out a plea… "Please, take my magic and let me love" … and tipped the liquid down her throat.

The potion was ice, traversing her whole body and mind. Coursing through her, reaching into every corner and hidden place, searching, seeking, sweeping, dragging out all the darkness and the light to scrutinise and bear witness. It held her immobile, frozen. And finally, when she felt it was almost beyond bearing, it drew from the ends of her arms and the crown of her head and the tip of her tail in a mighty rush that filled her heart almost to bursting. Then it exploded out of her chest and disappeared down into the void, leaving her empty and drained.

Serena fell back slightly, aware of a deep ache in her chest. Expecting only a feeling of sadness, she was surprised by the physical sensation of loss now her magic was gone. She felt half of what she had been, as if the void had entered her and left her hollowed out. She shivered as the Sea Witch raised the second door and drew her in front of it. A small orb of blue light hovered over the first vortex. The Witch handed her the second bottle, already open.

"Hold it out in front of you," she instructed. She began another invocation and the blue light drifted across to the second void. It shimmered and pulsed momentarily before dropping like a stone into the hole. The chant melded with a low thrum and Serena felt everything within her vibrating at that sacred frequency. She was aware of a soft rushing, like the whisper of a breeze or the ripple of a dolphin's wake and the bottle in her hands became suddenly warm.

"It is done," proclaimed the Sea Witch as she closed the doors.

Serena opened her eyes. The liquid in the bottle was now a deep transparent red, glowing richly where the light caught it. The Witch gave her a stopper with which to secure it and indicated that they should return to the benches.

Tia settled beside Serena, clasping her sister's hand tightly, her eyes huge. Serena's head was spinning with hope and loss, sadness and new possibilities. She had to focus hard on what the Sea Witch was saying.

"The transformation will be complete when you drink the second draught. Wait until the dark hours to do this so that you are not seen. Get as close to the shore as possible for although you will be able to swim as a human, you will be far less strong and agile in the water than you are now. You will have all that you need with you for your new life, and the knowledge and skills to help you fit in. The rest is up to you."

Serena nodded. "I understand. Thank you so much for helping me."

The Sea Witch smiled. "I wish you luck, child. And love and joy. Now go and embrace your new life and may it have a happy ending."

Tia and Serena left the cavern and swam through the wild ocean in silence, overawed. Tia was the first to speak.

"Did it hurt?" she asked. "When you gave up your magic?"

"A little," Serena said. "I feel empty now, hollow. Room for a soul, no doubt."

"Are you afraid?" Tia's eyes were worried.

"Yes," Serena confessed. "But I know this is the right thing to do. The only thing to do, for me. I'll never meet the expectations of the mer, I'll always be found wanting. At least this way I have a chance. I know you understand."

"I will miss you," said Tia.

"And I you," Serena replied. "But I will always remember, all of you but especially you, Tia. I think you're the only one that's really ever understood me. Don't think that some of the love I hope to find over there won't be held for you."

Tia said nothing but she didn't have to. The crystal tears that slipped from her eyes told their own tale. At the shore, in the quiet and the dark, they embraced fiercely before Serena unscrewed the bottle from its cap on the chain round her neck and took the contents in one swallow. As she screwed it back in place tingling ran through her in waves, warmth spreading gradually until it filled her whole being. Her tail became hot and there was a stretching, pulling sensation. Her heart filled and lightened, and yet her body felt increasingly heavy in the water. She went to kick upwards and discovered that she no longer had a tail. Instead she had legs, which did not have the same power.

Serena had a moment of panic before she realised that kicking them alternately was reasonably effective in keeping her afloat. Once she stabilised herself, she smiled one last time at her sister and moved in toward the beach, steering herself toward the small strip of sand that was hidden between two rocky outcrops. She swam until she realised that it was too shallow to continue and then got her new legs under her and stood unsteadily. Slowly she began to put one foot in front of the other, stepping out of the waves and onto the land. She turned to see her sister staring, hands over her mouth in shock at seeing her like that. She raised her hand. Tia waved back and then dived away with a flick of her tail. Serena sighed, turned and made her way slowly up the beach. With each step she grew more heavy and weary until she fell to the sand and sleep sucked her in.

When she woke the sky was paling into a wash of lilac and the stars were winking out one by one. She stretched and sat up, mentally examining her new body. It felt natural now, legs and feet, as if she had always had them. The heaviness had left her limbs and her heart felt light. She could see differently too, more clarity and less shimmer despite the dark, and she noticed a strange sensation which her new human wiring system told her was cold.

Knowing that that was partly why humans wore clothes Serena looked down, realising that she didn't have any on. The strap of a backpack was wound around her wrist. Remembering what the Sea Witch had said about having everything she needed, Serena flicked it open. Inside there was clothing, identification papers, money and various other bits and pieces. As she went through it her human story settled into her mind, just as real as her true story. It was the strangest feeling.

Serena put the papers back and took out some of the clothes, getting herself into a skirt, top and jumper. The clothing felt odd initially but she quickly became accustomed to it and appreciated the warmth it afforded. She stood and began to move, walking, spinning and running on the sand, getting used to the new sensations flooding through her from the ground and the air.

Eventually, as the sun rose higher and turned the sky from peach, pink and gold to a clear strong blue, she clambered across the rocks to the main part of the beach and found herself a sheltered place to sit and wait.

His group arrived mid-morning. She could feel his presence before she actually saw him, feel her heart quicken. She stayed where she was, watching, nerves overcoming her. She noticed that he was still searching the waves, the beach with restless eyes. As they finished a raucous game of Frisbee and his friends headed into the sea, she stood and climbed up onto the rocks, sat with the backpack beside her, looking out across the water. Surreptitiously glancing over, she noticed that he had decided not to swim but to wander along toward the place she was sitting.

Serena was acutely aware of her heartbeat thundering in her chest and the raw feelings created by her emotions. She was still getting used to the intensity with which humans felt things; even with her oversensitivity as a mer it had never come close to what she was experiencing now. She stared fixedly out across the sea, too scared to look over towards him, hoping desperately that he would notice her, recognise her. It seemed to take forever before she became aware of someone climbing up the rocks near her. She knew that it was him - she could sense it. She stood up.

He appeared in front of her, getting his balance and searching out over the water before turning to continue across the rocks. He saw her then, stopping in his tracks as sudden recognition flooded through him. He half raised a hand before dropping it to his side and moving across to her, his eyes locked with hers. He stopped in front of her. She could hardly breathe.

"Serena," he said quietly.

"You remembered," she whispered.

"I couldn't forget. I thought I'd dreamed you. But I was just as sure I hadn't."

"No. I'm real."

He reached out to take her hand. "I'm Steve. And I'm really glad."

Chapter 2

Seth put his mother's second suitcase onto the baggage trolley and slammed the boot of his car. They made their way toward the terminal without speaking, the easy conversation of the journey up now silenced by the weight of goodbye. Check in took a while, coffee a while longer and then it was time for her to go. She dug her passport out of her bag and turned toward him.

"You sure you're OK with this?" she asked him for the thousandth time.

"Mum. Stop worrying about me. Look after yourself for a change."

"Seth, I don't want to leave you. But…"

"Mum. Shh." He kissed her cheek. "You need to go. For Rachel and for you. And I need to stay for Auntie and for me. Be happy. You know it's the right thing to do. And I'll be out to visit before you know it. To make sure you're behaving yourself."

She smiled at that. "Pot calling the kettle black?"

He grinned back and shrugged, then hugged her tightly. "Have a safe journey. Be happy, Mum. You deserve it."

"And you," she said, her eyes blurred with tears. "I love you."

"Love you too."

"Right then," she said, moving away and shouldering her bag. "Here I go."

He gave her a last squeeze before she handed over her passport and disappeared through the gate into the departure lounge.

The journey back seemed even longer than the journey up and it was late when Seth got home. He thought briefly about going up to meet his friends and watch the bands but quickly decided that he couldn't face it. He was tired but too listless to relax. Stupidly, even though his mother had never lived in his flat, it seemed empty now that she was gone. Something ached inside him, dull and persistent. He went to put some music on then thought better of it, flicked off the light and headed out.

Everywhere in the town was busy during the tourist season. The Feathers was no exception, but it was still quieter and less chaotic than the Old Hare where he knew his friends would be. Seth got himself a drink and found a relatively peaceful corner to stand and contemplate while he watched the other punters laughing, talking and flirting. He lost track of time as his thoughts swung him away and it took him a while to realise that someone was speaking to him.

"Hey. Hello. Are you in there?"

Seth came back to the present with a lurch. A stunning blonde girl who looked vaguely familiar was standing in front of him, grinning.

"Sorry. I was…"

"On another planet. I could see," she laughed. "Seth, right? Can't be anyone else. You haven't changed much. Hardly at all. Still the long hair, still in black. It's good to see you."

Seth's mind was hunting desperately to put a name to her face. Remember where he knew her from.

"I'm…"

"Jessica." It hit him suddenly, full force. Jessica, the wild girl who'd joined them at college after GCSEs, who'd been brought down from London by her parents in an effort to tame her. Who liked to party and liked to be the centre of attention and who had created havoc amongst the boys and war amongst the girls before disappearing back to London after the end of A-levels. He hadn't seen her for five years. "I remember. You look different."

Her smile widened and lit up her whole face, brown eyes dancing with mirth. Her hair, which had been in a short bob and usually dyed any number of outlandish colours was now sleek and platinum blonde, hanging halfway down her back. She was wearing a fitted, knee length black dress, far more corporate and elegant than her previous mini-skirted appearance but no less eye catching. It was a very different image but still screamed 'look at me'.

"Yeah, well. Had to smarten up for work. So what are you doing in here on your own looking so glum?"

He shrugged.

"One of those days, huh? Well, let me see if I can cheer you up. Did you know…"

After a very short while Seth found his mood lifting. Jessica was funny and bright and he remembered back to their college days. He hadn't been directly in her social group but she had managed to keep everyone in her orbit anyway and he'd understood how she had ensnared so many of them. Her allure hadn't changed and he found himself drawn to her.

"So, what brings you back down here?" he asked. "Bright lights too much?"

"Hardly," she laughed. "No, I'm just down for a few months over the summer. Between contracts. Haven't had a holiday for four years. I thought I deserved a break." She looked him straight in the eyes. "Think I made a good decision there."

Seth felt his stomach flip. She looked… hungry.

"Hope so," he laughed a little nervously, leaning back against the wall. She moved towards him fractionally, close enough that her hair brushed his arm. He shivered inside.

"I know so." She bit her lip. "You going to tell me what's bugging you?"

"Nothing really. Just waved my mother off to Canada this morning."

"Oh. You have a problem with her holiday?"

"Not a holiday. Permanent." Seth sighed.

"Still. Is that a problem? I seem to remember she was really hard on you back when we were at college. Would've thought it might be good to get some distance."

Seth was amazed she remembered. Or had even noticed in the first place. "Yeah well, she had her reasons. And she was right."

"Hmm. Not convinced. You weren't that much of a bad boy, were you?" She moved so her arm rested against his. "Mind you, they do say it's the quiet ones you have to watch out for."

"Oh, do they?" Seth was reminded of what an incorrigible flirt she had been. Apparently still was. He didn't usually bother but somehow she was making him feel better. Less alone. He liked that. "Who says?"

"Now that would be telling," she said. He arched his eyebrow and she smiled coyly. "There's a cost for disclosure of secrets." She put her hand on his forearm, ran her fingers along it lightly. He caught her wrist in his hand, held her gently.

"What's your price?" he said quietly. She met his gaze.

"Walk me home to start with."

"Where are you staying?" Seth asked as they left The Feathers, her fingers twined with his.

"Same house we used to live in. Parents kept it as a bolthole when we moved back to London. It's mine this summer."

"Nice," he said. "I have a flat. Above my shop."

"Your shop?" She sounded impressed. "What shop?"

"The music shop on the front."

"I'm gonna have to check that out."

"Yes, you are."

They made their way across the High Street and down through the park toward a street of Victorian villas. She led him up the path of the second one in the row of six and into the porch, extracting her key from her bag and turning it in the lock without releasing his hand. The door swung open. She turned back to him, holding his gaze with a look that smouldered. His world trembled.

"You coming in?" she asked.

"I'm not sure I should," he said, reaching for her anyway. She came to him easily, arms sliding round him. "Not sure it's a good idea." He fitted her against him, holding her close. "Might not want to leave."

She looked up at him, laughed huskily. "Maybe that was my plan all along," she whispered. "It's not as if we're strangers."

He wasn't sure which one of them initiated the kiss, but once it started there was no stopping it. Somehow they stumbled into the house and Seth's world changed forever.

It was a magical summer. Seth had never been with anyone like Jessica and he was dazzled. She was demanding of his time and attention but so full of plans and ideas that he didn't really notice how possessive she was when they were out with his friends, or how increasingly difficult they found her. She could be entertaining and funny but equally dismissive and bossy. His two closest friends, whom he had known since school, remembered her well. They couldn't see, like he could, how much she had changed.

"She's still trouble, even if you can't see it." Ethan's voice was quiet. "I know that's not what you want to hear but I know it."

"Give her a…"

"I'm trying hard to give her a chance, Seth, but she worries me," Tallie said. "She always just took what she wanted, regardless, and I don't see that it's any different now." She held up her hand, forestalling Seth's interruption. "I'll be more than happy to be proved wrong. I just don't want you getting hurt."

Seth hugged her. He knew it was hard for her. Jessica had stolen her boyfriend back at college and so trust was a big ask. "You worry too much," he said. "But thanks."

As the weeks progressed, Tallie and Ethan saw less and less of Seth, and when they did meet up Jessica was almost invariably in tow. But Seth was besotted. He didn't see Jessica flirting while he was working or observe how she cut his friends dead when he wasn't around. He saw her vulnerability, her need to be cared for, her need for him and it drew him deeper and deeper under her spell. He craved her company, her touch, so badly it hurt.

"I'm so in love with you," he would whisper in the night, at which she would snuggle closer with her head on his chest.

Jessica was starting a new contract at the end of September and had to make a few trips up to London beforehand to prepare. Seth went with her the first time, leaving his assistant Tom in charge of the shop, but was secretly relieved when she didn't ask him to go again after that. He wasn't a great fan of the city.

He missed her dreadfully when she moved, but through October she came back every weekend. As November crept by though he noticed a change in her. Texts and phone calls diminished and she seemed to be working more and more. She did come down but it was for far shorter and more rushed visits. She declined his offer to come and see her instead.

"I'll be working anyway," she said, "and I know you hate it up there."

"Bring on Christmas," Seth said, pulling her close. "We'll have a whole week."

She smiled and kissed him. Then he didn't see her until halfway through December, when she whirled down to inform him that she was seeing someone else and whirled away again, all in the space of an hour and a half, leaving him shell shocked and silent, sitting amongst the fragments of his world.

It was a bleak Christmas, despite the efforts of Tallie, Ethan and his fiancée Gaia and Seth's Great Aunt Rose. He did his best to cover his hurt but they knew him too well.

"I hate to see you like this," Tallie said bitterly. "I so wanted you to be right."

They tried to make sure that he wasn't on his own too much, tried to fill the empty space she had left behind but he felt distanced from everything. Everyone. And even more acutely when he was out with the others. It was a relief when February arrived and he went out to Canada to visit his mother and sister and see his new niece.

Just before Easter, after locking up on a Friday evening, Seth entered his porch to let himself into the flat and saw a figure sitting on his doorstep, huddled in a big hooded jacket that he recognised as his. Before he could say anything, she looked up.

"Jessica," he breathed.

She scrambled to her feet, the hood falling back to reveal dishevelled hair and black tracks down her face where tears had carried the mascara from her eyes. There were still tears glimmering on her lashes. She looked a beautiful mess and despite himself he felt his heart quicken.

"What are you doing here?" he asked quietly.

"Hoping you'll forgive me." It came out as a sob. "I'm so sorry, I should never have broken up with you. He was a bastard but I didn't see it, didn't realise it 'til too late. I'm so sorry Seth."

"What happened? Did he hurt you? I mean..." Seth couldn't help it. As hurt as he had been by her, he hated to see anyone so upset, especially her.

"No, not like that. Just a manipulative bully. Control freak. Didn't want me to do anything on my own and then... then..." She put her hands over her face. "Please Seth. Please take me back. I don't know what I'll do if you won't. I..."

"Whoa. Slow down." He reached out and put his hand on her shoulder. "You're shivering," he said. "Come up and get warm."

Jessica dropped her hands and looked at him. She rubbed her eyes with her sleeve, smudging her makeup further. It made her look so vulnerable and he felt himself crumble.

"Really?" she asked.

He nodded. "I'll make coffee. Then we can talk."

"Thank you. So much." She reached up to touch his hand and instinctively he closed it around hers. "I promise I'll make it up to you."

He led her up the stairs and went into the kitchen. She left the jacket in the living room and followed him.

"I am really sorry," she said quietly. "If I hurt you."

He sighed and added milk to the mugs before turning. "There's no 'if', Jessica, surely you know that."

"I do, yes." She looked contrite. "But I am sorry. I just… I guess I lost my head there for a bit. I was wrong. I know what I want, who I want to be with. And it's you."

He was silent, just looking at her.

"You don't believe me?" Tears welled up again.

"Don't," he said, moving towards her.

"I do want to be with you." She walked over to him, put her arms around him. "Seth, please, let me show you."

The next thing he knew, she was kissing him and he was returning it fiercely. And Jessica was back in his life.

Chapter 3
Present Day

Serena sat on the rocks for hours, just staring out and remembering. By the time the chill became uncomfortable enough to make her rise and shake herself, the sky had turned a deep lavender blue and a scattering of stars sparked a trail for the moon to trace. She set off back down the beach, looking across to the parade of shops that ran along the front parallel to it, on the other side of the narrow road. They were all in darkness now, except for the fish and chip shop which still had visitors scurrying in and out like ants. Serena checked her watch. It was heading for eight o'clock. Somehow she'd lost four hours.

She shivered slightly as she made her way back through the town to the cottage. It was a fifteen minute walk and as soon as she got back she brewed a cup of tea and went upstairs to make the bed. Then she pulled the curtains and put the TV on, desperate for voices to fill the silence and the empty desolation of her heart, wondering how she could force herself through the days until her time came to an end.

The following morning she woke to the squabble of seagulls and the sunlight falling liquid across the floorboards.

"OK," she told herself. "Get on with it. Sarah'll be here at the weekend so make some effort."

She had met Sarah through Steve. It was her cottage that Serena had rented for the next year and a bit. Sarah owned two properties in the town and that was why Steve and his friends came down here; she gave them a special deal on summer rent. She was twenty years older than Serena but they had become very close and through all of Steve's appalling behaviour Sarah had stood by her and supported her, given her a place to stay and a shoulder to cry on. Once the divorce was almost through and Serena had decided to leave London, Sarah had insisted that she use one of the cottages for as long as she needed. She hadn't even wanted any rent but Serena was adamant.

Now it was the near the end of September. Not quite the end of the tourist season but Sarah usually took a week or two down here herself, which she had foregone for Serena.

"A long weekend will be great," she had said.

Serena hadn't had the strength to argue. She'd just been desperate to get away, from the city and Steve, from the people they had known together and from the memories that seemed to be everywhere. Although there were memories here as well they weren't the crushing, devastating same as in London. And at least here she could feel some connection, however tenuous, with her old life.

Sarah arrived late afternoon on Friday with wine and news.

"I can't believe it," Serena said. "That's amazing."

"Tell me about it," Sarah said. "Six months with the band, access to all areas for photography, information, comments and quotes. The biography of a European tour. It's going to be a massive amount of work, but what an opportunity."

"What does Lindy think? You'll miss each other horribly." Lindy was Sarah's other half, quite literally Serena had always thought.

"She's stoked for me. It'll be hard but she's trying to swing things so that she'll be able to come out a few times and travel with us." Lindy was a literary agent. In fact, that was how she and Sarah had met, a chance meeting at a literary festival years ago when Lindy was working for a publishing house and Sarah was flogging her self-published first book. The rest was history.

"So when do you leave?"

"Oh, not 'til the end of April next year, but I've got a few bits of preliminary stuff to do. Some interviews and bits and pieces. They're recording their album at the moment, which the tour will be promoting, and they want some of that included. And I've got a couple of other projects that I need to finish first, so next year is looking as though it's going to be pretty packed."

"I'll have to make the most of you in the next few months then," Serena said, her heart sinking as she realised that after April she wouldn't see her friend again.

Saturday whirled past. Sarah was on a mission to make Serena feel a part of the town where she had grown up and took her just about everywhere. By the time they reached The Old Hare, Sarah's favourite pub and the local live music venue, Serena was exhausted.

It was busy, all ages gathering to listen to the two bands that were playing. The place showcased a vast variety of music and attracted an eclectic mix of people. There were hippy types, couples, groups of workmates, half a rugby team, a hen party, and a lot more besides. Serena's gaze was frequently drawn to a particularly striking group tucked in the corner, not because they were noisy or badly behaved but because they were different from everyone else. It was a feeling she knew well.

She and Sarah got their drinks and found a table at the back. Sarah's old friends began to drift in and for a while she was distracted, though she couldn't help but keep glancing surreptitiously over at the little crowd in the corner. They were obviously at ease and having a great time in each other's company, talking and laughing animatedly. There was a guy who looked as though he'd walked straight out of a thrash metal band, with his big beard and leather jacket. One of the girls had dark red hair down to her waist, another, in a stunning steam punk style dress, had dyed her hair bright pink. A tall man with a plait down his back was talking to a guy who would have looked like a surfer dude were it not for the skinny black jeans and Iron Maiden T-shirt. They looked so relaxed and happy that Serena couldn't stop the ache of sadness spreading through her as yet again she felt separate and isolated from everyone around her. It was made more acute by the tall goth guy with long, dark hair and the biggest, warmest smile she had ever seen, who was dishing out hugs to the others, big friendly hugs that filled her with longing and envy. As the evening wore on and she struggled to keep the smile on her face and her conversation light, she wished that she could go over and be part of it, have one of those hugs for her own.

But she couldn't, so she tried and failed to ignore them, left with Sarah after the second band finished, said goodnight to her friend and then cried herself quietly to sleep.

Sarah left to return to London on Monday afternoon.

"It's been so great to see you," Serena said sadly as she hugged her.

"You too, lovely," Sarah smiled at her. "Keep your head up. He'll get his comeuppance eventually, you will glide gracefully on in your new, happy, fulfilled life with everything wonderful you deserve and karmic law will be satisfied."

Serena felt her eyes prickle. "You will come down again, won't you?" she begged. "I really can't face going back."

"Of course I will. And I'll bring Lindy next time." Sarah got into the car. "I'll see you really soon."

Serena waved until she turned the corner and disappeared. Then she went back into the cottage, almost wishing that the sea would take her there and then.

A week of fruitless job hunting followed. The tourist season was winding down and even expanding her search outside the town proved frustrating. It didn't help her mood when again and again her enquiries met a brick wall. October crept in and still she had found nothing. And then, to top it all off, an ominous white envelope dropped onto the doormat with the rest of the post. She picked it up, hands shaking, took it back to the kitchen and sat staring at it for long minutes. She knew what it was, had been expecting it, waiting for it. And finally it had arrived.

The decree absolute. Her death sentence.

After the way that she had been feeling since Steve had left, the crushing bitter weight of the sadness, she had almost expected to feel relieved when it arrived. And yet part of her, the human survival streak, was already screaming in fear.

She took a long shuddering breath and tore open the envelope, freeing the certificate from its confines. She cast her eye over it and then folded it up and stuck it in the middle of a random book about gardening that she pulled off one of Sarah's shelves. She re-shelved the book, tore the envelope into tiny shreds and then ran up the stairs to get dressed. In under five minutes she was out of the cottage and putting as much distance as she could between herself and the wretched piece of paper.

Seth was behind the counter serving a customer when the girl walked in. He looked up automatically as the bell above the door jangled. Her long, honey coloured hair had been tangled by the wind and she looked a little nervous. He caught her eye and smiled. She gave him a brief smile back before turning to look at the cork noticeboard on the left, which was festooned with flyers advertising music lessons and local gigs.

His customers left, leaving the shop empty apart from her, and he went over. She was looking systematically through the racks.

"Can I help you?" he asked, smiling again.

"I'm just kind of looking at the moment, thanks," she said. "This is a great shop."

"Thank you. Glad you like it."

"It's yours?"

"Yeah." He laughed, gesturing around. "My life's work."

"It's amazing. You must have every genre that's known to man in here. And more."

"You're very kind. Hey, risking a cliché here but haven't I seen you around town the last couple of weeks?"

"Yeah, probably. The one wandering cluelessly like a lost soul, that'd be me. I'm new here, still trying to get my bearings."

"Well it's nice to meet you." He extended his hand. "I'm Seth."

She shook it tentatively. "Serena."

"So what made you decide to move here?" he asked. Serena sighed and he saw something in her face, something that he recognised. Hurt. Sadness. He apologised immediately.

"Sorry. I shouldn't have asked. Forget it." But he found himself wanting to know.

"No, it's fine." She sighed again. "Had to move. I just got divorced. In fact that's why I came in here. My decree absolute arrived this morning and made me feel kinda ropey so I thought I'd buy myself a treat. Music therapy and all that."

"Aw man, that's rough. I'm sorry."

She shrugged. "It happens. Sometimes you just can't save it."

"I know where you're coming from." Memories of Jessica and how he'd felt the first time she left him resurfaced with alarming ease. "It sucks." He was sincere and it seemed to unnerve her. She turned towards the racks of CDs, her eyes a stormy grey.

"Yeah, it does," she agreed. "Anyway, unfortunately my ex has managed to gain custody of most of my CDs and I want to replace my favourites."

"Well, I can help you with that. You want to start with your number one. Fire away. This is going to be interesting." He rubbed his hands with glee and was pleased when she laughed.

"Oh dear. I'm going to disappoint you horribly now."

He shook his head. "How can music disappoint?"

"True," Serena said. "OK then, here goes. Alter Bridge."

Seth couldn't stop the look of delight from spreading across his face. "Can't fault your taste," he said. "Alter Bridge. Wow."

She couldn't help grinning. "You're surprised?"

"Shame on me but yes. Most people who come in here wouldn't know who they are."

"Well, ironically Fortress is the only one of theirs I managed to keep so any of their others... preferably all their others really."

"Oh." He knew the albums she was referring to, understood exactly what she was saying. "They are the masters."

She nodded. "There's no other band that can rip your heart out, break it, mend it and put it back where it belongs quite like Alter Bridge."

He looked at her intently, the delight replaced by a more serious expression. He wished he could change the sadness in her eyes but before he could think of what to say she spoke.

"Sorry." She shook her head. "Too much, I know."

"Actually, no. That is a perfect description."

They smiled at each other, a small moment of connection and understanding. Then she looked away.

"Sorry, too maudlin," she said. "Have you got any Avenged Sevenfold? Or Green Day's 21st Century Breakdown?"

"Really, a girl after my own heart," he said. "Let's see."

He led her over to the rock and metal section and located two for her. Then he excused himself as another customer came in, leaving her to look. Back behind the counter, he was caught with a phone query and it seemed that she lingered until the other person had left and the shop was empty again. Or maybe he was just imagining it. Hoping...

She brought her CDs up to pay. Seth put them through and took her money.

"Thanks," she said. "And sorry again if I was sounding like an idiot back there. I should learn to bite my tongue."

"Don't apologise," he said. "That's a crap thing to happen. But hopefully you'll be happy here, soon anyway." He smiled at her again, needing, though he didn't know why, to try and make her feel better. "Hey, have you heard Sylentium?"

"No, I haven't. Oh dear, lost a point there."

He laughed. "Hang on." Disappearing into the back room, he returned with a CD which he held out to her. "Borrow this and have a listen. It's Darkening Sky, their first album. I think you'll like them."

Serena took it uncertainly. "Are you sure?"

"Yeah, really. Drop it back whenever. No rush. I'd be interested to know what you think."

"Thank you. That's really kind. Especially since you don't even know me. I could be some crazy kleptomaniac person."

"I doubt it. I'm a reasonable judge of character," he said. "Well, in most cases. I'm sure you're not going to do a runner."

"Not for a while, no," she agreed. "Thanks so much. It was really good to meet you."

"Likewise," he said. "See you soon, I hope."

She looked back at him as she walked out of the door and as she smiled again he realised just how much he meant it.

Several days later, after more intensive but futile job hunting covering what felt like half the county, Serena decided to give herself a day off. Late morning saw her drawn, as she often was, to the sea, Seth's CD tucked in her bag to return. Now that it was halfway through October the number of tourists had reduced markedly and the town had a quieter, gentler feel. It was pleasantly busy but the beach was no longer heaving, giving the local couples room to stroll along it in straight lines rather than winding, spiralling paths between the towels, sand castles and fabric windbreaks. Serena still loved to see them walking hand in hand, even though each time it felt like a blade slicing off another piece of her heart.

Although the sun was out there were plenty of clouds moving swiftly across the faded blue of the sky, propelled by a wind that felt as if it could have come straight from the Arctic. The waves sucked hungrily at the sand, throwing themselves further and further up the beach towards her. As though they were reaching for her. She shivered and retreated rapidly back across the narrow roadway behind the front to the parade of shops on the other side. She walked past several of them and went into Seth's.

There were a few people browsing and Seth was deep in conversation with another man by the counter at the back of the shop. Serena made her way towards them and stopped at the end of the row of shelving, hovering uncertainly, not wanting to disturb them. Seth glanced up and an enormous smile spread across his face. It warmed her all the way to her toes.

"Serena. It's good to see you." He beckoned her over. "Ethan, this is Serena. She moved into town a few weeks ago."

"Hi." Ethan extended his hand, shaking long sand coloured hair out of his eyes. "Good to meet you." His handshake was firm and made her hand tingle. He obviously felt it too because a puzzled look passed fleetingly across his face, dissipating quickly as Seth spoke again.

"Ethan and I were at school together."

"Yeah, and I don't know who led who into worse ways," Ethan laughed.

"I do but I'm not going to comment," Seth shot back, grinning. "I'll only incriminate myself."

"I'm sure you were both just angelic," Serena said, trying to keep a straight face. Ethan let out a guffaw.

"Of course we were," Seth said. "Well, at least Ethan was."

"You wish. Or rather, the teachers wished."

"Well, those wings are heavy. And you know what they say, a halo's only six inches from a noose."

It was Serena's turn to laugh. "Never heard that one before," she said.

"Anyhow, I'd better get going," Ethan said. "Got to get back for my next client."

"I'll see you Friday," Seth said.

"Sure. Good to meet you, Serena. Catch you later." He raised his hand to them as he headed out.

Seth excused himself to go and deal with some customer queries and then served a couple of people at the counter. The shop quietened.

"Sorry," he said.

She grinned. "You should be. Imagine continuing to run your business when a semi stranger drops in unexpectedly to return a CD that you kindly loaned her."

He stared at her momentarily before he burst into laughter. "You're funny, you know that?"

"Really, I didn't come to hold you up, I…"

"You're not holding me up. It is good to see you."

She blushed slightly and rummaged in her bag, extracting the CD and handing it to him.

"Thanks again. It was really kind of you," she said. *It meant a lot* remained unspoken.

"What did you think?"

"You were right. I really liked it. Heavy but melodic."

"Great. I will savour this moment 'cos I don't get to be right that often." He was still smiling.

"I don't believe that."

"It's true. Ethan's the one that's nearly always right and he does like to rub my nose in it. But then, he has an unfair advantage, being psychic."

"Oh." Serena wondered if that had anything to do with the tingling she had felt. Then she dismissed it. She knew that humans couldn't access true magical energy.

"So, what have you been up to? Have you been OK? Or shouldn't I ask?"

"Massive amounts of unsuccessful job hunting," she said ruefully. "Wrong time of year, I s'pose."

He nodded. "What are you looking for? I'll keep my ears open."

She smiled gratefully. "Anything really, shop work, cleaning, basic clerical. I don't mind, I just need something. Partly for the money but partly 'cos I'll go stir crazy if I don't find something constructive to do."

He looked at her with such sympathy that she could have sworn he'd heard what she hadn't said. To block out the loneliness, to drown out the silence, to keep away the darkness that threatened to swallow her whole.

"OK. I'll ask around. How can I let you know if I hear of anything? Would you leave me your number, or is that too forward of me?" He looked a little unsure of himself suddenly.

"No, I'm really grateful for any help I can get," she said and dictated it to him so he could put it in his phone. "You wouldn't happen to know where I can get some logs for my wood burner, would you?"

"Actually, yeah." He scrolled through his contacts and wrote a name and number down for her. "This guy delivers to my great aunt. He's really good."

"Thanks," she said. There was a pause. "Well, after using you shamelessly, I guess I'd better go, let you get back to work."

"You can use me any time, shamelessly or not. You're not in the way, in case that's what you're thinking. I like it when friends drop in."

She looked at him. "But you hardly know me."

"Not yet. But I would like to think we could be friends. Couldn't we?"

She was somewhat taken aback by his directness, but there was no mistaking the sincerity in his eyes. She nodded.

"I'd really like that."

"How're you settling in?" he asked. "Is it a big change from where you were before?"

"I was in London," Serena said, "so yeah, it's a little different to say the least. But actually, I prefer it here. I love to be near the sea. I missed it when I was in the city, I didn't feel so at home there. Thought I'd come here for a year once the divorce was pretty much final, try and get my head together. I've rented a cottage from my friend. She grew up here." She clapped her hand to her mouth. "Sorry. Talking too much."

"No you're not," he said. "I asked. I want to know. Naturally nosy. Did you grow up on the coast?"

"You could say that," she agreed and decided to deflect the conversation. "What about you? Have you always lived here?"

"Pretty much. Since I was ten anyway," he said. "I moved away for a while when I left school, but I came back. I love it, my friends are here and my great aunt. The rest of my family's pretty far flung but I stick to my roots. Not very adventurous, huh?"

"I think it's great. I..." Serena stopped abruptly. He looked at her questioningly.

"What?" he asked, but she was shaking her head. "Go on, please. Tell me."

"You'll think I'm nuts," she said. "If you don't already."

"No, I won't." He was looking serious now.

"I don't feel like I have any. Roots. I'm still searching for home."

"Maybe you'll find it here." As more people came into the shop the bell made her jump. He smiled at her. "Things will get better."

"Are you sure it's Ethan that's psychic and not you?" she joked half-heartedly.

"I just know that..." He was interrupted by a couple of lads asking about an album they couldn't find. He went off to help them, gently touching her shoulder as he passed. It was a comforting, friendly contact but she was shocked at the jolt of emotion it sent through her. Being unexpected, she hadn't had her guard fully up and it made her realise how much she missed the closeness that she and Steve had shared. She realised suddenly that she had been able to talk to Seth so easily, more easily than most of the friends she had had in London. It was odd but she felt that somehow they had a connection beyond the polite conversation of acquaintances. It scared her. She took the opportunity to wave goodbye to him and leave, even though she wanted to stay. The look on his face told her that he wanted her to stay as well.

Serena took herself off along the beach and up the steep path to the cliffs. The wind was still keen despite the sunshine but she ignored it and walked and walked. As if walking, the constant rhythmic movement of muscles and bones, the steady monotony of one foot in front of the other, could somehow rub out all the emotion that that one gentle touch had brought back up to the surface. She struggled to understand what she was feeling, whether it was all just memories or something else, something new. For someone who wanted to be her friend but already seemed to read her better than anyone else. Including Steve.

"No. No. No." The word ran like a mantra through her mind. "Do not even go there."

She was trying so hard to block it all out that before she realised it she had walked the five miles along the coast path to the next village. She felt cold and tired and low. There was a little tea room halfway up the High Street, so she slipped inside and ordered herself a hot chocolate to warm up with. Then she sat at a small table in the bay window and stared out, watching the sunshine diminish as dark clouds rolled in slowly from the sea. Raindrops began to hit the glass.

"That's just great," Serena thought resignedly. She sat for a while longer but the rain showed no sign of abating. Eventually, when it became apparent that it was not even going to ease for the foreseeable future, she returned her cup to the counter and, finding that there was no bus for the next three hours, set off back the way she had come.

It took her twice as long to get home as it had to walk out, and by the time she got there she was drenched and shivering. The sky was so dark it felt like night time already, even though it was only a little after four. She dumped her sodden coat and jumper on the kitchen floor and hurried upstairs to run a bath.

A few hours later, having thawed out and feeling a little more relaxed, Serena was curled up in the big arm chair with her book when she heard her phone. There was a new text from a number she didn't recognise.

Am sorry if I upset you this morning. Will learn to keep my big mouth shut. Would really like to be friends. Pls? Seth

Momentarily she wondered how he'd got her number but then realised she'd given it to him herself when they'd been talking about jobs. That felt like an age ago. Still, it was kind of him to think about her feelings like that. She hesitated for a moment, then sent a reply.

No problem. Not you, it's me. Disconcerting to apparently have my mind read by someone I've only just met.

Moments later, something came back.

Sorry. Ethan's influence maybe? Will blame him as not here to defend himself!

Serena giggled. She liked his sense of humour. She pinged off another one.

Maybe you are psychic after all?

I wish but no chance, otherwise would have known what not to say.

"Oh," she thought. Humorous and self-deprecating.

Not your fault. Pls don't worry.

So you will come and say hi sometime? Soon?

Stupidly, Serena couldn't stop grinning.

Yes. Where else will I get my metal fix?

Over by the front, in his flat above the shop, Seth heaved a sigh of relief and grinned too.

Serena was walking along the esplanade the following week, window shopping and, as always, looking for job ads when the youngster on the bicycle flew past her on the pavement. Going far too fast, he swerved late and caught a frail looking elderly woman on the shoulder as he passed. He didn't stop, just bumped down onto the roadway and took off. She saw the lady teetering and leapt forward but wasn't able to reach her in time to stop her from crashing to the ground, her shopping bag spilling its contents around her.

"Oh my goodness," said Serena, throwing herself down next to the woman. "Are you OK? Have you hurt yourself?"

The lady looked dazed and was trying to push herself up but her shoulder seemed to be giving her trouble. She glanced at Serena.

"I think I'm alright, thank you dear. Ouch."

"Here, let me help you," Serena said. She slipped her arm round the woman's upper back and helped her into a sitting position, then sat beside her on the pavement. Another passer-by had stopped and was repacking the shopping. "Are you sure you shouldn't just stay still?"

"Thank you but I'm sure I'm OK."

"What can I do?" she asked. "Do you need a doctor? Or an ambulance?"

The lady was moving her shoulder around, wincing a little. "I don't think it's broken. I'm just a little shaken."

"Here, lean on me," Serena said, repositioning herself so that the lady could rest back against her. "Oh, your hand's bleeding. Wait, I've got a tissue." She wrestled one out of her bag.

"Is there someone we can phone for you?" the man asked.

"No, no," the lady said, "but my great nephew runs the shop a few doors down." She indicated behind her. "Perhaps you might be good enough to let him know I'm here. He's called Seth. He sells music."

"Oh," Serena thought. "Seth."

"Of course," the man said.

Serena looked up. "I'll stay here," she said.

"You're both very kind," said the lady as he hurried off. "My name is Rose."

"Serena."

Moments later Seth came hurrying up, concern written all over his face. He knelt on the pavement beside them. "Aunt Rose, what happened? Are you OK?" He noticed her suddenly and smiled warmly. "Oh, hi Serena."

"A cyclist bit me," his great aunt said drily. "And you two have apparently already met. I should have realised you'd know a pretty girl like this, Seth."

"Oh for heaven's sake Auntie, shush, you'll give me a bad name. Behave! Are you hurt?"

"No, dear, but I may need a hand to get up."

Between them Serena and Seth helped her to her feet. The other man hovered uncertainly as she thanked him.

"Yeah, thanks so much," Seth added as the man walked away. "Let's go back to the shop, you can sit down there for a bit."

Serena stayed on Rose's left side as Seth picked up the bag and took her right arm. She was a little unsteady as they helped her inside and Seth rushed off to get a chair. There were customers waiting.

"I'll make us all some tea in a minute," he said.

"Don't worry about me, see to your people," said Rose.

"I could do it," Serena volunteered. "If you like."

He gave her a grateful look and indicated a room behind the counter. "Kettle and stuff's back there," he said. "Thanks."

Making sure that Rose was comfortable, Serena went into the back room and made three mugs of tea. Carrying them out, she put two on the counter and took one round to Rose.

"How are you feeling?" she asked.

"Better, thank you. After this I'll be fine to get the bus home."

"Don't be daft," Seth interjected. "I'll close the shop and drive you."

"No, dear, you won't. You're not losing business because of me."

"Auntie, you're really pale and I don't want you taking another tumble. The bus driver wouldn't thank you either."

"He'd never let me live it down. But you're not…"

Serena couldn't help smiling as they bickered good-naturedly back and forth, but eventually she broke in.

"I have a solution that may suit both of you," she said.

They looked at her.

"I'd be very happy to drive you home, Rose," she continued. "That way you don't have to fight with the bus and Seth doesn't have to shut the shop."

"I can't put you out like that."

"I can't expect you to do that."

They both spoke at the same time and then grinned, at each other and at her.

"Really, it's fine," she reassured them. "I've nothing else on today. I could offer to stay and look after the shop but that would be worse for business than closing."

"You've been so kind, dear, but I feel that would be too much of an imposition." Rose sounded unsure.

Serena shook her head. "Honestly, not at all. Well, unless you're about to tell me that you actually live a hundred miles away."

Rose laughed. "Now that really would be taking advantage."

Another customer came up to the counter and Seth went to serve her. He took a moment to watch Serena and his aunt laughing together.

"I'm going to get the car then," Serena said. "I'll come and park outside."

"Are you sure?" Seth was still looking uncertain.

"Absolutely," she confirmed. "It makes sense. And I promise I won't drive like a maniac. Rose will be perfectly safe."

"Thank you," he said. "Really."

Once Rose had left with Serena, Seth returned to the shop, the germ of an idea forming in his mind. He'd noticed how easy the conversation had been between Serena and his aunt which told him that Rose had liked her instantly. Just as he had. He knew his aunt needed some help around the house although she was reticent to take just anyone on. Maybe, just maybe…

And the smile that Serena had, that she had given him as she left had made him feel slightly light headed. It was more than just liking her. He felt a connection with her.

Seth crushed that thought immediately, consigning it to the box in his mind marked DON'T EVEN THINK ABOUT IT. It was no coincidence that it was next to the box labelled JESSICA.

When Rose was settled into the car, she directed Serena through the town and up the hill to the west side. Her home was in a lane off the main road, the third of four large detached houses with a view out over the sea. Serena pulled into the drive and switched off the engine.

"It's beautiful up here," she said.

"Isn't it?" Rose agreed. "I'm very lucky." She unclipped her seatbelt as Serena slipped out of the car and came round to open the door.

"Shall I bring your shopping in for you?" she asked.

"That would be very kind, thank you." Rose managed to get out of the car, but Serena saw her wince as she pushed through her arm to stand up.

"If your shoulder doesn't settle down in a day or two, you will get it checked, won't you?" Serena was concerned.

Rose nodded. "I'm sure it will be fine. I'm a lot tougher than I look. Tough as old boots, in fact."

"Glad to hear it."

Rose took her key and opened the door. She indicated a door leading off the hall to the back of the house. "If you'd be kind enough to leave it in the kitchen I'd be grateful.'

"Would you like me to put it away for you?"

"No thank you. I shall do it later."

"I'll just pop the cold stuff in the fridge then."

"That would be kind. I'm going to sit down in the living room.'

Serena put the shopping on the wooden table in the kitchen. The window looked out onto a large garden with an area of lawn and flowerbeds full of colour. A wooden bench sat beneath a twisted apple tree.

"Your garden is beautiful," she commented as she returned.

"It is, isn't it?" Rose looked pleased that she'd noticed. "I've spent many happy hours out there playing with the plants. I find I can't really do it now though. Sore knees and bad balance make it difficult."

"That's a shame," Serena agreed. "But at least you can enjoy all the work that you've put into it."

"Very true." Rose pushed her glasses more firmly onto her nose. "And for that I am grateful.'

"Is there anything else I can do before I go? Will you be OK?"

"It's good of you to offer, but no, I'll be absolutely fine. And no doubt Seth will be along to check on me this evening when he closes up. He's very good to me like that."

"You seem very close."

"Yes. I'm very lucky to have that."

"Well, I guess I'll head off then, if there's nothing else I can do. It was so nice to meet you. And if I can do anything, like if you do need to get your arm checked, I'd be really happy to drive you, if the bus times don't suit. Here, I'll leave my number just in case."

"You've been so kind, my dear, I can't thank you enough. I hope I see you again."

"I hope so too."

Seth went straight up to his Aunt's when he closed that evening. He couldn't help worrying about her. As fiercely independent and strong minded as Rose was, he could see how much more fragile she was becoming. She would admit to tiring more easily and struggling to cope with the housework but since her two forays into finding help had not ended well, she remained resistant to looking for anyone else and she limited the amount of assistance that she would accept from him.

"You do enough already dear," she would say, shooing him off. "You're too busy to do more."

Now he was worried that the fall might have affected her worse than she had let on and had half decided by the time he got there that he might have to persuade her to go to A and E. So he was pleasantly surprised to find her in the kitchen stirring something that smelled delicious, the shopping already having been put away.

"You're feeling a bit better then?" he asked.

"I'm fine," Rose said, smiling at him pointedly. "Shaken but not stirred. I did tell you this morning but I might have known that you wouldn't believe me."

"Yes, well." Seth looked slightly abashed. "Just wanted to make sure."

"I knew you would dear." Rose turned back to the stove. "Even if I'd told you not to. So I've made us something to eat."

"Oh Auntie, you shouldn't have. I could've done that."

"You've been working all day. Besides, I'm a better cook." She laughed drily. "But you can dish it up if you like."

Seth got out two plates and served the food as his aunt took a seat at the kitchen table. They talked as they ate and inevitably the conversation turned to Serena.

"The girl this morning, Serena, she's very nice isn't she? Very helpful. Do you know her well?"

"I've only met her a couple of times. She seems really nice, but I don't know her that well," Seth replied. "Not as well as I'd like," he thought to himself.

"Has she been living here long?"

"No, only a few weeks. She's had a rough time recently."

"That's a shame."

"Yeah, I think it's been tough. Just got divorced."

"Dear oh dear. She seems too young for that."

"Yeah, well." Seth shrugged. "Anyway she's rented a cottage down in town. Trying to get back on her feet, I guess.'"

"Where's she moved from?"

"London. She says she liked it there but she prefers to be near the sea. Says she feels more at home."

Rose's eyes twinkled. "For not knowing her very well, you seem to know an awful lot."

Seth looked at her sharply, then smiled. "I suppose."

"I don't blame you for liking her, dear. She's delightful. A big improvement on the other, if you'll forgive me saying so. She has gone again, hasn't she?"

"Yes, Auntie, she has." Seth sighed, memories of Jessica's most recent departure still raw. "Anyhow, Serena and I aren't going out, we're just friends. I'm not planning to get involved again any time soon and I don't think she is either."

"Hmm, well, if you say so. But you seem to have an understanding."

"I guess so. I hadn't really thought about it." The lurching feeling of delight in Seth's gut when he realised the truth behind his Aunt's words took him pleasantly by surprise. "But I do know that she's looking for work."

"Oh. What does she do?"

"I think she'd be happy to do anything really. Shop work, housework, clerical. She said she's not looking for anything specific."

"Do you think she might be able to help me sort through the papers and do my typing for me? My eyes aren't so good now and I'll never get this book finished if I have to do it myself, I'm so slow."

"You seemed to get on well this morning. Do you think it would work if she was here all day?"

"I think she might just be perfect."

Seth smiled. He thought his aunt was probably right.

The following morning Serena had just made herself a cup of tea when her phone rang. At first she didn't recognise the voice, but Rose introduced herself quickly.

"Oh, hi," Serena said. "How are you today? How's your shoulder?"

"Better thank you, but still sore and stiff. I wanted to thank you again for your kindness yesterday. I appreciated it very much and I know Seth did too."

"Honestly, it was no bother," Serena said, blushing even though she was alone in her kitchen.

"Well, I could argue that you put yourself out for me et cetera but still. The other reason I'm calling is because I have a question for you. When Seth came up to see me last night, he told me that you were looking for work. Is that correct?"

"Yes," Serena replied. "I am."

"Do you have a particular thing in mind?"

"No not really. I'm happy to do pretty much anything." Serena couldn't help but wonder where the conversation was going.

"In that case, would you be interested in working for me? I need someone to help me collate and type papers for a book and also to do a bit of housework. I can't seem to manage it all now."

"Wow," Serena said, her heart lifting. "That sounds great. I'm definitely interested."

"Good," Rose replied. "Perhaps you could come up to the house today or tomorrow, whenever you're free, and I can show you what I have in mind before you commit yourself."

"Brilliant." Serena couldn't keep the enthusiasm out of her voice. "I had nothing planned today except more job hunting. What time would suit you?"

Having arranged to go up and meet Rose at eleven thirty, Serena threw herself into the shower, got dressed and walked down to the front. She wanted to thank Seth. He was kneeling on the floor unpacking a delivery of CDs when she entered the shop, which was empty. He looked up as the bell rang and that wide smile spread across his face when he saw her.

"Hi," she said.

"Hi yourself," he replied, pushing himself to his feet. "You OK?"

She nodded. "I just came to thank you. For whatever you said to your aunt."

"I only told her you were looking for a job. She phoned you then?"

"Yeah, this morning. I'm going up to see her later to find out more about what she wants.'"

"That's good." Seth looked really pleased. "I'm the one who should be thanking you. You were great yesterday."

"Oh good grief Seth, I did what anyone else would have done. It was nothing."

"Actually it meant a lot to me. To both of us." He paused, then continued. "It's so quiet this morning. Do you have time for a coffee before you go?"

She checked her watch and nodded.

Serena pulled into Rose's drive and got out of the car, admiring the view before she rang the bell. It took a few moments for Rose to reach the door but she smiled widely at Serena.

"I'm so pleased to see you dear. Come in."

Serena followed Rose into the living room and took a seat where she indicated.

"Would you like a cup of coffee or tea?" Rose enquired.

"No thanks, I'm fine."

"Right then, to business." The smile on Rose's face belied the seriousness of her words. "If you're still interested."

"Oh yes," Serena said. "I'm really excited to hear about your book."

Rose explained that she needed help to sort through and collate a vast number of papers and then type up the appropriate ones into a manuscript that would potentially become the book. They went to the study, which was chaotic to say the least, and while Serena was a little daunted by the number of documents that were involved, she was fascinated by the subject and the detail. Rose had always been interested in plants and healing and had gathered together a huge number of tips, recipes and facts about botanical medicine and other uses for common plants.

"As you can see," Rose said, sweeping her arm in an arc across the room, "I have a piling system rather than a filing system and unfortunately it has got a little beyond me. I also need a bit of help around the house. I did have a lady who came for a while but she didn't really understand what I needed. Wanted to tidy me up completely and I'm afraid I disappointed her by not maintaining her standards." She smiled wryly. "In my own home! So what do you think dear? Do you think you could cope with a somewhat disorderly old lady and her odd ways?"

"I think," Serena said slowly, "that I may just have found the perfect job."

Serena went home elated, having agreed hours and terms with Rose. She was tempted to call in and tell Seth, but decided it might be a bit much. She was touched later that afternoon when a text came in from him.

Aunt Rose told me you're going to help with her book. So glad. Will definitely be constructive but may still send you stir crazy!

Very excited. Starting tomorrow! Am a bit crazy anyway so probably won't make much difference after all.

Crazy is good. All the best people are crazy. See you soon.

She couldn't help giving her phone a hug, thinking that Seth and his aunt were two of the nicest people she had ever met.

Chapter 4

It was more than a week before Seth saw Serena again, although he knew that things seemed to be working out well. Rose was full of praise for her.

"She's so quick," she said. "Quick to understand what I want and quick to sort it out. And all without any drama or making me feel like a naughty schoolgirl like that other one did."

Seth grinned and arched his eyebrow. Rose batted him lightly on the arm.

"Fine. Maybe I do misbehave. But I always intended to grow old disgracefully and that's exactly what I'm doing."

"No kidding."

So when Serena dropped in a few days later just as he was closing, he was keen to find out how she felt.

"It's great," she said enthusiastically as he flipped the sign to 'Closed' and began switching things off. "We get the housework out of the way first thing and then dig into the boxes and files. I can't believe the amount of stuff she knows, has written about. Your aunt really is extraordinary."

"Don't I know it," he laughed. "In so many ways."

"Oh?" Serena's curiosity was piqued. "I was thinking about her knowledge of plants, but that's not what you meant, is it?"

"No." Seth shook his head. He was still laughing. "It's certainly not."

"You're going to have to tell me now," she smiled. His laughter was infectious.

He switched the lights off. "How long have you got?"

She raised her eyebrows.

"Actually, if you're not in a rush, do you want to come up to mine for a coffee and I'll tell you about Auntie? Only if you've got time."

"I'd love to."

They left the shop and Seth locked up. Then he unlocked the door just to the left, which was sheltered and set slightly further back from the street. It opened onto a narrow hallway and a flight of stairs. He motioned her in ahead of him. "I live above the shop," he explained.

The stairs led them up into the sitting room. "I'm really messy, so apologies in advance," he said. "I guess it runs in the family."

Serena took in the room with its two seater sofa and two armchairs, a wooden coffee table, a TV, a music system and lots of full bookcases. It was comfortable and unpretentious and she liked it. He headed across to the kitchen to put the kettle on and she stopped part way over to look at some of the books. He was soon back with two steaming mugs.

"Thanks," she said, accepting hers. "You like to read, I see. You've got more books in here than the average library."

"I know," he agreed. "I can't help myself. You?"

"Yeah," she nodded enthusiastically. "First thing I unpacked when I got down here, my books. Stupid really but they're like a security blanket. You can always rely on a good book."

"Not so much 'home is where the heart is' as 'home is where the books are'."

"Something like that, yeah."

He saw something, sadness maybe, pass fleetingly across her face as she spoke, but then it was gone and she was pointing to a book on the shelf.

"Hey, I love this guy's stuff, but when I mention him, most people look at me blankly. Crazy, 'cos he's a genius."

"Totally," Seth agreed. "Have you read…?"

After a while they sat to finish the mugs of coffee.

"So," Serena said. "Tell me about Rose."

"Where do I start?" Seth replied with a grin. "Well, where *do* I start? She's always been a bit of a rebel. By all accounts she was the black sheep in her family, wouldn't toe the line and do what her father decided was appropriate. He thought that his three girls should learn to type and do secretarial work until they snagged a husband. My Gran and her other sister did just that but not Rose. She managed to get herself a tutoring post with a family in London, and discovered Kew Gardens. That was where she got so interested in plants. She met a botanist who was researching the medical uses of plants in other countries, started working for him. They ended up travelling the world together. And getting married."

Serena smiled. That did seem like typical Rose. "Good for her."

"My great grandparents apparently came to terms with their rebel daughter in the end. And her sisters were always close. My grandmother though, I think she was always slightly scandalised by Rose, always thought her behaviour was rather… improper. I remember how horrified she used to be on Sunday afternoons when my sister and I were little, when all the adults were sitting around talking but Auntie would be out in the garden with me and Rachel, prowling around looking for insects behind the shed and digging up worms."

That made Serena giggle. "I can imagine that," she said.

"She's always been fun," Seth said. "You could never tell what she was likely to do next. And that hasn't changed."

"You're very close, aren't you?" Serena observed.

"Yeah. I'm lucky. It's funny because I've always felt closer to her than my Gran but there you go."

"Is your Gran…?"

"She passed away eight years ago. She was the middle sister. Her older sister passed two years later."

"I'm sorry."

Seth shrugged. "It's one of life's certainties, isn't it? Death?"

"I guess."

"That's what they say about life. No one gets out alive." He shook his head. "Sorry. Dark ramblings. Must stop." He smiled at her.

"We all do the dark ramblings thing," she said. "It's another certainty. Well, unless you're unbelievably lucky."

"Yeah." He met her eyes. "I know you know about that. I'm sorry, I didn't mean to bring up dark stuff."

She shook her head. "It's actually good to know someone who's not afraid to talk about dark stuff. Most people won't, well, most that I know. I don't understand it really. Maybe denial, or fear? They'd rather do the ostrich thing but it doesn't work for long. If you don't try and deal with it, sooner or later it'll come back and bite you."

"I know what you mean," he said. "It eats you from the inside."

He could see she understood. They were both quiet for a while. Then, somewhat hesitantly, she spoke.

"Feel free to tell me to sod off if I'm being too pushy, but do you want to swap a demon with me? Shine a light on one of the little sods and scare it for a while?"

Something in her eyes told Seth that this was a big step for her. As it would be for him if he agreed. But maybe she realised that.

"Yeah, OK," he said slowly after a few moments. "After you."

Serena stared at her hands. "Steve, my ex, when he and I broke up I thought I was going insane. It was as though the whole world had shifted, fallen apart, like it wasn't quite real any more. As if I was isolated from everything by this glass wall around me that I couldn't seem to get past. It hurt so much. That's partly why I left London, to see if leaving the immediacy of the memories for a different place and different people would help me reconnect." She looked back over at Seth. "But when I moved down here I kind of made a pact with myself that I'd only stay for a year and then move on. So if my world shifts again it'll be on my terms and not someone else's."

"Is it working? Are you feeling any less alone?" He sounded genuinely upset for her. "Because you're not. I know we don't know each other that well, but you're not alone here. You can always talk to me if you want."

She smiled wanly at him. "I know. I find it really easy to say stuff to you. God, I'd told you my divorce sob story within two minutes of meeting you. You must have thought I was nuts."

"No. I thought how brave you are. And strong. Moving somewhere new and so far away from everyone you know at a time like that."

"I don't feel brave or strong. But I don't feel so isolated and that's mainly thanks to you and Rose."

"I'm glad it's getting better. I'm glad you can talk to me. Because I can talk to you too."

"Go on then. Your turn."

He leaned back on the sofa, fingers drumming on the arm.

"My parents divorced years ago. My mother brought me and my older sister up on her own, here near Gran, Aunt Rose and Aunt Louisa. I gave her so much trouble when I was in my teens. Going out, getting drunk, playing truant. And yet she stuck by me through all of it when she could so easily have given up on me. Especially since she'd had enough crap already to last a lifetime. Now she's in Canada with my sister and really happy, but I still feel guilty."

"She's your mother and she loves you. And you love her. Just because you were acting out, it doesn't change that. And you're such a kind and generous person Seth, I may not know you very well either but that much is obvious. Just because you lost sight of that for a while doesn't mean she did."

He was shaking his head. "I should have known better."

"If other people make mistakes, do you hold it against them for years? Think that they did it on purpose and they should have known better?"

He shook his head. "Of course not."

"So why do you still hold your mistakes against yourself?"

He opened his mouth to speak, then closed it again and shrugged his shoulders.

"You shouldn't judge yourself so harshly. There are plenty of people out there'll do that for you, *and* find you wanting. Believe me, I do know that." Serena grinned at him ruefully. "But really, it was a long time ago. You're different now. I get the feeling you're an awful lot kinder to other people than you are to yourself. You and your aunt, you are two of the loveliest people I've ever met. So please don't doubt yourself. And if your torch isn't bright enough to get rid of the guilt demon, I'll bring my floodlight and flush him out for you."

"Now there's an offer I don't get every day."

Serena and Rose spent a lot of time laughing as they worked together. The structure of Rose's book was beginning to become apparent as Serena worked further and further through the papers. The amount of documentation was immense and Serena was fascinated by all of it; Rose had collected not just botanical information, herbal lore and remedies but recipes, dyes, regional uses, superstitions, magical correspondences and all sorts of other anecdotes. Rose's friend Sheila often dropped in. She and Rose were obviously very close and Serena couldn't help feeling a small pang of envy as she observed the depth of their friendship.

She had been sorting papers into sections, and one afternoon brought a whole ream of them downstairs to the sitting room to ask Rose some questions. She hesitated in the doorway when she realised that Sheila was there as well. Rose beckoned her in.

"Come and join us, dear."

"I don't want to interrupt. I just had some questions about these but it can wait 'til tomorrow."

"Nonsense," Sheila said. "If you need to make Rose do some work for a change, I won't stop you."

Serena giggled as Rose tsked. "Ask away," she insisted. "But do come and sit down first."

"I've been trying to get all the recipes for remedies together. I think I've got most of them." She put the pile down on the table and another sheet of paper beside it. "There are some repeats though, with small variations. So at some point you need to go through this list to choose which ones you want to include, and if they're duplicated, which recipe."

"My, you're organised." Sheila sounded impressed.

"She certainly is," Rose agreed. She picked up the top two documents from the pile and looked over them, a smile creeping across her face. "Linden tea – I remember picking those blossoms for hours and getting unbelievably sticky in the process."

"Have you made these all things?" Serena asked. "These tinctures and teas and syrups and balms?"

"Probably two thirds of them over the years," Rose said. "Some of them work really well. Some are really nice. And some are foul. Unspeakably foul."

"Are the health benefits proportional to the foulness?" Serena laughed.

"Possibly, but I didn't test that hypothesis. If they were that disgusting, they were consigned immediately to the compost."

"Not before you tested them out on the unsuspecting," Sheila said wryly. "There are some that I'll never forget."

Rose couldn't help laughing. "Sorry. But they weren't all bad."

"There's so much information here, it's unbelievable. And fascinating. And so much could be lost," said Serena.

"I know and I'm so glad you decided to take this on and help me. You've got further in three weeks than I've got in three decades."

The next time Serena dropped into Seth's shop she couldn't stop talking about it.

"I feel horribly in awe of Rose," she confessed to Seth and to Ethan who also happened to be there. "There's just a mountain of information and knowledge that she has. The amount of research and writing she's done over the years is unbelievable. And the really scary thing? It seems any random set of notes or piece of paper that I pull out and start reading to her, she usually remembers and quotes to me and tells me where and when she wrote it. I think she's actually a super being and not entirely human at all."

Ethan and Seth both laughed at that.

"SuperGrantie," Ethan said.

"Great and Aunt," Seth explained in answer to Serena's puzzled look. "Grant."

"OK," she said. "That's a new one."

"You think that's bad?" Ethan grinned. "Her husband was always called Gruncle."

"Yeah, Gruncle Gregory."

"No way," Serena said mirthfully.

"I swear," Seth said. "It's true."

"Seth, before I forget, Gaia wants to know…" Ethan began. Leaving them talking, Serena wandered over to look through the albums. She had remembered another one that she wanted but it wasn't on the shelf.

"What are you looking for?" Ethan asked, coming up beside her. "Don't tell me you're into screams and growling as well."

Seth rolled his eyes while Serena laughed. "You're not, I take it."

"Some's OK. Less growling, more singing's OK."

"Fair comment. Actually I like all sorts of music, but this is my favourite."

"So what you looking for?"

"Nightwish's Imaginaerum. But I can't see it."

"Darn, am I out?" Seth disappeared out the back and his disembodied voice floated out to them. "Yes, I am." He reappeared. "I'll order it for you Serena, it shouldn't take long."

"Thanks."

Ethan left the shop with his psychic antennae on full alert. He wasn't sure what it was about Serena but there was definitely something. He'd noticed it the first time he'd met her and again just now. An otherness, a wild emptiness and an aura like he'd never seen before. And yet she seemed ordinary in every other way. He was intrigued. He had seen many things that most other people would be blind to, met magic more than once. He couldn't help wondering…

Seth called in to see Serena on the following Saturday afternoon to deliver her CD. As he walked through the little courtyard beside her kitchen door he heard a dull thump from the small garden beyond and an exclamation.

"Oh for crying out loud." There was some scraping and clunking. "Right, this time you *will* capitulate, you little horror." Another thump was followed by a shout of exasperation.

"Grrr!"

He left the package by the door and continued on past the cottage into the garden. Serena had her back to him, wrestling a log back into position for chopping.

"I've had it with you," she growled angrily, swinging the axe. "Split, dammit."

The axe landed on the top of the log, embedding itself firmly into the wood.

"Aahh!" she yelled in frustration, letting go of the handle. She spun round and saw him there, her hands flying to her face in embarrassment.

"Having some trouble?" he asked mischievously. The look of horror on her face slowly gave way to a smile and then she burst into laughter.

"You could say that, yes," she agreed. "Damn things won't cooperate. Mind you, I'm so hot now I don't think I'll need a fire." He walked over as she continued. "I don't know what I'm doing wrong. I managed the first lot alright," she indicated some split pieces to their left, "and then it all went to pot."

"It's not your technique," he assured her. "Yes, I did see that last one. It's because you're…"

"I'm what?" she broke in, voice dangerous, eyes flashing. He grinned at her again, completely disarming her.

"So little. You've not got enough weight behind you to get through those big ones. And maybe confidence, if you haven't done this much before. Nothing to do with being female, really. It's a question of size."

Her eyes softened. "Oh."

"Here, let me have a go," he said, stepping forward and disengaging the axe. She stopped him.

"I'm sure you've got better things to do with your day off."

He looked quizzically at the sky for a moment, then shook his head.

"Nope, can't think of any. I left your CD by the kitchen door." He repositioned the log.

"Thank you," she said.

"No problem."

"Can I make you some tea?"

He smiled at her. "That'd be great."

She went in to boil the kettle and he set about the logs. She was soon back with two steaming mugs.

"You make it look so easy," she said wistfully.

"Thanks." He paused to take the mug from her. "I've had lots of practice, that's all. I do Auntie's wood for her every year and there's a couple of her friends who need a hand too. Plus I'm quite a bit taller and heavier than you, so more whack for the same effort."

"Well, I appreciate it," she said, "but I really hate being beaten by inanimate objects."

He finished his tea and hefted the axe again. They talked while he made his way through the pile, despite her protestations. Then he insisted on helping her carry them round to the log store to stack them.

"I don't know how to thank you," she said when they had finished. It was getting dark, past five o'clock already. He shook his head.

"No need," he said. "Coffee would be nice though."

They sat in her kitchen and the time disappeared. Before they knew it, it was after six.

"I'm going to make us an omelette," she said, getting up. "If that's OK with you?"

"I'd really like that, but you don't have to," he said.

"I know, but I'd like to," she said. She smiled at him, feeling suddenly shy. "Another thank you. Just don't have great expectations 'cos I'm a fairly basic cook."

He shook his head but she was already rattling around the kitchen in cupboards and the fridge.

"I'm going to the Old Hare tonight, there's bands playing and I'm meeting some friends. Why don't you come up?" he asked. "If you've not got anything else planned."

She was chopping a pepper and some mushrooms as she spoke. "I'd love to as long as your friends won't mind."

"They won't. And I've heard these guys before, they're heavier than the usual pub band, you'll like them. Well, I hope you will. Otherwise I'll owe you."

"Yeah, really," she laughed, tipping the vegetables into the frying pan to cook and starting to whisk the eggs. "After doing all that chopping for me, you really will."

After they had eaten he excused himself, needing to go and shower before heading out.

"Do you want me to come back for you?" he asked her, not wanting to make any assumptions.

"No thanks, it's fine, I can meet you there," she assured him, but he thought he saw a little nervousness in her face.

"Are you sure? Or you can meet me at mine if you prefer. I know it can be difficult walking into a place full of strangers on your own."

"No really, it's OK. It's kind of you but I'm having to get used to it. I won't say it doesn't still faze me at times, but it's getting better."

He looked at her. He wanted to tell her that she didn't have to do this thing on her own, not if she didn't want to, but his courage failed him.

"If you're sure. I should be there from about half eight."

"OK." She walked over to the door. "I'll see you later."

"Thanks for dinner." He paused and looked at her directly. "If you change your mind, if you want to meet before, text me, OK?"

She smiled and nodded. "Thanks."

When Serena reached the pub it was already full and the first band were starting their set. She took a deep breath, feeling daunted; despite what she'd told Seth, she still hated walking into crowded places alone.

She slipped through the door and stood looking around. She couldn't see anyone she knew, but she recognised Ethan on the far side of the room, standing with a small group of others. She realised that he was beside the girl with long red hair and the steam punk girl that had caught her eye when she had been in with Sarah.

"Oh," she thought, suddenly realising why Seth had seemed so familiar when she saw him that first time in his shop. The hugs guy.

Anxiety gnawed at the pit of her stomach. She didn't have the nerve to go over and speak to Ethan, even though she was certain that that was who Seth was meeting. She started to make her way to the bar, thinking she'd get herself a drink and hope that he arrived in the meantime.

"Hi." A hand touched her elbow and she looked round to see him standing there. He had, apparently, just appeared out of nowhere. Relief flooded through her as she smiled back.

"Hi. I was just going to get a drink. You want one?"

"Got one thanks." He held up his glass. "Only just got here myself. But I'll come with you."

He guided her through the throng. He was tall and fairly broad and she noticed that people tended to move aside for him, which amused her. She was tall but slight and getting through a crowd felt like fighting her way through the love children of a rugby scrum and a brick wall.

"Come over and meet the others," he said when she had got her drink, leading her, as she had correctly guessed, towards Ethan and his group.

"Seth!" The girl with pink hair leapt up from the edge of the cushioned bench. "We were beginning to think you weren't going to make it. Give me a special."

Seth opened his arms and she flung herself into his mammoth hug.

"Mm, better." She was laughing.

"Hey, my turn," said the auburn haired girl who was holding Ethan's hand. Seth hugged her too.

"Anyone else?" he asked.

"I'll have one." That was from the girl with dark hair who was leaning against the wall.

Ethan spotted Serena standing behind Seth and took a couple of steps forward.

"Hi Serena," he said. "It's good to see you."

"Hi," she responded.

"Don't mind the hug therapy," he said, gesturing at Seth. "That's what Gaia calls it. It's a bit of a Saturday night ritual."

"I'm lucky 'cos I have your hugs on tap, my love." The auburn girl had put her arms round Ethan. "Hi," she said to Serena.

"This is Gaia, my wife," Ethan said. Serena smiled.

"Serena," she said.

"Oh, you're the one who's helping Rose with her book," Gaia said, smiling enthusiastically. "Seth told us about you. All good," she added hastily, noticing Serena's worried look. "It's really nice to meet you. Are you settling in OK? It must be a hell of a change from London."

Gaia's brown eyes were warm and interested. Serena felt strangely at ease with both her and Ethan.

"Yeah, thanks," she said. "I prefer it to the city. It's quiet and so beautiful. And everyone I've met has been so lovely."

"We are lucky," Gaia agreed. "I've been here four years and I wouldn't want to be anywhere else. Hey, let me tell you who's who." She beckoned the pink haired girl over. "This is Tallie. She was at school with Ethan and Seth and Nikki." She gestured to the tall brunette who was talking animatedly to Seth.

"Hi," Tallie bubbled enthusiastically. "You're Serena, right? Actually, I think I've seen you a few times round town. You go in the library quite often, don't you?"

Serena nodded, surprised.

"Thought so. Before you get worried, I'm not some weirdo stalker. I work opposite, in the alternative clothes shop. Well, not always in the shop. I'm often in the workshop above. Can't help staring out every now and then."

"You mean most of the time," Gaia teased. Tallie grinned impishly.

"I'm just interested," she said.

"Just plain nosey, more like," the surfer dude guy said, putting his arm round Tallie and extending the other hand to Serena. "Rob," he continued as Tallie flapped him lightly. "Other half of the nut case here."

"I shall treat that with the disdain it deserves." Tallie stuck her tongue out at him. "As usual."

Gaia was laughing. "Welcome to the cabaret," she said.

"Anyway," said Tallie loudly, "as I was saying before I was so rudely interrupted," she poked Rob in the ribs, which just made him grin, "I'm often working upstairs and as I'm naturally observant, unlike *some* round here, I do notice people." Gaia and Rob exchanged a knowing glance before descending into laughter again. "Oh for goodness sake you two, stop picking on me." Tallie looked over at Serena. "See what I have to put up with?"

Serena couldn't help smiling back at her.

"Right," Tallie said decisively. She disentangled herself from Rob. "I'm going to have a sensible conversation with a sane person while you two lunatics try and gather yourselves back together." She sat down on the bench seat next to the tall black guy and motioned Serena to join her. "Serena, this is Howie. He can be sane sometimes so I think we're fairly safe."

Tallie was full of questions about what it was like to live in London and Serena found it quite easy to talk about for a change, about the general hustle and bustle, the markets and places to go out, the art galleries and museums.

"I wanted to go and study there," Tallie said ruefully, "but it didn't happen. Went to uni elsewhere. Oh well."

"What did you take?"

"Art and design," Tallie said. "That's what I do at Velvet Graveyard. Design and make their special range."

"Wow." Serena was impressed. "I love that shop. It's amazing."

Tallie smiled appreciatively. "Thanks. Hey, pop in sometime and I'll show you the workshop if you like."

"That'd be great."

Seth sat down opposite them and leaned forward.

"Great band, huh?" he said. Serena nodded.

"If you like them, you should come up next week as well," Howie said. "It's metal night. Going to be heavy."

"That sounds amazing." Serena was enthusiastic. "They have all sorts on here, don't they?"

Serena was swept along as the conversation turned to music and bands. As the next band started most of them ended up on their feet, close together in the dancing crowd. She caught Seth looking at her and grinned at him widely, glad that he had invited her. He smiled back and she remained aware of his gaze as she turned back to the stage and allowed herself to disappear into the music.

When the band finished Tallie insisted they sit for a while longer. Gaia asked for Serena's phone and fed all their numbers into it. When they finally left, Serena and Seth walked back toward the front with Nikki and Howie who both peeled off to his house part way down the road.

"Your friends are so lovely," she sighed.

"That's why they're my friends," he laughed.

She rolled her eyes. "Well, duh."

"Duh yourself." He nudged her elbow. "So, will you come up to the metal night next weekend?"

"Yeah," she said. "Sounds great."

Seth stopped as they reached Serena's turning. "Shall I walk up with you?"

She stopped too, shaking her head. "Thanks but I'll be fine. Thank you for inviting me tonight. It's been a while since… well, since I've had fun like that." "Felt that included," she finished silently.

"I'm glad you said yes." Seth looked genuinely pleased. "So… I'll see you soon then?"

"See you soon."

Chapter 5

Serena found herself invited to Tallie's place one evening the following week. Gaia was there too.

"Ethan and Rob are out. Some boy stuff," Gaia said. "It's a good excuse for a get together."

"Not that we really need an excuse." Tallie brought a big bowl of salted popcorn into the living room. Serena was looking at drawings that were spread across the coffee table.

"Are these yours?" she asked. Tallie nodded.

"New designs for the shop, mainly," she said. "I was playing earlier."

Gaia picked up a couple of sheets from the other side of the table. "This looks more like Storm," she said. "It is, isn't it?"

Tallie nodded again, then caught Serena's mystified look. Gaia handed over the papers so Serena could see.

"I draw comic strips," Tallie explained. "And I've finished a graphic novel about this character, Storm. I've been working on a sequel."

Serena studied the detailed pictures. Tallie certainly had talent.

"The local paper published some of the comic strips last year," Gaia said, sitting down and helping herself to popcorn. "They were really good."

"It was great to see them in print," Tallie said. "Maybe I need to serialise Storm. I'd love to get that published."

"It'd be too frustrating," Gaia said. "I read it in virtually one sitting. I couldn't have waited a week for each new instalment. It's addictive."

"You're so kind," Tallie said. "Well, I can dream."

"Could I read it?" Serena asked.

"If you really want to," Tallie said. Serena nodded. "I scanned all the strips and Rob magically made them into a coherent document so I'll email you a copy. It's probably easier that way." She looked pleased.

"Perfect," Serena said happily. "Can't wait."

"Rob's a computer wizard," Gaia said.

"A veritable one stop shop for all your technology needs," Tallie laughed. "Which is great for me because I have the technological ability of an eighteenth century dormouse."

"That much, huh?" Gaia smirked. Tallie threw a piece of popcorn at her.

"Like you're so up on it, missy."

"True. Without Rob, my website wouldn't exist."

"You have a website?" Serena was intrigued.

"Gaia makes the most stunning jewellery," Tallie told her. "Silver Wings. Here, I'll show you."

The three of them were still talking animatedly when Rob and Ethan got back. As Serena said goodbye and walked home she was hit with the realisation that this was what she had been looking for, been longing for since she had left the sea. Not just true love but to feel included, close to others, to be a real part of something bigger than her. It was bittersweet – to have found it, experienced it but to know that it would be hers only for the shortest of times.

It was a couple of days later that she settled down to read Tallie's book. Just as Gaia had warned, she couldn't stop, staying up ridiculously late to finish it. The next morning she phoned Lindy.

"Would you have a look at something for me?" she asked. "Sarah too. And tell me honestly whether you think it's got potential. A friend of mine wrote it. Drew it. Both. I couldn't leave it alone."

"Of course," Lindy said. "I'm intrigued. But I will be honest, so be prepared."

"Definitely. Thanks Lindy."

"You must have a Christmas tree." At the beginning of December, Tallie was clearly horrified that Serena was even considering not having one. "I'll go and dig it up myself if I have to! And put it up."

"I wouldn't argue if I were you," Rob said. "It'd be a lost cause."

"I agree," Gaia chimed in. "With both of you. You can't not have a tree. We'll do it for you. Go on Serena, you'll let us, won't you? It'll be fun."

"Do you really want to?" Serena sounded doubtful.

"Yeah." Tallie was nodding enthusiastically.

"In fact," Ethan said, "cheekily inviting myself, we could have a tree party. That's if you don't mind, Serena?"

"Sounds great. Are you sure..."

Tallie gave her a squeeze. "Definitely. It'll be great. Stop stressing. When? Saturday? Sunday? Soon, before you have a chance to change your mind."

"Just nod," Seth laughed. "Resistance is futile. And yes, Tallie, before you ask, I know where to find the perfect tree."

Saturday evening saw the six of them in Serena's living room, Rob and Seth stabilising the tree while Ethan and Serena sorted out the string of lights and Gaia and Tallie laid out the decorations they'd brought. It didn't take long to decorate and Tallie hugged Serena.

"Happy early Christmas," she said.

"Indeed," said Ethan, also giving her a squeeze. A static shock passed between them, making them both jump.

"Feeling electric tonight?" Rob quipped.

"Funny," Ethan replied. He smiled at Serena but there was a question in his eyes. He knew she'd seen it because she looked away quickly, and in that moment his suspicions were confirmed. She was different. Having to hide something. It reminded him of when he had met friends of Gaia's; how one of them had turned out to be very different indeed. One of the fey, in fact. A magical being, who had affected him in the same way Serena did. He wondered again just what he was picking up.

Serena moved over to re-examine the tree, disconcerted by Ethan's apparent intuition. It was almost as if he *knew*... Shrugging the thought off, she went out into the kitchen to get them all a drink. The phone rang.

"Hello my lovely." It was Sarah's voice. "How are you?"

"Great. You? We've just put up a tree..."

They chatted for a while and then Sarah said "Lindy's got something to tell you," and passed the phone over.

"Hi Serena, how're you? Your friend's book; I loved it. Would she like me to take it on?"

"Oh! Lindy, that's fantastic. I haven't even told her I sent it to you. She'll be so excited. Do you want to speak to her? She's in the other room."

"Great."

Serena hurried through and beckoned Tallie out, leaving the others mystified.

"Got an early Christmas present for you," she said. Tallie raised an eyebrow as Serena brandished the phone. "I sent Storm to my friend Lindy. She's a literary agent. She wants to take it on. Here." She thrust the phone into Tallie's hand. "Talk to her. I'm not kidding."

Serena took the drinks through, leaving Tallie in the kitchen and stalwartly refusing to say anything.

"She'll tell you in a minute," was all she'd give them.

Tallie came tearing through five minutes later and nearly knocked her over with a flying hug. "Thank you, thank you, thank you," she squealed. "Oh my God, thank you so much."

"You deserve it," Serena said.

"Would someone please put us all out of our misery," Rob interjected, "and tell us what the heck's going on?"

Tallie grabbed him next. "I have an agent," she yelled. "For Storm."

"It's really nearly Christmas!" Tallie flung herself down next to Gaia at the Old Hare the following Saturday. "When it gets to the middle of December, I feel like a kid again."

"Tallie, you are a kid," Seth said. Tallie stuck her tongue out at him. "My point exactly."

"Well, it's why you all love me," she pouted.

"Of course it is," Ethan said.

"We wouldn't want you any other way," Seth agreed.

"Have you lot finally decided what you're doing for Christmas?" Tallie went on.

"We're going up to Gaia's parents," Ethan said. "Christmas Eve, then coming back the day after Boxing Day."

"Can't wait," Gaia said, rubbing her hands together. "My sister's coming down too and I haven't seen her for nearly six months."

"I'm going to my Mum's," said Nikki. "Then my sister and I are going to meet her boyfriend and Howie, we've booked a cottage for four days down near the Lizard."

"We've got my parents coming to stay." That was Rob. "And then we're all going to Tallie's parents on Christmas Day."

"Yeah, and it'll be the first time that Gran's met your Mum and Dad," Tallie said, hugging Rob excitedly.

"Are you going up to Rose's, Seth?" Nikki asked. He nodded.

"Yes, and Sheila's coming over as well," he said. "It'll be a riot, especially by the evening when they're both a bit tipsy."

"I can't imagine Rose tipsy," Serena said.

"She's like Dennis the Menace's Granny," Ethan laughed.

"Believe me, she doesn't need to be tipsy for that." Seth was laughing too.

"What about you, Serena?" Gaia asked.

Serena swallowed. "Oh. Sarah's invited me to spend it with her and Lindy so... I was kind of hoping they might come down, but they're too busy. They do sometimes at Christmas, Sarah grew up here so she likes to catch up."

"Fab. I know I've never met them but they've been so nice to me on the phone," Tallie chipped in enthusiastically.

"And she escaped to London," Nikki said. "Lucky her."

"Well, I escaped a city to live down here, and I know where I'd rather be," Gaia commented.

"Yeah, London's fun, but it kinda makes you feel like you're on a treadmill after a while," Rob agreed.

Serena slipped away at that point, pretending she needed the ladies room, but really to avoid any more questions. She thought her real answer "I'm staying home alone with a bottle of wine and lots of chocolate" might cause some consternation, but she didn't want to become an object of pity. Sarah had in fact invited her to spend it with them, but she really couldn't face going back to London. Not because she thought she was likely to bump into Steve, but because even her friends there all had some link to him. It was just too emotive.

She stayed out of the way until the second band came on and most of her friends were on their feet, distracted by the music. It was a lively set and the whole place was stomping. Tallie and Gaia whirled her round with them until she was breathless and she felt the heaviness lift.

"This is my Christmas," she thought. "Early, with my friends."

Seth was unusually quiet as they walked home together. He continued along with her even when they got to where they normally parted company to go in different directions.

"Seth, you live over there, not up here," she said.

"I know," he replied.

"So why are you walking away from your place and not towards it?"

She made her voice light, but he looked serious. Worried. He shrugged. She stopped in front of him.

"Seth, what's bothering you? You've hardly said two words since we left the Hare. And now you're not going home."

"What are you doing for Christmas?" he asked.

"I already told you," she said, heart sinking.

"No, you didn't. You didn't answer the question."

"Sarah's asked me…"

"Yes, but you didn't say you were going. And the way you said it made me think you'd already decided not to. Which then made me think that you'll be on your own."

Serena's cheeks burned, the fragile happiness that she'd felt earlier evaporating. She turned away from him and started walking again, faster this time, fighting the urge to run. He kept pace with her easily.

"You don't need to say anything. You're not going, are you?" he continued.

"Get out of my head, Seth."

"I'm right, aren't I?"

"So what if you are?" she snapped.

"Whoa," he said. "Easy. I'm not trying to upset you."

"Fine. So go home."

But he didn't. They reached her cottage and he followed her through the courtyard.

"Serena. Please. It's just a question."

"Leave it alone."

"I just want to know if you're going to be on your own. And if you're happy with it. 'Cos if you're not…"

"If I'm not, what're you going to do?" she hissed.

"I could speak to…"

"Don't you dare say anything to Rose," Serena flared. "Just don't. I'm fine. I'm ecstatic in fact. I don't need pity and I don't need rescuing, thanks."

"That wasn't what I meant. I…"

But Serena had her door open and was half way through it. "Great evening. Thanks Seth."

"Serena…"

The door slammed shut. He saw the hall light go on as she left the kitchen and headed up the stairs.

"Damn," he thought and headed dejectedly home.

Serena unlaced her boots and flung them furiously into the corner. Her clothes flew angrily onto the chair as she got changed. It wasn't Seth she was mad at, it was herself. She knew she'd been nasty, when all he'd been trying to do was look out for her. And much as she hated to admit it, she would have loved to be with him and Rose and Sheila. In fact, just him... she crushed that thought quickly. By the time she'd been in the bathroom her anger had cooled and sadness was replacing it. She picked up her phone, thinking she would text him but she couldn't bring herself to. She didn't know what to say, where to even begin. Loneliness crashed over her once more and she climbed into bed, pulled the duvet up over her head and cried.

A few minutes later, the phone pinged, making her jump. Rubbing tears away, she checked the message.

I'm sorry. Didn't mean to upset you. Just want you to be OK.

"Oh, Seth," she thought. "I really don't deserve a friend like you."

No, I'm sorry, I was out of order. Please forgive me. Just took me by surprise is all.

It's fine. Serena, you're my friend. Can't help worrying about my friends. Don't like to think of you being on your own.

I'd rather that than go back to London. I can't face it. I'll be perfectly OK with wine and chocolate, honestly. Please don't say anything to Rose.

OK, I won't. Talk soon?

Really soon.

Two days later, in the late afternoon, Serena was typing in Rose's study when she heard the doorbell ring and a commotion in the hallway. Worried about Rose, she hurried to the top of the stairs to see Seth wrestling a large Christmas tree through the front door. She ran down.

"Need a hand?" she asked.

He looked round. "Oh, hi Serena. I think I've got it but if you wouldn't mind steering the top while I take it into the sitting room, that'd be great."

Once the tree was in Seth secured it upright in its heavy container.

"Phew," he said.

"That looked like a bit of a struggle," Rose commented drily.

"It's a big one this year," Seth said, standing back and looking at it.

"It's gonna look great."

"Do you want any tea first, or shall we begin?" Rose asked.

"Let's get to it," Seth said, rubbing his hands together. There were a couple of boxes in the corner which he lifted onto the table and opened. "Now, where're the lights?"

Rose went over to look with him, as Serena stood there feeling slightly awkward. "Rose, I'll just go and finish off and then I'll head home."

"Oh. Must you dear? Or would you stay a bit and help us with the tree? I'm not tall enough to be much use with the lights so I just have to watch while he ties himself in knots.'"

Seth rolled his eyes and laughed. "Of course. Because I'm that incompetent."

"Do you have other plans this evening, Serena? If not, would you stay and do the tree and eat with us? We'd both really like it if you would." Rose was sincere and Serena couldn't help herself.

"I'd love to," she said.

She went to save her document and shut down the computer. By the time she returned Seth had located the lights, so she helped him loop them round the tree. Then the three of them unwrapped the decorations and arranged them carefully. When it was done, Seth moved the tree back into the bay window and they all sat down to admire it.

"That looks gorgeous," Serena said.

"Yes it does. It never loses its magic," sighed Rose.

Seth just smiled.

Shortly after, they all went into the kitchen to eat.

"Sheila will be over tomorrow no doubt, when she sees it in the window," Rose said. "She'll want to do a full inspection."

"Let's hope it's up to scratch, otherwise I'll be for it on Christmas day," said Seth.

"I suspect you'll be for it anyway, dear." Rose was laughing. "You usually are."

He raised his eyebrows. "Nice to know there are some things you can rely on."

"Hmphh. So, Serena, what are you up to for Christmas?" Rose asked.

Serena shot Seth a sharp glare. He held his hands up, shaking his head.

"I didn't say anything, I swear," he said.

"Oh dear, have I spoken out of turn?" Rose looked really worried.

"No, no," Serena said quickly. "I'm sorry, Rose, it's fine. Seth and I were talking about it the other day, that's all."

"I just wondered if your friend was coming down. Or if you were going away? To see family."

"No," Serena said uncomfortably. "Family's not an option. Sarah and Lindy are at home, and Lindy's parents are visiting. They invited me to go." She stopped.

Rose looked at her sympathetically. "I hear a 'but' coming."

Serena looked down at her plate. She couldn't lie. "I've decided not to. Too many bad memories in London. Maybe it makes me a coward but I just don't want to go back." She looked back up at them. "So I'm not." Her voice held more than a little defiance.

"That's not cowardice, dear, that's self-preservation," Rose said. "We both understand that, really we do. You don't have to justify yourself. But it still begs the question, what are you going to do on Christmas day?"

Serena felt mortified, but she smiled over it and answered steadily. "Bottle of wine, big bar of chocolate, rubbish TV and pyjamas all day."

"Well," said Seth. "It's a plan."

"It is," said Rose. "And if it's what you want, that's fine. But if you'd like some company, I'd be delighted if you'd come and join us for Christmas. And I'm sure Seth would be too."

"Rose, you're so kind, but I can't take advantage of you like that. Both of you. It wouldn't be right."

"I don't understand. What advantage would you be taking exactly?"

"You and Seth already have plans and I know Sheila's coming. It's a family time. I wouldn't intrude on that."

Rose and Seth looked at each other and smiled.

"My dear, family is wonderful, but friends are the family that we choose for ourselves. That's why Sheila comes over at Christmas, because she's my closest friend and we like to spend time together. Seth and I are lucky to have you as a friend as well. That makes you part of our family. You wouldn't be intruding. We'd love to share Christmas with you."

"It's true," Seth said. "All Aunt Rose said. She's better with words than me but please, at least think about it."

Serena stared hard at the table, biting back tears. Antagonism and cruelty she could fight, but kindness tore her to shreds.

"I'm sorry, dear, I didn't mean to upset you." Rose sounded genuinely anxious, reaching out to take Serena's hand. Serena shook her head mutely, taking a deep breath.

"You haven't," she said after a moment. "But you're both so kind, it sort of overwhelms me."

"You're kind. And what you give out is what you get back, sooner or later. It's a rule of karma," Seth said. "Ethan's always going on about it."

"So's Sarah," Serena replied and smiled.

"So you will think about it?" Rose confirmed. Serena nodded.

"I will. And thank you."

Chapter 6

Serena woke early on Christmas morning. It was still dark outside and she was warm under her duvet but there was a restlessness within her that refused to let her go back to sleep. She felt such a strong pull from the sea and whether it was real or just sentimentality, because so many people were with families and loved ones at this time of year and she still missed hers, she couldn't deny it. In the shorter, darker days of winter when the beach was often empty at dawn and dusk, she was more likely to catch a glimpse.

"I miss you, Tia," she thought.

Throwing back the cover, she slipped out of bed and padded down to the kitchen to make a drink. She switched on the Christmas tree lights, enjoying the soft coloured glow that warmed the shadows. Then, having made up her mind, she went back upstairs to dress in warm layers before lacing herself into her boots, putting on her coat and hat and heading down to the beach. She left the tree on, shining in the window.

The sky was almost imperceptibly lightening as she reached the sea. It was still only seven and most of the houses remained in darkness. She hurried down onto the sand and across to the rocks, absentmindedly playing with the little potion bottle that she still wore on its chain round her neck. Clambering up to a high point she sat, wrapping the heavy fabric of her skirt round her legs. The waxing half moon glinted on cresting waves and the stars began to dim and fade as she scoured the horizon for signs of her kindred.

She lost track of time as she watched and waited, the sky reddening and then paling through pink to soft blue. Clouds ribboned across, dove grey and ivory in the low sun, while the silver of the moon on the water was replaced by mellow gold. Serena sighed.

"I love you," she called to them silently. "I don't forget."

She stretched her cold fingers and hugged her knees a little longer. Just as she was thinking that she really ought to get back, she heard someone call her name. She recognised Seth's tall frame, bundled up as he was in coat and hat.

"Happy Christmas," he said, waving.

She stood up and scrambled down from her perch back onto the beach.

"Happy Christmas to you," she said. He hugged her quickly.

"You're freezing," he noted. "How long have you been here?"

Serena looked at her watch. It was twenty past nine.

"Two hours, near enough," she said. "I woke up early and got the fidgets."

"You're lucky you're not a block of ice," he said. "Your fingers are blue."

She looked down. He was right and she hadn't even noticed. She was starting to shiver.

"You need to warm up," he said. "Come and have coffee with me."

"I should go home really," she said, her teeth chattering now.

"And you will – after. I'm glad I decided not to go running this morning and just come out for a blast of air or I wouldn't have seen you up here. You're in serious need of defrosting. Come on."

She had stuck her hands deep into her coat pockets, so he linked his arm through hers, tugged her back to his flat and sat her in front of the radiator. He disappeared into the kitchen and reappeared ten minutes later with tea and two plates of toast and scrambled eggs which he put on the coffee table. He pulled her to her feet.

"Come and eat something."

"You didn't have to do that," she muttered, embarrassed.

"Yeah, but I wanted to. I'm hungry and I bet you didn't eat before you came out, did you?"

She shook her head. He nudged her shoulder with his.

"Well then."

By the time they had eaten and talked for a while Serena had stopped shivering and the restless sadness that had filled her had dissipated. Seth was easy company and she was looking forward to going up to Rose's. She looked at the time, realising that it was heading for eleven thirty.

"I'd better get moving," she said. "I told Rose I'd be up about half past one to start cooking."

"I'll be up then as well. I can help."

She smiled, standing and putting her coat on. "Thanks. And thanks for breakfast."

"No problem."

"See you later then."

"Yeah." He walked down the stairs with her. "Umm, Serena?"

She turned, the question on her face.

"Aunt Rose was serious when she said you're welcome to stay over tonight. She wasn't just saying it because she thought she ought to."

Serena's cheeks burned. "She's been so kind to me. You both have. But I kind of feel I'm gate crashing your Christmas as it is. I don't want to…"

"…be in the way," he finished for her. "How did I know that was coming? Don't be daft. Do you really think Rose invites people if she doesn't want to?"

Serena shook her head, remaining mute.

"We'd both like it if you stayed. There's loads of room, you know that. Then you'll be able to relax and have a drink and not have to worry about driving back. Just think about it, OK? Bring your toothbrush and give yourself the option." He ducked down so he could look at her. "OK?" He was grinning like a loon.

"OK," she relented as she stepped out the door. "OK. I'll see you later."

Seth's candour and humour had lifted Serena's mood and she couldn't get the smile off her face as she showered, dressed and loaded the car. In spite of herself, she packed a small overnight bag, telling herself that she wouldn't use it but at least she could tell Seth honestly that she had considered his aunt's invitation. Even as she told herself that, she could feel her resolve wavering. It would be so nice not to be alone.

Sheila had already arrived when Serena got to Rose's and the two of them welcomed her in as though she was family.

"I'm so, so glad to see you dear," Rose said, hugging her. "Happy Christmas."

"And to both of you," Serena replied. She hung up her coat. "Right. I'll get cracking."

"Have something to drink first," Rose said. "There's no rush."

"You look beautiful," Sheila commented. "Tall and elegant. That dress is gorgeous on you."

Serena blushed. Rose prodded her friend.

"Not like us, eh?" she laughed. "Short and stout. Like two teapots."

"Neither of you are stout," Serena scolded them, smiling. "Look at you. Like two birds, you are. Just willow... wands rather than trees."

Sheila laughed. "Aren't you a gem?"

"I already told you that," Rose said.

"Right, that's it," Serena said. "I am unloading the car and going to the kitchen before you embarrass me anymore."

She left the two of them chatting in the sitting room and brought the boxes in. Putting the parcels under the tree, she took the others through to the kitchen and began to sort out the dinner. Rose had already put the turkey in the oven and Serena added the potatoes and parsnips she had prepared the previous day. She heard the door open and voices raised in greeting and knew that Seth had arrived. She busied herself putting fresh water on the vegetables, suddenly feeling shy and overwhelmed at being included in the Christmas that Seth and Rose and Sheila usually shared. Minutes later, Rose came through to find her.

"You're not supposed to be slaving in here while we're all enjoying ourselves out there. Do you need a hand with anything right now or can you come through?"

Serena nodded. "It's all OK for now."

"Good. I've got some wine to toast the day."

"I might just stick to soft drinks, thanks. Got to drive later."

Rose looked at her. "You don't, you know. There's plenty of room. I wish you'd stay. And not feel awkward about it."

"I... Seth said..."

"I told Seth I thought I might have upset you by extending that invitation. He said it was more likely that you thought you'd be in the way. You're not. You're far more than an employee Serena, I hope you know that."

"Thank you," Serena whispered. Rose came over and gave her a squeeze.

"Go on, stay. It'd make my day, and Seth's."

Serena hesitated. "OK," she said finally. "If you're sure."

"Good." Rose smiled. "Now would you kindly get four glasses out of the cupboard and bring them through while I procure the wine."

Seth and Sheila were laughing as Rose and Serena returned to the sitting room. Seth came and took the glasses from Serena.

"Hi again," he said. His gaze made Sheila laugh.

"Yes, she is gorgeous, isn't she?"

"Sheila, stop it," Serena said, reddening furiously. Sheila laughed even harder.

"It's the truth."

"Well," Seth said, grinning. "I'm surrounded by three beautiful women all day. I must've been good this year because Santa's been really kind."

Now glassless, Serena put her hands to her flaming cheeks and shook her head. Seth opened the bottle and started to pour. He looked up when only the fourth glass was empty.

"Er, Serena, what do you want to drink?"

"Keep pouring, Seth," Rose said. "She's staying."

And although she tried desperately to fight it, the look of delight on his face swept Serena's breath away.

A little later, Serena was busy in the kitchen, turning the roast and topping up the water around the steaming Christmas pudding. She was liquidizing the soup that she'd made for a starter the day before when Seth appeared.

"Can I help?" he asked. "The three of us are feeling very guilty that you're in here on your own."

"I'm quite happy, honestly," she said, giving the soup a last blast before she decanted it into a saucepan. "I'm just glad to be here."

"We're all glad you're here," he said sincerely. "Here, let me wash that up at least. And then give me something useful to do."

They cooked the rest together and eventually Rose and Sheila migrated through to sit at the kitchen table, sipping sparkling wine and talking. Dinner was hilarious. Rose and Sheila teased Seth mercilessly but he clearly didn't mind, batting most of it back at them and generally giving as good as he got. Serena spent a lot of time laughing. She couldn't remember the last time she'd laughed like that; in fact, she couldn't remember ever laughing like that at all. The mer didn't laugh. And Christmas with Steve's family, though pleasant, had been a fairly staid affair. She'd always had to be on her best behaviour.

Afterwards, Seth and Serena cleared up and then he insisted that she go and sit with Sheila and Rose while he finished off. She tried to argue but he hustled her out.

"You've done most of the work. Go, sit, it's my turn."

They opened parcels next. Sheila rubbed her hand together with glee as Seth unwrapped the one from his sister. Rachel apparently had a wicked sense of humour, and even now liked to wind him up. A bright orange tie with a moose on it and a personal CD compilation of girly pop and trance were amongst the delights she had included. Seth just raised his eyebrows and laughed.

"It goes both ways," Rose assured Serena.

"Yeah, she's gonna love the cocoa and the slippers," Seth agreed. "Just a reminder that she'll always be older than me."

"You will have to play that CD before seven, dear," Rose said. Seth shuddered.

"One track. Now. To get it over with." He got up and went over to his aunt's CD player.

"What happens at seven?" Serena wondered aloud.

"Oh, we Skype Diana and Rachel and the rest of the family. It's late morning for them but it's a good time all round," Rose said.

Seth pressed play. "Apologies in advance," he said.

They managed a couple of tracks but it was obvious that Rachel had selected the most formulaic, synthesised and repetitive songs that she could possibly find.

"Please, put on something that we can dance to," Sheila said. "A waltz, preferably."

Seth quickly located a CD from Rose's collection and put it on.

"Ah, that's better," said Rose as Strauss filled the room.

"Madam," Seth said, extending his hand to Sheila. "Would you care to dance?"

It made Serena smile as she watched him whirl first Sheila and then Rose expertly round the room. The he came over to her. "Would you?" he asked.

"I have no idea how," Serena said in horror. "I've never waltzed in my life and I've got two left feet."

"Don't look so terrified," he grinned. "It's easy, I'll show you. If I can, you can."

"Absolutely, dear," agreed Sheila. "One, two, three, step back, side, together. Follow Seth, you'll be fine."

Reluctantly she stood and he began to move, instructing her gently as they went. She did get the hang of it fairly quickly and Sheila and Rose began to applaud.

"So how come you waltz so well?" she asked.

"My Gran insisted," Seth told her.

"Yes, she was a bit of a stickler for correctness, my sister," Rose said. "All gentlemen should know the waltz was what she always used to say."

"And ladies," Seth reminded her. "I haven't forgotten all the times she made Rachel and me waltz round her kitchen."

Serena couldn't help laughing at that. The waltz ended. "You learn fast," Seth said. His arm lingered round her waist. She didn't move either, trying to ignore how it made her feel.

"I'm impressed," said Rose.

Serena pursed her lips, an idea springing to mind.

"Since I've just learned the way you like to dance," she said thoughtfully to the two ladies, "perhaps you'd like to learn how we do."

Such a look of incredulity crossed their faces that Seth collapsed into a chair laughing. Serena stood there, grinning.

"You know," Seth said finally, "I think that's a really good idea. It's only fair. Hang on."

He disappeared into the hall and returned with his MP3 which he plugged into the CD player. "What do you think?" he asked Serena mischievously. "Machine Head? Metallica?"

"Be kind," said Serena. "Nice bit of Bullet, I reckon."

"Oh yeah." He set it up. "We'll show you first."

Serena and Seth swung their heads down, hair flying as they started a modified form of headbanging to the screaming guitars. Then they both started laughing again at the horrified look on Sheila's face. Rose, however, was grinning. She stood up.

"Right. I'll try anything once. Any advice?"

"Don't try and move your neck too far. Start gently and slowly, like this." Serena demonstrated. "And when you're comfortable with that, you can add a bit of a swing side to side."

Rose tried, somewhat stiffly but to Seth's great approval. "Come on Sheila," she said. "My head hasn't fallen off yet."

"Oh, fine, but expect an earful tomorrow if it starts my arthritis up," Sheila grumbled, but she got up and had a go.

Seth went over and hugged them both afterwards. "I love you two so much," he said. "You are so awesome."

Serena watched, her heart overflowing, especially when he met her eyes over the tops of their heads and smiled.

"Right," Sheila said, sitting down. "I think I need another glass of wine."

"Coming up," said Serena and headed for the kitchen.

"Goodness, look at the time," she heard Rose exclaim.

When she returned, Seth had set his laptop up on the coffee table and was sitting on the sofa between the other two making the connection to his family. Serena poured them all a drink and then sat in the armchair out of the way.

"Happy Christmas!" came a disembodied chorus from the laptop.

"And you!"

"Oh my goodness gracious, Scarlett, look how you've grown."

"How are you all? It's lovely to see you there, Sheila."

"Thanks so much for the music, Rache, just my thing as always!"

"Oh, you're so welcome, little bro. See, I've got my ultra-sexy slippers on."

"They're so you. What do you reckon, Chris?"

"Oh yeah, Can't wait to get 'em off later."

"How's your new job, Diana?"

"Good thanks, very different but lovely people. Starting to get to grips with it now."

"Have you finished your book yet, Aunt Rose? Or shouldn't I ask?"

"Well actually, it's coming on in leaps and bounds thanks to Serena. Oh."

Serena suddenly found herself the focus of three pairs of eyes.

"Oh my dear, I'm so sorry, we got quite carried away there."

"Yeah," Seth said contritely. He stood up and beckoned her over. "Come and meet my family."

Serena had been shaking her head, indicating that she was fine, but she didn't want to turn Seth's invitation down and appear rude. Rose and Sheila shifted in opposite directions leaving her a space next to him.

"Hi," she said self-consciously to the four faces on the screen.

"This is Serena," Rose said. "That's Diana, Rachel, Chris and Scarlett."

"Hi," they said.

"Have you actually managed to make sense of Auntie's study?" Rachel asked. "Good grief, you're brave to take that on."

"You'd be amazed if you saw what Serena's managed to do," Sheila sniggered. Seth was nodding emphatically.

"Don't tell me you've actually managed to find the files?" Diana said. "They've been AWOL for years."

"Not only has she found them, she's sorted through a lot of them and is typing them into manuscript form," Rose said delightedly.

"Lord, you must be an angel. Or a saint."

"No, she's my elf," Rose said, giving Serena an affectionate squeeze.

Once the Canadian contingent had signed off Rose and Sheila leant back, looking tired.

"I'm going to make us a cup of tea and some nibbles," Serena said, jumping up and heading for the kitchen. Seth disconnected his laptop.

"I'll go and give her a hand," he said.

"Thanks dear," Rose replied. She and Sheila smiled at each other as he left the room.

"Tell me again why they aren't together," Sheila said.

"I have no idea," Rose sighed.

Once they had eaten, Sheila headed home. After she had hugged them all, Seth insisted on walking her back up the road and seeing her into her house, despite her protestations. When he returned they sat talking until Rose said she had to go to bed.

"Thank you so much for such a lovely day," Serena said.

"I'm so glad you were here, dear," Rose replied. "And that you decided to stay. Please don't feel you have to get up early. We certainly won't be."

Seth enfolded his aunt in a massive hug. "Thanks, Auntie," he said and followed her out of the room. He returned shortly after with two glasses and some red wine.

Serena was sitting at the end of the sofa with her legs curled under her. The light was soft in the room, just a small lamp and the Christmas tree glowing in the window. She looked so peaceful, so stunning that he stopped in the doorway just to gaze at her. He was so glad she was there and yet a little melancholy was creeping in. He wasn't ready to feel how she made him feel and yet he didn't want to stop feeling it. It had been a perfect day and he really didn't want it to end. Eventually he walked over.

"Can I tempt you?" he said.

She smiled and nodded. "Thanks."

He handed her a glass and sat down on the sofa with her.

"It's been a perfect day," she said, echoing his thoughts.

"Yeah, it has. Best Christmas for a long, long time."

"Your family are so lovely. So much fun."

He smiled with a sigh. "Yeah. They are. Most of them anyway."

"Oh." Serena stared at him intensely and he could somehow sense that she felt the same melancholy that he did. He felt her watching him as he looked away, gazing at the tree, his long fingers playing restlessly with the stem of the glass. She continued. "That kind of invites questions, but I don't want to ask if it's something you'd rather not go into. Christmas can be hard enough, even when it's great."

"You can ask. You understand what it's like to have sad things round your edges."

"Is it something to do with why your Mum and sister are in Canada and you're here? Trouble between you?"

"No. Not with them." Seth's face tightened. "With my father. The distance helps them, I think. My sister's been in Canada for eight years, she met Chris at university and went out there with him after they graduated. They got married three years later. My mother emigrated three years ago, give or take. Just before Scarlett was born."

"You miss them." Serena was sympathetic.

"Yeah, I do," he agreed, "but I went out for the wedding and again after Mum moved. Scarlett must've been about six months old then."

"Weren't you tempted to stay? Out there, I mean."

"Not really," Seth said contemplatively. "It's lovely where they are near the Rockies, really spectacular, but I like it here."

"Hard not seeing them though. Especially when you're so obviously close."

"Yeah, but we Skype each other fairly often. It's good."

"It must've been tough for your mum. With you and your sister on opposite sides of the Atlantic."

He nodded. "It was. It took her a while to decide to go out there but I think it was the best thing for her. I told you that she divorced my father. She couldn't put all the crap behind her when she was still here, and God knows she coped with it long enough."

"That doesn't sound good."

Seth looked at her. "Sorry. Moaning."

"Please. That's hardly a moan. You can try a rant if you want."

"My father was a bastard. Really nasty. Not to Rachel and me so much, he pretty much ignored us as long as we kept quiet, so that's what Mum made sure of, that we were otherwise occupied most of the time. But to her he was a total control freak, manipulative, emotionally and verbally abusive. I didn't realise how bad it was for her until much later. She left him when I was ten and Rache was fourteen, and he took her to the cleaners, made the divorce unbelievably difficult, left us with pretty much nothing. She built a life for us here but put herself on hold until we were both adults. And really settled. Which took a while in my case. It's her turn now."

"I'm sorry," Serena said, horrified. "That's awful. Your father... do you...?"

"No. Haven't seen or spoken to him since the day we left and I have no desire to either." Seth spoke vehemently, feeling the old anger rising even now, so many years later. "He could be dead for all I care."

"Seth, I'm so sorry," Serena said quietly. "It must be so hard."

Seth felt his face soften at her words, allowing her presence to calm him, bring him back to himself and the present. "No, I'm sorry," he said. "Shouldn't have been raising my voice to you."

"I did say you could rant," she reassured him. "And that's just crap. No one should have to go through that."

He shrugged and gave her a half smile. "We all have baggage," he said. "And I had it easy really. Don't know why I still let him get to me, but hey."

"He was your father and he wasn't a father. That'd get to anybody."

He shrugged. "I suppose. Families, relationships, they're tough, I know you know the score. And thanks for letting me vent. Now it's your turn."

She looked at him, puzzled.

"I know about your divorce, but you never mention your family. Well, only the once and it was obviously difficult for you. It's fine if you want to tell me to sod off, but I just get the feeling sometimes that whatever it is about them really gets to you."

"Oh." Serena was obviously flustered. "Um, I don't really know where to start."

Her eyes were a dark blue-grey that he wanted to swim in, but she looked so desperate that he put his hand out and squeezed hers. "I'm sorry. Forget it."

"No, it's OK." She hesitated. "It sounds bizarre and it's hard to explain. Let's just say that I grew up in a pretty insular community and their beliefs and lifestyle just didn't... well I didn't fit with them from a fairly young age. I was always a bit of a disappointment to them, especially when I fell for Steve. Outsiders are rarely welcomed and then only if they fully accept the creed and live according to the code."

"Was it like a cult or something?"

"Not a cult, no, just a very closed group with rigid opinions and closed minds. So when I decided to leave and chose to marry Steve, well, that was the final nail in the coffin. We haven't spoken since."

"Because you married someone they didn't like?"

"Not just that. I think some of them tried to understand but in the end my leaving was really a betrayal of everything they believe and hold dear. I'm a disturbing presence to them. They can't change and I can't go back. It's easier for everyone that we disown each other. So that's what we've done."

"That's harsh." Seth ran his hands through his hair. "That's really harsh."

"I miss them. And I still love them, and I'm sure they feel the same about me. But some things are insurmountable, and we just disappoint each other when we're together. So in a lot of ways it's better like this."

She seemed so calm but he could see that she hurt, even though she covered it well.

"You're a braver and better person than I am," he said.

She shook her head. "No. It's totally different. There was no abuse for a start, and also I made the decision to leave, not them. My choice, my responsibility. As was my marriage. What happened to your family was not your fault at all."

"Yeah, maybe, but I didn't handle it well. Not like you have. I was hideous to my mother when I was in my teens." The regret and guilt still bit as deeply as ever. "Staying out late, coming home drunk, with a police escort on a few occasions. Blaming her when it wasn't her fault at all. I should have been better. I was as bad as him."

"No Seth, you weren't. You were young and your father let you down, all of you." Serena turned on the sofa to face him. She leaned forward, her face sincere. "Even though your mother was the one who left, it doesn't sound like he was ever there for any of you like he should have been. That's going to cause issues and everyone deals with it differently. Anyhow, teens are supposed to rebel, it's in the rules. And now it's in the past. You're all still so close, I can see how much you love each other. That's what's important."

Seth sighed. She seemed to know just what to say, seemed to know him almost better than he knew himself. "Serena, how are you such a good, kind person after all the crap you've been through?"

"I could ask you exactly the same thing. Especially since your father was such a toad. You don't take after him at all."

"I'm not that great. Really. Even now. But I don't ever want to be like him. It's my worst nightmare that I'll end up like him."

The thought was a heavy weight that hung on him, pulling him down. Evidently she could see that and she reached out to him this time.

"That'll never happen. You're not like that, you're not that person, Seth. You couldn't be if you made it your life's mission. You're kind and thoughtful and generous. You don't manipulate and use people, you look out for them and take care of them. You aren't your father, you're you."

He looked at her, light pouring out of her and enveloping him. Tentatively he took her hand, wanting to be closer. "You're magic, did you know that? I think I need to hug you. That is, if you'll let me."

"Tallie and Gaia will be jealous," she said, obviously trying to make him smile. It worked.

"They'll get over it." He moved toward her, put his arms round her. "Thank you."

They stayed like that, talking quietly until the early hours, finally heading up to bed at about one thirty. He kissed her cheek.

"Happy Boxing Day," he said. "Sleep well."

New Year's Eve saw them all at the Old Hare after a raucous dinner at Tallie and Rob's. The place was crammed and dancing was reduced to bouncing on the spot, given that they were packed tighter than sardines. Somehow they had managed to secure a table and eventually Gaia, Tallie, Serena and Nikki ended up standing on the bench seat at the back, partly to be able to see the band and partly to stop themselves from getting flattened.

"It's alright for you lot," Tallie said to the guys. "You're all really tall and people don't tread on you."

Howie laughed. At six foot two he was the tallest but the other three weren't that far short of him.

"Shouldn't have stopped growing so quickly then, should you? Only got yourselves to blame."

Nikki put her arms round his neck from behind. "Suddenly I feel a whole lot steadier," she said. "How hard do you think I should grip?"

"You grip, you get flipped," Howie threatened with a grin. "Don't tempt me."

"Still, it's a better view from up here," Gaia said. "And at least we can breathe."

"Maybe we should come up there with you," Ethan suggested.

"Hey, no fair, we'd be squished again *and* lose our height advantage," Tallie said. "This is the only way I ever get to feel tall. You lot stay down there where you belong."

"Fighting talk sweetie? I might just have to tickle you for that." Rob grabbed Tallie round the waist and made her squirm.

"I'm going to brave going to the bar now," said Seth. "It may only be eleven fifteen but it could take half an hour. What does everyone want for New Year?"

"I'll come and give you a hand," Howie said.

Serena stood swaying to the music and looking out across the room. It was full of laughter and excitement, people singing and stomping and talking, greeting each other, shaking hands, embracing, kissing. It reminded her exactly why she was here. What she had coveted so much when she was still mer. Companionship, affection, love.

Excitement was building as midnight approached, the band whipping everyone up into a frenzy. Someone had hooked up the radio to the PA system so that they could all count down and hear Big Ben ring in the New Year. As it struck, the cheers and whistles broke out and Serena found herself hugging Tallie and Nikki and Howie all at once before Ethan grabbed her, then Gaia. Then Rob and Tallie were kissing, and Nikki and Howie, and Gaia and Ethan and she was standing there in between them all with Seth looking at her from the other side of the table. His eyes burned into her. Her heart turned over but she tried to ignore it, saw him come towards her, reaching out a hand to her. He steadied her as she stepped onto the table and over to him. The next thing she knew, he had lifted her down and enfolded her in his arms.

"Happy New Year," he said and didn't let go.

Chapter 7

The Christmas and New Year celebrations shook Seth. Not the festivities so much as the way he suddenly found himself thinking about Serena; almost wishing that the friendship they had could become something else. He banished those thoughts immediately but they had a nasty habit of sneaking back in when he wasn't completely focussed on something else. And on the occasions that he allowed himself to follow the path they took, things inevitably ended badly. He didn't want to go there again. He decided to give himself a bit of space to get his head round it all.

After New Year Serena buried herself in work. January was hard because no matter how she tried to ignore it, she and Steve had got married at the beginning of February and the memory of her wedding day haunted her more and more as it approached. Helping Rose to sort through her recipes and pick the best ones was a good distraction. They did a lot of experimenting, mixing, cooking and testing. Sheila found herself the recipient of some interesting food while Gaia and Tallie were willing guinea pigs in some alternative spa days.

"I could eat this lip gloss," Tallie said.

"If you must, dear," Rose laughed. "It's only glycerine and juice from some frozen blackberries.'"

Serena saw very little of Seth for a few weeks, bumping into him a few times on the beach in the early mornings when she had gone down to the sea and he had been out for a run and meeting up at The Old Hare on Saturdays. He had also been roped in as a test subject and she had to laugh at his descriptions of what Rose had insisted he try.

She missed him more than she was prepared to admit to herself and that didn't help her mood. It was another good reason to hide in Rose's

paper mountain. Out of the blue one Sunday morning he texted her.
Want to go for a walk?
Would love to but I'm up to my ears in half chopped vegetation.
Another test of Auntie's alchemy?
How did you guess?
Need a hand?
That'd be great. I'll pay you in tea!

Seth appeared about twenty minutes later and couldn't help laughing as he came in. Every surface in her kitchen was covered in bottles, jars, bowls, implements and the remains of multiple peelings and choppings.

"Holy crap, it looks like a battleground in here," he said. "Did you take on the Triffids and lose? Or are you trying to create a monster?"

"If I had the energy I'd make a very rude sign at you right now," Serena grimaced. "But I don't, so I won't."

"I'm not really laughing," he said. "Well, I am, but I brought chocolate biscuits so I've earned the right."

"Lifesaver," Serena said. "You're forgiven. I'll put the kettle on." She held up stained and sticky hands.

"*I'll* put the kettle on." Seth headed for the sink. "And then you can enlighten me as to exactly what it is you're trying to do."

Later, after he had helped her with the infused honey, the cough syrup, the preserved lemons and the clean up, they sat down at the kitchen table to have a sandwich.

"I know Rose appreciates you, but you really do go above and beyond the call of duty," he said.

"Actually it's good fun," she replied sincerely. "And I've learned so much. It's not just the remedies and recipes but all the folklore that's just fascinating. And the more I learn the more I realise I don't know. There's even a language of flowers. The Victorians used to use flowers to send secret messages to each other. Like love letters but with petals, not ink."

"Wow," he said. "Well, it's a fairly safe bet what a rose would mean. Or a forget-me-not. What do you suppose a Venus fly trap would stand for?"

"Hmm, not sure, but I know someone I'd like to send one to. That or a Titan Arum."

"Are they those stinking ones that smell like rotting flesh?"

"Yup."

"I wonder who that would be heading for."

"I'd like to aim it at his head," she said vehemently. "And the Venus fly trap could deal with another part of his anatomy."

"Remind me not to cross you. You can be quite scary."

"Oh, ha, funny. 'Cos I'm so fierce."

"I'm not going to test that statement."

"Best not." She shook her head, wishing that Steve hadn't entered her head. Her mood fell. Seth seemed to sense it because his voice became serious.

"I've no doubt he deserves worse than a Venus Fly Trap. Want to tell me what happened? Put some light on the dark stuff?"

It still disconcerted her how easily he could read her thoughts. "You really want to know?"

"It hurts you. It matters to me."

"OK. I guess." She hesitated. "I met him here. He had an accident and I helped him. We fell for each other then, it was very fast, very intense. He's that sort of person, all or nothing. We got married about six months later. And it was great for a year and then not so great. He met someone and had an affair. We managed to get past that, just, but then he realised that monogamy was not for him. He wanted his freedom so he could be with other people, well, other girls and I realised that I'd made a mistake."

"A big mistake," she thought. "One so huge you can't imagine it."

"His loss," Seth said. "Some people just don't know when they're lucky. If it was me, I would have stayed fallen." He smiled but his eyes were serious, intense. She felt her colour rise and laughed a little desperately.

"Oh for goodness sake stop it, you're making me blush. Anyway we split after that, he was with someone else anyhow, but because we had so many mutual friends I knew that he was still screwing around behind her back too. He filed for divorce so that was the end of it. And that was really why I needed to get away from London. To get away from all of that."

"He must be really stupid." Seth's voice was quiet as he shook his head. "Really, really stupid."

Serena felt she needed to break the seriousness. And what Seth's genuine concern was making her feel. "Yeah, well. What about you? A string of gorgeous girls at your beck and call?"

He shouted with laughter at that. "Oh, I wish. Hardly. No. I have," he corrected himself, "had a girlfriend. On and off, but we're not seeing each other now. For the moment anyway. Or possibly for good. Who knows?"

"That sounds…" She paused, searching for the right word.

"Complicated," he finished for her. "Yeah, it is."

"Why is it?" she asked. He stared at her. "Sorry. I shouldn't have asked. It's none of my business."

"No, it's a fair question," he said. "I've asked myself the same thing on more than one occasion."

"Did you find an answer? You don't have to tell me if you don't want to."

He sighed. "You really sure you want to be my ear? Again? You'll probably think I'm an idiot."

She moved round the table to sit next to him. "Hey, you've just listened to me moan and groan, not that I expect you to do that. The moaning and groaning that is. But isn't that what friends do? Listen? Swap demons. And that particular demon, you know, the love one, it makes fools out of most of us. I guess we both know that."

So he told her about Jessica, and how she had whirled into his life like a tornado and set him spinning, then dropped him like a stone for some other guy. And then come running back, begging forgiveness when it fell apart, only to do the same again a few months later, reappearing just as he'd got himself together and met someone else. She had wreaked havoc with that relationship and with him, leaving him again when something better came along. And how she lived in London now but when she came back she would usually expect to be with him if it suited her.

"It's been the same for nearly three years," he said, "on, off, on, off, and I don't seem to be able to stop myself. It's like an addiction. Even though I know it's not good and it's not going to end well, I can't seem to say no to her. She's like a drug. God, that sounds pathetic." He sighed, drumming on the table with long fingers. Tentatively Serena reached out and put her hand over his.

"Not pathetic, no," she disagreed. "That sounds like someone who really cares and someone who maybe doesn't care quite so much. I'm sorry," she added, as a shadow crossed his face. "But she doesn't seem to appreciate how much it costs you to be there for her like that, over and over again."

"That's what Ethan tells me. He finds her really hard to tolerate, in fact all the others do," Seth said. "Maybe I'm just a mug."

"No, you're a kind and open hearted person," she dissented. "Don't you think you deserve better?"

He shrugged and looked away, though he left his hand where it was under hers.

"Who knows?"

"Ethan. Me. You." There was silence for a moment. "How does she make you feel? What makes you want to go back even when you know what's likely to happen?"

"How does she make me feel? Hmm. Excited, desired, on edge, off balance. We have a very, umm, physical chemistry." He stopped. "Now I'm blushing, but it's the truth. And she's so wild but she can be so fragile. I can't help but look after her. It kinda hurts but it's good too. Sometimes. And when I've tried to step away, say no, well, the spirit is willing but the flesh is weak. She knows how to hook me back in. And I'm still blushing."

"Yeah, right, 'cos I'm so innocent I don't know what you're talking about." Serena smiled at him before she continued. "Does she make you feel loved?"

"You ask some tough questions.'"

"Sorry. I'll stop."

"No, it's good. Makes me honest about things that I lie to myself about. No, she doesn't make me feel loved. And I know she doesn't love me. She doesn't settle or get tied down. She's a butterfly."

"One more question?" she asked. He nodded. "Do you love her?"

It took him a while to process that one. Eventually he moved his hand but only to wind his fingers through hers.

"I don't know," he said. "I told her I did, back when we were first together. I thought I did, but now I really don't know."

He was studying her as he spoke and there was something in his look that made shivers run through her. Good shivers. She looked down at their hands, still entwined.

"See, what I feel... felt for her was more of a head rush. No time to think. She's there and then she's not. The first time, and the second, I really wanted her back. Maybe that was love. But now, I don't know. She's difficult and unpredictable and it feels more like a game than anything real. I don't think it's enough anymore. I want more than that. I feel different now, I'm not really sure about anything since..." He stopped. "I'm sorry, going on like that."

"You're not," she said, wishing that he'd finished the sentence. That the end had been "since I met you."

As the end of January approached, despite her efforts Serena could feel her mood slipping. She felt more and more despondent, not just because her anniversary was another reminder of her doom but also because it made her think more of her sea family and she missed them keenly. Their calm objectivity, their measured responses, their cool detachment yet unfailing constancy. No matter how she had longed for human emotion, at times it was overwhelming. She made a little posy of rosemary, the herb for remembrance, and took it down to the beach. It was a wild evening, the waves wind tossed and white as she stood up on the rocks, remembering how she and her sisters had danced through the water laughing, catching the currents and riding the rip tides. She threw the rosemary as far as she could.

"I still remember," she whispered. She made her way across the rocks to sit above the hidden cove where she had come ashore. When she closed her eyes she could almost feel Tia close by.

She was glad that the anniversary fell on a weekday so that she could lose herself in work. She started early and finished late, but despite her best efforts, she couldn't keep the melancholy at bay and it only increased as she drove home. She only realised that she'd left her laptop at Rose's when she picked up the message on her land line. She half contemplated going back, but couldn't face it.

"I won't need it tonight," she told herself. "Bath, food, film, bed. Tomorrow will be better. Damn Steve. Damn our wedding day."

She went up and had a hot shower, got into some clean clothes and tried to decide what film to watch. Some of her DVDs were still in a box in the living room, so she put on some music and started to look through. She had forgotten that the photos were in with them.

Against her better judgement and wishing she had the strength not to, Serena pulled the photo album out of the box and flicked through it. Even though she was disillusioned and hurt by what Steve had done and angry at the way he had betrayed her, she couldn't help that falling, heartsick sensation when she saw the pictures of them together, with friends, holding hands, smiling. The pain of her abandonment came crashing over her like a wave once more. Forcing herself to her feet, she stumbled into the kitchen, slamming the album onto the table and blindly putting the kettle on in an attempt to recreate normality and stave off the desolation that threatened to overwhelm her.

"Dammit," she yelled, wiping away the tears that would no longer be denied. "He's not worth it. You know that. Get a grip." Her hands tightened instinctively on the edge of the counter and she stood frozen as the kettle sang through its boiling and then switched itself off. She remained there, unable to do anything but breathe and cry, the ocean pouring from her as she cursed her foolish heart and wished that it didn't hurt so much. It was then that the knock came at the kitchen door.

"Damn," Serena thought, frantically trying to dry her eyes. She couldn't pretend she wasn't there; the door was half glass and she was clearly visible. Taking a deep breath and swiping away the remaining tears, she turned around and headed over to open it.

Seth was on the other side of it smiling, with her laptop in his hands.

"Hi," he said as the door opened. "I promised Auntie that I'd drop this off. Hey, what's wrong?"

"Thanks," Serena managed to get out.

"Serena, what's the matter? What's happened?"

She took the laptop and put it on the kitchen table. "I'm OK. Bad day, that's all."

He stepped in and saw the photo album. Something clicked. "Past catching up with you?"

She nodded and took a deep breath. He heard it catch. He took a step closer to stand beside her.

"Want to talk about it?" he asked gently. She shook her head, wrapping her arms around herself as if they were the only thing holding her together.

"That's OK," he said. "Here. Come here." He put his arms around her, hugging her gently. "I know it hurts. I know. But it will get better."

She started to cry then, silent sobs racking through her, but all she could say was "Sorry."

"You don't have to say sorry," he murmured, stroking her hair. "It's OK."

Gradually her tears subsided. It was a while before she could speak.

"Seth, I'm so sorry. I didn't mean for you to see this," she said eventually. "Damn, I'm such an idiot. Such a cry baby."

"No, you're not," he said. He hadn't released her and she hadn't moved away. "You're hurt. He hurt you. That makes him the idiot."

She did move then, giving him a weak smile and reaching for another tissue to mop at her eyes.

"How did you know...? You are psychic. Thank you. And now I've wasted half your evening."

"Hey. Don't say that. You're my friend. That's not wasted time. I'm not going to leave you when you're so upset."

She looked at him, her eyes full of shadows. He wanted to put his arms round her again and try and shield her from them.

"In fact," he went on, "if you've got nothing better to do, maybe we could drink coffee or go for a walk or something. Have another hug. You can talk if you want. If it would help."

His eyes were kind. His gentleness made her want to weep again. She turned resolutely away and flicked the kettle back on. "Coffee sounds good," she said. When she turned back she saw him looking down at the album on the table.

"Is this what upset you?"

"Partly," she said hoarsely. "You can look if you want."

"Really? I don't want to pry."

"It's fine." She started to make the drinks, stirring slowly, taking her time with the milk. He was still looking when she took the mugs over to the table. He closed it as she got there.

"That's tough," he said. "You looked so happy."

"We were, to start with." She took a deep breath. "It would have been our third wedding anniversary today." She could feel tears prickling.

"I'm sorry."

"Not your fault," she said. "It is what it is." She sat down and pushed her knuckles into her eyes, trying to stop herself from crying again. It was a vain attempt as the tears spilled over anyway. "Damn. Why can't I just feel angry? Why does it hurt so much? Even now?"

Seth pulled a chair next to hers and sat close to her, putting his arm round her. He felt her stiffen, start to draw away, but he didn't let go.

"You don't have to stay." She wiped more tears away and turned to look at him. "I'm OK. Really."

He held her gently but firmly. "Yeah. I know. I say that too sometimes when it's not true. Sometimes I think if I say it enough I'll believe it. And just so you know, I'm not staying because I have to. I'm staying because I want to. It's OK," he said. "It's OK to cry, it's OK to hurt. You don't have to hide it. Just let me stay, be your friend. He's a damn idiot and he didn't treat you right. You're better off without him so you can find someone who'll be true, who will love you truly. And you will."

Serena felt herself break then. She was so tired, tired of pretending that everything was all right, that she was coping, that she wasn't lonely and afraid and cursed. She didn't have the energy to try and push him away; she didn't want to. Instead she took him at his word and let go, holding on to him as she fell helplessly apart.

Seth hurt for her. He knew how she felt, still remembered the first time that Jessica had left him, how it had felt as though she had taken his world with her. How there just seemed to be nothing left. And he had had his friends around him, and his family, from a distance but still there. Serena seemed to have no one from her old life except Sarah, who was miles away.

He pulled her closer, held her head against his shoulder until her tears abated and her breathing calmed and eventually he felt her begin to relax.

"Thank you," she whispered. He felt her move and tightened his arms round her.

"Stay," he said. "Just a little while longer."

Then she put her head back down and did as he had asked.

Chapter 8

Serena found the rest of February a struggle despite her best efforts to put the past back into its box, but she realised just how close she had become to the friends she had made. Her understanding of friendship changed completely. The social circle she had been part of in London had involved clubs, parties, big social events and going out and, fun as that had been, she had never felt very close to anyone apart from Sarah and Lindy. Here, things were completely different. Seth, Tallie and Rob, Gaia and Ethan, Nikki and Howie all just seemed to be happy to share each other's company, whether having a raucous night at the Old Hare, eating chips on the beach or sitting at each other's houses having a cup of coffee. And they had accepted her into that with no hesitation and no question. As she dragged herself through the seemingly endless days, they were all there with a smile or a hug, things to distract her and an ear when she needed it.

Rose had an uncanny knack of teasing information out of her and then making her feel so much better. In fact, Serena was surprised at how much Rose could make her laugh with her humorous observations and bone dry one liners.

And Seth texted her every day. He also seemed to manage to appear at moments when she was feeling alone and small, when everything was crumbling around her and it was just too overwhelming to bear. And when he walked with her, talked to her, drank tea with her and then hugged her close, somehow the darkness retreated a little and she could breathe. If he hadn't been so human she would have sworn he was a guardian angel. Her guardian angel.

"Not just yours," the little voice in her mind said, and when she thought about how he looked out for Rose and Sheila, his friends and, in fact, anyone who needed help, she knew it was true.

It was her birthday in early March and she was lifted when Sarah and Lindy managed to free up the weekend to come down and stay.

"I am so glad to see you," said Sarah, getting out of the car when they arrived late on Friday afternoon and hugging her so hard that she almost couldn't breathe.

"Well, don't asphyxiate the poor girl then." Lindy was smiling widely at Serena, giving her a hug as soon as Sarah let her go. "It is really good to see you, she's right. How are you?"

Friday evening passed in a whirl of catching up and laughing. Serena woke on her birthday to Sarah bounding in with hugs and gifts, followed a little more sedately by Lindy with tea and croissants.

"Happy birthday," Sarah sang as she grabbed Serena in a hug.

"Ditto," Lindy grinned, setting the tray on the bedside table. "Now eat while these are warm and then you can unwrap."

It wasn't long after that Serena's phone pinged. There was a text from Ethan and Gaia wishing her happy birthday, and as she sent one back to thank them and that she'd see them later, another one came in.

Happy Birthday. Big birthday hug ready for you. Will give to you this evening, unless you want to collect it earlier. Actually that's a better idea. Then you can have another one this evening!

Seth. She smiled.

Thank you, crazy person.

Projecting, are we?

Maybe. More than likely. Not sure what we're doing this afternoon, but will try and drop in. Want you to meet Sarah and Lindy.

Me too. See you later!

Serena had arranged for Tallie to come over for lunch. Lindy wanted to talk to her about her book and she knew that it would be impossible later when they were at the Old Hare.

"Books seem to be the theme," Serena laughed as she told them about the work she was doing, and some of the mad concoctions she had cooked up as a result.

"Yeah, some of those 'cures' are fantastic but some have been, well…" Tallie left the rest unspoken but the expression she pulled was explanation enough.

"You're not kidding," Serena said.

"Speaking of fantastic, I have some news for you, Tallie," Lindy said.

"One of the publishing houses I work with, they're a small outfit but very organised, I sent them three chapters of Storm and they want to see the rest. They're definitely interested and they came back to me really quickly, which is a very good sign."

"Oh wow," Serena whooped. "That's... wow!" But Tallie just sat there, her eyes huge, completely stunned. She tried to speak but nothing came out. Serena jumped up and hugged her, shaking her gently.

"Goodness, Lindy, you've managed the impossible," she said.

"That's unfair. The book's amazing," said Lindy, shocked.

"No, no." Serena couldn't contain her mirth. "I know how good the book is. But rendering Tallie speechless? That really is a miracle."

Once Tallie had recovered, she had to call Rob and her parents and her Gran. She was nearly beside herself with excitement.

"It's your birthday, Serena, but it feels like mine," she said. "Times about a gazillion."

"I'm so glad for you," Serena replied. "It's so exciting."

"Let's have a wander around and down to the beach," Sarah suggested. "I feel like calling in at a few old haunts."

"Yeah. Let's go tell Seth. He'll want to wish you happy birthday anyway," Tallie enthused. "Oh, I'm just going to call Gaia."

They wrapped up against the cold wind and set off into town.

"Where first?" Serena asked.

Sarah took one look at Tallie and said "Shall we call in and see your other friend? Otherwise I think she may explode."

"You're right." Tallie was nearly skipping. "Sorry to be such a kid but..."

"That's why we love you," Serena finished off.

Tallie bowled into Seth's like a small hurricane and the other three couldn't help laughing as the news tumbled out in a somewhat random order. Seth looked a little confused but unfazed and when he finally got to grips with what she was saying, picked her up and whirled her around in his excitement for her. Then he came out from behind the counter to greet Sarah and Lindy and pick Serena up in a big hug as well.

"Happy birthday," he said. "That feels better."

Sarah and Lindy stopped to chat with Seth, while Tallie excused herself and scampered off home to see Rob.

"She was actually speechless earlier," said Serena.

"Would love to have been there for that," Seth said.

"I hear it doesn't happen often," Lindy commented.

"I've known her since we were eleven," Seth grinned, "and I've never seen it."

The shop was beginning to get busier so Serena, Sarah and Lindy headed off and left Seth to it.

"We'll see you later at the Hare," Sarah said in parting.

Serena couldn't help feeling excited as they got to the Old Hare. She had her old friends and her new ones together in the same place on her birthday and she felt that that was the greatest gift of all. But Gaia had made her a birthday cake and there were cards and presents that told her how well they really knew her. She still couldn't quite believe how amazing it felt to be this included, this at ease. Banishing any thoughts of the future firmly from her mind, she got up when the bands came on and threw herself into the melee.

Seth was talking to Lindy on the way back home and Sarah linked her arm through Serena's.

"I'm so glad to see you like this," she said. "With such good friends around you. I was worried about you being down here on your own but you were right."

Serena squeezed her arm. "It's because of you I'm here," she said. "And I don't just mean the cottage. I never would have survived last year if it wasn't for you. I'll always be grateful to you, Sarah. You know how much you mean to me, you and Lindy."

"Don't be silly. We support each other. You've helped us pick up the pieces before. You're part of our family, you always will be."

Lindy and Seth had come to a stop where he and Serena usually parted to go home, but after saying goodnight to the others, he asked Serena if he could borrow her for a few minutes. Mystified, she followed him back to his flat, glaring daggers at Sarah and her knowing smile as she and Lindy headed back to the cottage.

"Are you OK?" she asked, a little concerned.

"Yeah, I just... I have something for you but it's... oh, I don't know. A bit silly, I guess. I didn't want to give it to you with all the others there. It's only little but I hope you'll like it."

"Seth, you gave me a present already. You didn't need to get me anything, let alone something else."

"I wanted to, so hush."

He opened the door and pulled her upstairs. "I know you need to get back so ...'

"They won't mind," Serena said.

"Hang on." He snapped on the light and hurried across the room, returning with a small envelope. "Wrapping's not great but hey! Happy birthday."

"Thank you. Again."

There was a little blue velvet pouch in the envelope. She sat down on the sofa to open it, drawing out a small silver charm.

"Oh," she breathed.

It rested on her palm, a delicate and detailed starfish, glinting in the light. He sat down next to her, looking at her intently. When she didn't speak or move he spoke, concerned.

"If you don't like it, I can change it. I won't be offended. It just made me think of you."

Serena shook her head. "It's beautiful. Why?" It was hard to speak past the lump in her throat.

"Oh, because you love the sea so much. And because you've shone light for me and that's what stars do. Sea star. Seemed like the best of both worlds. Oh, no, Serena, it wasn't supposed to make you cry. I'm sorry."

"It's beautiful. Thank you," she said again.

"Please don't cry. I didn't mean to upset you."

"You didn't, Seth. People cry when they're happy, too. Well, at least, I do."

"So you do like it?"

"I love it. In fact," she took off the chain with the little bottle on it, "it's going on here right now next to this." But her hands were shaking so much she couldn't thread it. Seth took it from her and did it himself, moving her hair out of the way so he could put it back in position. His touch made her ache, his breath warm on the back of her neck as he refastened the chain and she hugged him afterwards, wishing... just wishing.

"Happy birthday," he said again as she left.

Seth had just finished serving a customer late the following Saturday morning when Tallie flew in. The shop was fairly busy but one look at her and the tears pouring down her face put that straight out of his head.

"Tallie, what's happened? Are you hurt?"

Tallie shook her head, unable to speak. Seth hugged her tightly.

"Do you want me to call Rob? Ah, hell, it's his reunion weekend. He's miles away, isn't he? Here, come back here where it's quiet. Don't worry, Tallie, I'll do whatever you need. It's going to be OK." He drew her into the back room.

"It's Gran," Tallie choked out. "She's had a stroke. She's in the hospital and I don't know how bad it is but I need to get there. But Rob's got the car and I can't think what…" She gave up talking as the tears took over again.

"It's OK, it's OK." Seth tried to soothe her. "Don't worry, I'll sort something out." He sat her down on a chair. "Stay here for a moment. I'll be back."

He hurried out to the shop again. There were still several customers browsing, so he went to the door first and flipped the sign to "Closed'. Then he went round to each one to tell them that he was closing because of an emergency. Once the shop emptied he locked the door and returned to Tallie who was fumbling with her phone, almost blinded by her tears. He took it from her gently.

"Who can I call for you? Rob?"

"I've already spoken to him. He's coming back but he won't get here 'til this evening, late. I was trying to call Serena. I was going to stay at hers tonight."

"I'll do it. And then I'll take you to the hospital."

"Seth, you can't. You can't close on Saturday, it's your busiest. I'll get a taxi."

"It's already done. You will not, no way, get a taxi. Give me a minute to call Serena and then we'll go."

Seth located his keys and his jacket as he phoned Serena. "Hi, Serena, you OK? Tallie's Gran's in hospital, had a stroke, so I'm closing and taking her over there. She won't be around tonight."

Serena sounded concerned. "Oh no. Is she OK? I can take her if you want, then you can reopen. I know Rose won't mind."

"No, it's fine. She's really upset, I'd rather stick around. No offence."

"None taken, but let me come as well then. If you think it would help."

"I'm sure she'd appreciate that. I'll pick you up on the way. You're at Auntie's? Fifteen minutes then?"

"I'll be waiting outside."

Seth stuck his phone in his pocket, put his arm round Tallie and steered her out of the door and over to his car. When they turned into Rose's lane, Serena was standing on the pavement. She rushed round to give Tallie a squeeze and then climbed into the back seat. Seth set off and between them, they managed to calm Tallie down a little and to ease her anxiety. Serena hugged her from behind.

"I know I'm not Seth," she said, "but you'll just have to take what you can get." Tallie even managed a smile at that.

By the time they reached A and E, Tallie's gran had been moved to a ward.

"That's a good sign," Seth said comfortingly. "A ward, not intensive care or high dependency, that's got to be good."

Tallie smiled at him gratefully but Serena could still feel how badly she was shaking. She kept her arm firmly linked with her friend's as the three of them made their way down the corridor to the ward. One of the nurses took Tallie off to see her Gran and Serena and Seth waited in the day room. They sat together talking quietly.

"Poor Tallie," Seth said. "I can't imagine how... if it was Aunt Rose, I don't know what I'd do."

"I know," Serena agreed. "I hope it's not as serious as she thought."

It was a long time until Tallie reappeared. Her mother was with her. Serena and Seth both stood up hurriedly, the question obvious on both their faces.

"She's stable," Tallie said. "And they've got her on the right meds so they think they can minimize any further damage."

"So she's out of danger?" Serena asked.

Tallie nodded. "They think so. She's still drifting in and out of consciousness but the doctors are pretty sure she'll improve now." Her eyes filled up again and Seth drew her into another hug while Serena squeezed her hand.

"Thank you so much for bringing Tallie down, Seth." Tallie's mum spoke then. "Jon and I felt we couldn't leave at the time, just in case. And Serena, I've heard so much about you, it's so nice to meet you. Thank you too."

"It's no problem," Seth said and Serena nodded agreement.

"Yeah, I can't thank you guys enough." Tallie's voice was muffled by Seth's shoulder. She moved away, wiping her eyes. "For everything."

"Any time. Always," Seth said quietly. "You know that."

"Is there anything else you need? Anything we can do?" Serena asked.

"No, thanks," Tallie said. "You've both been amazing, but I just need to stay here now."

"Do you want us to stay?" Serena checked. "Or go and get you some clothes or anything?"

"No, honestly, thanks but I'll be fine. And Rob'll be here later with the car so..." She shrugged. "Do you mind if I go back to Gran now?"

"Of course not," Seth said. "I guess we'll head off if you're sure there's nothing else."

Tallie hugged them both again.

"You will let us know how she's doing, won't you?" Serena said.

"Of course. I'll see you soon."

Serena and Seth headed out of the hospital and got into the car, both quiet and thoughtful.

"Well," Serena said uncertainly. "It sounds more positive than Tallie thought earlier."

"Thank goodness," Seth agreed. He was gripping the steering wheel so hard that his knuckles were white as he steered the car out of the space.

"Are you alright?" Serena asked.

"Yeah. Just can't get Auntie out of my head. It brings it home, you know? I never think of her as old and frail, but she is. And I know something'll happen one day but I can hardly bear to think about it." Seth could hear the tension in his voice.

"Do you want to go and see her? Or stop and phone her? Hey, we're still in the car park, pull over for a mo."

"Why?"

"Please. You'll see."

He drew in to the side and put the handbrake on, then turned to face her, feeling irritated, not at her but at the helplessness washing through him. She thrust her phone into his hand, dialling tone already sounding.

"Hello," came Rose's voice. Seth started and a strange sense of relief flooded through him.

"Hi, Auntie," he said. "Just thought we'd tell you that Tallie's Gran is stable and..."

After a short conversation Seth handed the phone back. "Thanks," he said.

Serena smiled. "Should we go back? You could just about reopen if you wanted."

"For half an hour?" Seth shook his head. He looked at Serena, feeling a rush of gratitude. And more. Much more. He crushed it quickly but it hovered there in the back of his conscious. "No. I think I'm going to play truant this afternoon. It's three o'clock. Are you in a hurry or shall we go find something to eat?"

"Sounds good."

It was very much later when Seth dropped Serena off at Rose's to pick up her car. They had eaten and then got waylaid by a notice advertising a Battle of the Bands that night at one of the numerous venues in the city. It had been a really good evening, especially when Tallie had texted them to say that her gran had woken for a few minutes and recognised her. Rose's house was in darkness and Serena opened her door to get out.

"Serena." Seth didn't know what he wanted to say, just that he wanted to say something. She paused, turning toward him. "Thanks for coming today. It really helped, you being there. Not just Tallie either."

She looked puzzled. "I didn't do anything."

He reached out and squeezed her shoulder quickly.

"You'd be surprised."

She smiled. "It was good fun after we knew Tallie's gran was improving." She slipped out of the car. "See you soon."

"You know the answer to that."

Chapter 9

Seth knew that Jessica was back before he saw her. Tallie had come into the shop and warned him and he'd decided to stay out of her way. She confused him. If he was honest he didn't really miss her anymore and, although it hurt him sometimes to think about her, that was more to do with the way she had behaved than him wanting her back. He didn't. Life was good and he didn't want to change that. He liked being with his friends, liked spending time with Serena. Really liked Serena, if he was honest, but after seeing how devastated she had been, he was cautious about pushing their relationship beyond friendship.

He had no desire to be sucked back into the drama that was Jessica's world so while he knew he probably wouldn't be able to avoid her completely, he planned to keep any conversation brief and business like and to ignore the flirting that was her norm. That was the difficult bit. Because much as he hated to admit it, she still had a hold over him.

When he did see her first it was at a distance. She was on the beach in a group of people, flirting madly and lapping up the attention as usual. He couldn't help but smile wryly. Some things would never change.

He saw her at the Old Hare the next Saturday and she came over to talk. He knew she was sizing him up so he stayed friendly but casual and eventually she went back to her own friends. His relief was tinged with melancholy but he felt better when Ethan gave him a thumbs up and Serena, realising who she was, came and gave his hand a sympathetic squeeze. He liked that more than he would have cared to admit.

He decided to forgo his usual night out with Ethan and Rob the following week. He knew Jessica would most likely be at the Feathers and despite himself, he'd been thinking about her. He'd been thinking about Serena too, about the discussion they'd had and what she'd said to him about deserving better, how kind and sincere her eyes had been when she'd said it. How much he liked being in her company. They were so different, Jessica and Serena, and the way he felt about both of them only added to his confusion. He was tired anyway; it had been a hectic couple of days and he felt like staying in with a beer and some music and just chilling out.

There was a knock at his door, late that night. His heart reacted when he saw Jessica standing there on the doorstep, but instead of the lightning flutter of anticipation that she used to cause, it was a jumpy lurch of panic, a desperate fall against his will.

"Hi," she said.

"Hi."

"Aren't you pleased to see me?"

Seth forced a smile to his face, trying to cover his mixed feelings. He said nothing.

"I thought I'd see you down at the pub."

He shrugged. "Knackered. Thought I'd give it a miss.'"

"Too tired to ask me in?" She had that look on her face, all wide eyed innocence, the one he found impossible to say no to. And although he knew she knew that, he relented.

"Come on up," he said, as nonchalantly as he could manage.

"How've you been?" she asked, looking around his flat for changes. Signs of another female presence, most likely. "Any gossip I should know about."

"I'm good, actually. And I'm sure you know far more gossip than I do."

"Touché," she said.

"So," he went on, heading into the kitchen to put the kettle on and gain a little more distance between them. "What brings you back this time?"

"Oh, you know, this and that. Little hiatus with work, end of one contract and a while before the next begins. Guy who doesn't know what he wants, needs some space he says. Thought I'd come back and catch up."

She was standing in the kitchen doorway now, looking as gorgeous as ever, thick blonde hair falling down her back, brown eyes wide.

"Of course there are some things I want to catch up with more than others," she said, biting her lip.

Seth turned away and busied himself with mugs, hating himself for the effect she still had on him.

"Yeah, well, lots of people to hang out with here. Must be boring after London tho'. There's not much to do." His voice failed as he felt her behind him, felt her pressing herself against his back as her arms wound round his waist.

"I can think of things I'd like to do right now. You have to make your own fun here and we're good at that, aren't we?"

He didn't move, summoning all his willpower. "Jessica, I don't think I..."

But she had slipped round in front of him, her hand sliding under his T-shirt and across his skin. He drew in a sharp breath as she reached up and began to kiss his neck, her hair brushing against his arm. He couldn't help himself; he put his hand up to stroke the silky strands. Serena's face appeared in his mind, and a desperate longing for...

"Mmm," she purred.

"Jess, please, I don't..."

"Oh Seth, don't fight." She was kissing his mouth now, soft kisses that coaxed and teased. "Do you really want me to stop?"

She looked at him with those big eyes and he was lost once more. Winding his hand through her hair, he pulled her head back and kissed her hard as he felt himself drown.

Rose was less than delighted to hear that Jessica was back in Seth's life.

"Hasn't she caused you enough heartbreak?" she asked.

Seth shrugged. "I know. You're probably right. You and Ethan and most of the others. But I hope it might be different this time." Even as he said it, it sounded hollow. And he wasn't even sure that it was true. For some reason Serena was always in his head.

"Well, I'll be polite if you bring her to see me, but be wary Seth. She's trouble with a capital T, that one. I'm afraid I don't trust her and I'm not sure you should either."

"Auntie, stop worrying about me. I'm a big boy now. I know what I'm doing." He wasn't sure who he was trying to convince. He could tell by her face that she wasn't either but thankfully she let it go.

"The book's coming on in leaps and bounds," she said, changing the subject. "Serena's a marvel. She's got me beyond organised."

Seth laughed. It had always been a standing joke amongst his family just how chaotic Rose was.

"Bet you never thought you'd see the day," he teased. She batted him gently with the back of her hand.

"That's enough of your cheek," she said. "I don't know. Youngsters today."

"I'm twenty six, Auntie. Not sure that classifies me as a youngster."

She looked at him over the top of her glasses. "Believe me dear, when you get to my age, everyone under sixty is classified as a youngster."

"Oh Auntie, you know you're only twenty three."

"I may act like it sometimes, but the old bones remind me otherwise. Go on, scoot, you've got better things to do than hang around with an old fogey like me."

"Old fogey, my…'

"Now then, language, you'll make me blush."

Seth kissed her cheek. "Of course I will.'

Seth found himself spending a lot of time with Jessica and much less with his friends. He didn't intend it to be that way but it was just easier; Jessica was possessive and had a tendency to try to dominate any situation she found herself in. He had suggested that when she met her friends he'd go out with his but she was pretty resistant to that idea, insisting that they go out together almost all the time. He didn't really have much in common with most of the people she liked to hang out with but he made the effort anyway. That way he didn't have to deal with her sulks or wheedling or ill temper. And although a few times he had said no and endured the result, she always seemed to find her way back in just before he told her where to go. He knew she didn't really like his friends and that was why she was so overbearing but she seemed determined to go with him anyway. Ethan, Gaia and Rob tolerated her for his sake while Tallie pretty much ignored her. Serena was friendly but he did catch her looking at him once or twice with a worried expression. She seemed reassured when he smiled at her, but he was touched by her concern. He missed seeing her, talking to her. Texting wasn't the same.

So one evening when he had just locked up and was heading back to his flat he was glad to see her coming out of the fish and chip shop.

"Hi," he said. She grinned and looked down at her chips.

"Caught in the act," she said. "Want one?" She offered him the packet. The smell wafted up, tantalising him.

"You know, one's not going to be enough. Think I might get some myself. Where are you headed?"

"I was going to make the most of the sunshine," she said, pointing at one of the benches situated above the beach. "The clocks may only just have gone back but it makes so much difference."

"Mind if I join you? Feel like I haven't seen you in days.'"

"Great."

Once he had got his chips he sat beside her on the bench and told her how pleased Rose was with what she'd done.

"It's been a revelation, going through those papers," she said. "All that knowledge. And Rose's drawings are amazing. Have you seen them?"

"One or two," he replied. "Landscapes."

"These are botanical studies, so detailed. I found them in a box under the bed in the blue spare room. They're stunning. I'm going to start scanning them onto the computer. She wasn't going to use them in the book but it would be a crime not to."

Seth watched Serena as she spoke excitedly about his aunt and her book. Her eyes seemed to be an even deeper blue than usual as she described the different sections she and Rose had planned and put in order, laughing as she described her struggle to find some other papers that Rose had feared lost and how they had inexplicably turned up in the airing cupboard.

"Strangely, that doesn't surprise me at all," he said.

"She's a great lady, your Aunt." Serena was sincere.

Seth smiled. "Yeah, she is." He felt guilty when he caught himself thinking how pretty she was and couldn't help reaching for her hand. "And so are you. You've really helped her and she and I both appreciate it."

Serena blushed slightly. "I really enjoy her company. I'm the lucky one."

Jessica stood watching them from the other side of the street, a dark frown hardening her usually soft features. Having had no reply when she had knocked at Seth's door, she had been about to text him when his laughter had drifted across from the front. That was when she had noticed them sitting together. She didn't like it. Didn't like the relaxed way they were talking, the way they were laughing, the way the girl smiled at him and especially the way he was looking at her. She recognised that look; she had been the recipient of it once upon a time, a tender caring look of wonder. He probably wasn't even aware of it. The way he looked at her now was different, guarded and wary, but he still had the kind and generous heart that she had been attracted to in the first place. She liked being with Seth because he made her feel special, and she needed to be his one and only. For the time that she was here, anyway. She needed him to make her the centre of his world and that left no room for anyone else. And what she wanted she would get, one way or another.

Jessica put on her brightest smile and headed across the street. Bending down, she slid her arms round Seth from behind, running her hands provocatively under his jacket.

"Hey there," she said right by his ear. "I was wondering where you'd got to."

"Here all the time," Seth said, a hint of irritation in his voice which both girls picked up on. He leaned forward, away from her, but undeterred she slipped round to sit close to him on the bench, resting her hand on his thigh.

"Have I met your friend?" she asked, the emphasis on the last word belying the sweetness of her tone.

"You know you have, Jessica." Seth sounded annoyed now. "You've met Serena at the Hare and in the shop."

Jessica delicately furrowed her brow and then cleared her expression. "Yes of course. You're Rose's cleaner, aren't you?" The honey still dripped from her voice, but Serena clearly made out the intended put down. She decided to ignore it for Seth's sake.

"That's right," she agreed. "Amongst other things. I'm helping her collate material for her book."

"How fascinating," Jessica said, then turned and addressed herself to Seth. "Perhaps she'll show me when you take me to see her, baby."

"I'm sure she'd be delighted to," Serena said calmly. She could see that Seth was becoming uncomfortable and decided to remove herself from the situation.

"I'm going to head home," she said. "See you soon, Seth. It was nice meeting you again, Jessica.'

"Yeah," Jessica replied.

"See you soon," Seth said. She couldn't quite read his expression as she walked past and set off along the road.

Jessica and Seth sat in silence for a few moments.

"She seems... nice," Jessica commented after a while.

"She is. She's lovely. And she deserves far more respect than you just gave her."

"I don't know what you mean. We were just talking."

"No, you were putting her down. Don't bother to deny it," he continued quickly as she began to speak. "I know you, remember."

"You do, baby," she said breathily. "And you're right. But I can't help being jealous when I see you with a pretty girl."

Seth was about to retort that maybe now she understood how he felt most of the time but she leaned forward and brushed his lips with hers. Standing up and taking his hands, she tugged gently but insistently until he stood up.

"I'm sorry," she said. "Let me make it up to you."

Against his better judgement, Seth let her lead him back to his flat.

Serena walked home feeling ill at ease. She didn't like the way Jessica behaved around Seth, and not just this evening; it clearly made him uncomfortable but Jessica was either completely oblivious to or really didn't care about the way he was feeling. Serena couldn't understand that. She could see why the others found her so difficult and she could also see how much Seth was affected by her; the combination of attention and neediness Jessica displayed was the perfect hook for a kind man like him. She wanted to shake Jessica hard, tell her to open her eyes and look at what she had with him, to treasure it rather than throw it away and break him again.

"Stupid girl doesn't know how lucky she is," Serena muttered crossly to herself. She made herself a drink when she got home and sat in the living room watching the TV, unable to shake off the unease or the knowledge that Jessica and Seth were together now and what she felt for him would have to remain hidden.

She was still feeling out of sorts the next morning and threw herself into her work at Rose's, spending the morning scanning the drawings to create a new file. She didn't think she could concentrate on writing up notes. She was cross with herself when Rose came into the study to bring her coffee at half past eleven.

"Rose, I'm so sorry," she apologised. "I should have made that. I lost track of time."

"Nonsense, dear, it's about time I made you a drink. You do so much for me." She put the mug down and came round to see what Serena was doing. "Gosh, they look alright, don't they?"

"They look better than alright. They're going to look amazing in print. Seth said he's not seen them. You must show them to him, Rose. He'll be blown away."

"They're only pictures. And he's somewhat distracted at the moment."

"Hmm, yes, he is." Serena was unable to keep the distaste out of her voice and Rose was sharp enough to pick up on it.

"So you've met her then? Jessica?"

Serena looked at her and tried to be polite. "Yes. She's charming."

"Please dear, you don't have to pretend. I can see you don't like her much. I can't stand her myself."

"Oh."

"Sorry, have I shocked you?" Rose's eyes were twinkling and Serena couldn't help grinning back at her. "I'd better not say anything else."

"Please feel free," Serena said. "I get the feeling she's not that popular with a lot of people around here. And seeing the way she is with…" She stopped, blushing slightly.

"With Seth? I know. Don't get me started. She thinks she owns him. I don't know why he keeps letting her take advantage like she does."

"He said…" Serena hesitated, not sure whether to continue, but then went on anyway. "He said it's like an addiction. She's like a drug."

"Don't worry dear, I won't say anything. It makes sense though. But I wish he could give her up. He never looks really happy when she's around. He knows what's coming, every time, and he still lets her wind him round her little finger."

"He's too good hearted," Serena observed. "He wouldn't hurt anyone, we all know that, and she plays needy too well. He'd never want to let her down, I'm sure that's how she hooks him in."

"You're right, I'm sure. That and the chemistry between them." Rose laughed as Serena's eyebrows shot up. "I may be old but I was married. And that girl is not ashamed of using her, let's call them feminine wiles, to manipulate the opposite sex. I think she's used to getting her own way and will do anything to ensure it."

Two days later Serena, coming back late from Rose's, knocked on Seth's door to drop off the MP3 player that he had left there the evening before and also a memory stick onto which she had uploaded Rose's scanned drawings. She stood for a while and was just about to knock again when the door opened. Jessica stood there barefoot in a bathrobe.

"Oh. It's you," she said. She didn't bother to hide the disdain in her voice since Seth was apparently out of earshot.

Serena bit back a sharp retort. "Yes," she said evenly. "Rose asked me to return this." She held up the MP3 player. "He left it there yesterday. And also to give him this which has the files he wanted on it."

"Fine." Jessica reluctantly took the two items, staring hard at Serena. "Is that it?"

Serena nodded. "Yes thanks. I'll..." Jessica slammed the door in her face, "be going then. Charming."

She walked home, getting there just as Tallie arrived. "Sorry, running late," she apologised. "Had to drop something off at Seth's."

Tallie followed her into the kitchen. "How is he?"

"Don't know. She opened the door. I assume he's OK."

"Hmmph." Tallie sat down and opened the wine she'd brought, pouring it into the glasses Serena put in front of her. "I doubt it. If he is it won't be for long."

"Well..." Serena began, but Tallie went on.

"I can't believe he's let her back in." She was more upset than angry. "When he knows damn well what'll happen."

"Maybe it'll be different this time." The words almost choked Serena, cut like pieces of glass.

"It won't be." Tallie looked at her. "He's told you about her then?"

"Some. There's obviously something between them. Neither of them can stay away."

"Yeah, there's something all right," Tallie spat out. "She likes to wring every last drop out of her victims and he tries to assuage his guilt mountain by letting her. Self-flagellation, that's why he does it."

"He doesn't see himself like we all see him, does he?"

"No." Tallie sighed heavily. Serena had never seen her deflated like this; she was usually so relentlessly positive. "He never has. Ever." She looked questioningly at Serena. "Has he told you anything about when he was younger?"

"About his parents, you mean? Yeah, some. His father sounds hateful and I know he feels bad about how he reacted – how it affected his mum." She sat down next to her friend.

"When I first met him, when we started senior school together, he was so quiet and withdrawn," Tallie said. "Most people thought he was really unfriendly but he and Ethan and I all kind of fell together really quickly. Maybe 'cos we're all a bit weird." She roused half a smile at that. "And yes, he did have a couple of wild years, but he wasn't really any worse than the rest of us. And he was never mean, never spiteful; even then he was the one that picked us up when we fell, physically and metaphorically. He still does it now, for everyone but himself. Still punishing himself and I don't know how to help him. Neither does Ethan."

Serena was horrified to see tears in her friend's eyes. Until that moment she hadn't fully realised the bond between Tallie, Ethan and Seth.

"Meanwhile that... bitch takes full advantage," Tallie went on. "Just uses him as a pick me up when she's got nothing better to do. That's just like her. And she's too stupid to realise that there is nothing better. She doesn't care about him and he doesn't love her, not any more but he still lets her get to him somehow, lets her in enough to hurt him. God, I hate her." She reached for a tissue. "I know I shouldn't but I do."

"You're allowed," Serena said. "Just as long as you don't make a little wax doll and stick it full of pins."

Tallie giggled at that, mopping her eyes. "Oh, for heaven's sake," she said as the tissue came away black with eyeliner. "Now I look like a panda."

Serena smiled sympathetically. "She seems to unsettle everyone. I gather she's not been very nice to you."

"Not when we were at college, no," Tallie agreed. "But I could forgive her that if she was kind in the way she treats Seth. If they were genuinely together. But..." She tailed off, tears rising again. "Dammit, Rob's my soulmate but Seth's my best friend. Him and Ethan. I hate to see this happening again."

Serena hugged her, feeling helpless.

"And you know what's worse?" Tallie went on. "I thought there was something happening between you and Seth. I so hoped there was... is." She looked at Serena, whose heart had jumped into her throat. "He's different when you're around, and the way he looks at you... I've never seen that before, not even with her when it all started. You seem to have a connection that... oh, I don't know, you just seem to light each other up. You'd be so good for each other. I'm right, aren't I?" She looked hard at Serena. "You do have feelings for each other? And now she's back, in the way."

Serena scrambled for words among the seething thoughts raging through her head.

"I do really like him, yes," she said carefully. "And I don't like to see him like this. But I want him to be happy and if it's with her, then at least he's my friend." She shrugged. "And don't you dare say anything to him about what I just said. You would regret it. Because I am fierce and dangerous and as scary as the night." The face she pulled lightened the moment and they both started laughing.

"You're about as scary and fierce as the bunny I had when I was nine," Tallie giggled. "But I won't say anything, I promise."

Inside though they were both still thinking, Serena trying to fight down her feelings for Seth and Tallie wondering how she could magic them together.

Chapter 10

The following morning Serena drove Rose into town to do her shopping and meet a friend for coffee.

"I'm quite happy," she insisted, batting away Rose's reservations. "I'll wander on the beach. Maybe pop in and see Seth. Call me when you're ready to go."

She started onto the beach but the wind was hard and cold, turning the drizzle into arrows of ice. She thought better of it and headed across to the record store. It was empty apart from Seth who was studying a magazine as he sat behind the counter.

"Hi," he said, smiling widely. "It's good to see you."

"You too," Serena replied. "I brought Rose into town and she's having coffee with a friend so I thought I'd…'

"Sorry I missed you last night."

"'s OK. I only dropped some things off."

"Still would have liked to have said hi. And thank you. But I guess better late than never. So hi. And thank you."

Serena giggled. "You're welcome."

"Have you got to go anywhere else? Or can I offer you coffee and refuge from the weather 'til Auntie's finished?"

"I don't want to get in your way."

Seth laughed, looking round the shop. "Oh yes, because I'm *so* busy today."

"OK then." Serena slipped off her coat. "Thanks, that'd be really great."

He found another stool and they sat behind the counter talking about an article in the magazine and Rose's drawings.

"I was blown away by them," Seth confessed. "She used to belong to an art group and I've seen her paintings and a couple of drawings, but nothing like those. The detail is incredible."

"She's a bit of a dark horse, your aunt," Serena said affectionately. "Some of the things she comes out with stop me in my tracks."

"Tell me about it." Seth was laughing. "I told you some of the stories but believe me, there are others. She was, is and always will be a rebel."

"Good for her," Serena said.

"Great, isn't it? She's led me into mischief many times, much to my grandmother's disgust. Not just what I told you before. I'm not talking about hunting worms behind the shed."

Serena was about to ask what he was talking about when her phone rang. Rose was ready to go.

"You'll have to tell me the gory details next time I see you. Thanks for the coffee."

"No bother." Seth's smile always made her heart jump. "Catch up soon?" She nodded.

Serena was shrugging into her coat and Seth had taken the cups out to the back to wash them when the door opened and an icy blast blew in.

"You!"

Serena looked up to see Jessica glaring angrily at her.

"What are you doing here?" There was the slightest pause but just as Serena began to speak the other girl launched into a tirade. "Don't bother, I know what you're trying to do and you might as well give up now. It's pathetic the way you're throwing yourself at Seth but I'm warning you, stay out of the way. He's not going to be interested in someone like you. Ever. And in case you hadn't noticed, he's mine."

"Jessica." Seth sounded livid. He had come out in response to the bell when the door had opened and had heard most of the rant. "What the hell? You don't come in here and speak to my friend like that."

Jessica hurried over to him. "Baby, I'm sorry. I didn't mean to… but she's always hanging around you. She…"

"I enjoy her company." Seth stepped back, away from her. "She's my friend, for God's sake. She's got every right to be here and you have some damn nerve telling her otherwise."

"I'm sorry, but it really bothers me when she's coming on to you all the time."

"Don't be so stupid, of course she's not. Serena, I'm so…" Seth looked across and realised that Serena had slipped out quietly while he and Jessica had been arguing. "Damn."

"Well, at least now I've got you to myself," Jessica said softly, sidling closer to Seth and slipping her arms round his waist. "That's what I wanted."

But Seth was rigid with anger. He took hold of Jessica's upper arms and moved her away from him.

"Don't," he growled. "I'm not in the mood."

"I can fix that," she wheedled.

"No." It was just short of a shout. "I can't believe how you spoke to her. I can't believe you would do that."

"I'm sorry Seth. I don't want to fight with you. Please let me make it up to you." Jessica made to move forward but Seth held up his hand. Her eyes widened as she realised that she may well have overstepped the mark.

"You know what, you need to go. I can't talk to you right now."

"Seth, please." Jessica's face fell. She was actually staring to worry. He had never spoken to her like that before, never sounded so angry or so cold. "Don't be like that. It's only because I want you all to myself, I can't help..." Her voice faded, and she put on the hurt look that she knew always worked on him. "I'm sorry."

"It's not me you should be apologising to," he said gruffly. "Look Jess, I'm at work. I can't do this now."

"Later then," Jessica whispered. "Talk about it later. We could go out for dinner and talk."

Seth glared at her for a long moment. Then he sighed, running his hand through his hair.

"Fine," he said, with an edge of despair.

Seth paced round the shop, furious. Jessica had left quietly in the end, which was unusual for her, but he was too angry to notice. He felt like punching something but knew that wouldn't serve any purpose, so instead he went and rearranged the store room, taking his frustration out on the heavy boxes and bins. The shop remained quiet so he had time to think about what had happened and why he was feeling the way he was.

Jessica had always been jealous and in the beginning he'd found it quite flattering. That was when he'd felt so strongly about her, when he thought he'd fallen in love. But he'd realised the hard way that her possessiveness had nothing to do with her heart and everything to do with appearance and ego. He'd deflected and tempered her comments to others before and warned her off in the same way. But he had never heard her go for someone like she had gone for Serena, and he had never raised his voice to her like that either.

Seth finished re-stacking the boxes and took two full of older stock out to the front to sort through for the sales bins. He still felt angry and confused. Furious that Jessica would speak to his friend like that, that she never really tried to fit in with his friends at all, resentful that she still expected him to drop everything and everyone for her at a moment's notice. Confused because right now he was worried about Serena, cared more about how she was feeling than about Jessica. And because he was wishing that Jessica had been right about how Serena might feel about him.

Seth swore silently to himself and tried to focus on the CDs. It was impossible. He was already regretting agreeing to see Jessica that evening and he desperately wanted to speak to Serena, to apologise and make sure she was OK. But something held him back. He picked up his phone three times with the intention of calling her but couldn't quite bring himself to dial. Eventually he texted her.

I'm so sorry. Don't know what to say.

He continued to label stock and add it to the racks, the monotony of the task poor comfort for his agitation. He nearly dropped the pile he was carrying when his phone buzzed.

Don't apologise. Not your fault. I'm sorry I caused a problem. Will try and stay out of the way. Are you sure you're OK? Because we are friends, aren't we?

Seth groaned, his heart falling. Friends. "Yes," he thought. "Just friends, dammit."

Don't stay away, she had no right to speak to you like that. She knows it. I...

Seth hesitated, his fingers hovering over the letters. Miss you. Want to see you. Wish it was you not her.

... want my friends around me. She'll have to live with that or...

Or what, he thought. And he knew Serena would be asking herself the same thing.

That evening, having agreed to meet Jessica at the restaurant at eight thirty, he was surprised when she turned up on his doorstep twenty minutes early.

"I thought we were meeting there," he said.

"I'm sorry. I thought we would be better here. Without lots of people around." She did look genuinely concerned and he could feel himself softening. "Please? I brought dinner." She held up a bag of takeaway food.

Seth sighed and opened the door to let her in. "Fine. If that's what you really want. But we need to talk."

"I know," she said quietly and because she was ahead of him, he didn't see the little smile that danced over her lips.

They sat and ate in the living room, the conversation polite and stilted. It was as though neither of them really wanted to start and the food was a good distraction. Eventually though it was finished. Seth took the plates into the kitchen, coming back to find Jessica sitting on the sofa with her legs tucked under her. Ignoring the obvious invitation to sit next to her, he sat in the arm chair at the other end, turning it slightly more toward her. He studied her. She looked so innocent and vulnerable.

"So," he said.

"Seth, I'm sorry about earlier. I shouldn't have lost it like that. But when I'm with you, I don't want to share you."

"Jessica, I have other people in my life. Always have, always will. And they're here a lot more than you are."

"Exactly. I have to make the most of you while I can."

"That's not working for me anymore."

Jessica put her feet down and moved to the edge of the sofa. She stared at him intently. "What do you mean?"

"Exactly that. You come back, you go. We pick up and then you drop me. Again and again. Each time you think it's OK but it isn't. Have you ever thought that maybe I want more than that? Someone who really cares? That I don't want to do this anymore?"

"Seth, we're good together. We have fun together. It doesn't have to be any more difficult or complicated than that. Why can't we enjoy this for what it is?" He just looked at her. She got up and walked over to him, sat on his lap, put her arms round him. She felt him sigh. "Please Seth. You know how I need you."

"You don't need me. You just..." The rest of his words were lost as she kissed him. "Damn, Jess, we're supposed to be talking."

"I know. But I know what I want. And it's you."

"For now."

"Now is all we have. Seize the day, Seth, stop worrying about tomorrow." She was kissing him again and he tried to fight off the dizzying rush she created.

"You're going to leave again. I don't, can't…"

She silenced him with her mouth, running her hands over him. "Shh. Make the most of now. Please."

Serena barely saw Seth over the following week and a half. She missed him, but after Jessica had made it so plain that he was off limits and despite his text, she had stayed away, just because she thought it would be easier for him. They texted though. He had phoned her once, the day after the debacle in the shop to apologise again for Jessica's behaviour, but she had told him not to worry about it.

"That's her, not you," she had said. "As long as you're happy, that's what matters to me. Just be careful, won't you?"

"Thanks," he had answered. He sounded tired. "For caring. I'm lucky to have you as my friend."

"You know where I am. If…" If you need me hung silently between them.

"I know."

She went up to the Hare on Saturday to watch the band, thinking that she would see him but that Jessica couldn't have a problem with it if she was with Ethan and Gaia and the others. But neither of them were in evidence, and Ethan soon filled her in.

"She's gone off back to London, left this morning. Did her usual, dished out the nasty stuff and just went. She's such a bitch. Sorry, but she is."

"Poor Seth," Serena said, horrified. "Not again."

"Oh yeah. She's always bad news and he knows it but there's just something about her that…"

"How is he? Have you seen him?"

"He's not good. We went over earlier but he couldn't face coming out, even though we did our best to persuade him," Gaia told her. "Just wanted to be on his own."

Serena watched the first set, but she couldn't get Seth out of her head. She knew what it felt like and she hurt for him. As the band took a break, she decided.

"I'm going to go and see him," she told Gaia. "He may not want company but I know what it feels like."

"I think that would mean a lot," Gaia said. Ethan nodded in agreement.

"See you," she said and slipped out of the pub.

She walked down the hill and knocked on the door of his flat. No reply, but she could see low lamplight emanating from his window. She knocked again and waited. She was just reaching for her phone to text him when she heard him coming down the stairs. She heard the bolt being drawn and the door opened. He looked rough.

"Hi," she said. "I just came to say I'm sorry about what happened. Ethan told me."

"Thanks," he said. His eyes were sad.

"Oh, Seth, I really am sorry." She wanted to hug him the way he had held her in her similar situation, but she didn't have the nerve. She reached out to him instead and he took the hand she offered. "You deserve so much more." She squeezed his hand. "I know you told the others you didn't want company, but you don't have to be alone. I know what it feels like."

"It's my own stupid fault," he said. "I should have, no, I *did* know better and I just let it happen anyway. I have to live with it, not land it on anyone else. I'm fine."

"I knew you'd say that but I'm pretty sure you're not. I'm your friend. That's what you told me when you came round and found me upset. Please, just make me a cup of tea and let me *be* your friend for a while. Then you can kick me out. But one cup of tea, can you do that?"

He hesitated for a long moment, then sighed and stood back. "OK. Thanks."

They went up to the flat and he asked her about Rose and how they were getting on with the book, the other things she had been up to, kept talking fast, filling every pause with something. Eventually she rose from the armchair she was in and sat next to him on the sofa.

"Stop, Seth," she said gently. "You don't have to keep making conversation. You don't have to pretend that everything's OK when I know it's not."

"Don't," he said gruffly. "I can't talk about it now."

"You don't have to. You don't have to talk. You don't have to do anything. Just don't be alone. Unless you really want to."

There was a long silence, then he sighed and looked at her. He took her hand. "I don't want to be alone. I thought I did but I was wrong. I'm glad you're here. But I don't want to talk about it. Can we just sit?"

"Whatever you want," she said. "We can sit, walk, watch a film, whatever."

"Yeah, let's watch a film. And a hug would be great."

After she hugged him, he put a DVD in and sat back down beside her, his face still set hard. She rested her head against his shoulder for a moment and was surprised when he lifted his arm and put it round her.

"Do you mind?" he asked.

"No," she said, putting her arm round him. They sat close together quietly and it was well into the early hours when the third film finished.

Serena yawned. "I'd better go home."

"I'll walk with you," he said.

"There's no need," she said. "Really, I'll be fine. I've survived London streets on my own. And here."

"No, I'll walk home with you. Don't argue," he said as she began to speak again. "I can be very determined and you won't win." He gave her half a smile.

"Well, OK then," she smiled back.

They walked in silence through the shadowed streets, the cool and quiet of the night broken only by the rush of the sea. They stopped outside Serena's door.

"Thank you," he said.

"I didn't do anything."

"You did. You were there. I don't know what I did to deserve a friend like you, but there must have been something good somewhere."

"Seth, you deserve the best of everything. I'm glad I'm your friend."

He put his arms round her and hugged her hard and long. "So am I.'

Serena watched him head off home before letting herself into her house. She played absentmindedly with the starfish on the chain round her neck as she thought about Jessica. She wondered what she could do to make him feel better.

She texted him on the Sunday morning to see how he was.

Not bad thanks. Taking myself off to the wilds for the day. Need time to think.

As long as you're OK. Sending hugs.

Can I have them next time I see you?

She laughed to herself.

They'll be waiting for you.

It was late that evening when he appeared to collect them. He still didn't want to talk and although he seemed less shadowed she could see the hurt in his eyes. She wished she could make it go away.

At work the following day, working through Rose's documents as usual, an idea struck her. She went back to the file about the language and symbolism of flowers.

"He may not want to talk, but at least I can send him a message," she thought.

She trawled through the information, noting down the flowers that seemed to fit best with what she wanted to say. Then she slipped the piece of paper into her bag so that she could think over them again later.

Rose was upset about what had happened but unsurprised.

"He came in to see me yesterday on his way back from wherever he'd been," she told Serena as they drank their morning coffee together. "I hate to see him so unhappy. Especially when we all knew how it was going to end. Every time that girl comes back it's like watching an accident in slow motion and not being able to stop it. It may be wrong but I so dislike her."

"Me too," Serena agreed. "But I doubt we've seen the last of her."

"More's the pity," Rose said glumly. Then she brightened slightly. "Let's talk about cheerier matters. I see you were working on chapters rather than just sections last week."

"Yes," Serena agreed. "Actually, if you're free this afternoon, maybe we could go through some of it."

Serena took a walk along the beach that evening, enjoying the early spring sunshine and disregarding the chilly breeze that was blowing in off the waves. There was something in the air that she couldn't quite identify, a sensation around her of excitement, almost as if the world was holding its breath. She looked out to sea for the longest time, just wondering if it was a call from the deep she was hearing, translated differently by her human neurology. The sea was ruffled by the wind, but she could make out flashes in the far distance and couldn't help wondering whether Tia and her sisters had come by. She waved anyway.

"I love you," she thought as loudly as she could. As she continued to walk something made her look down to the sand beneath her feet and she couldn't help smiling. There were four small shells lying there in a circle around a delicate little piece of driftwood. She picked them up, knowing that they were a gift to her from the sea. Treasures from the deep. A shell for each of her sisters and the driftwood was her.

"Thank you, Tia," she murmured as she slipped them into her pocket.

When Serena reached home, she placed the shells and the wood in the blue glass bowl that she kept on the windowsill of her bedroom. As she made herself something to eat she was thinking over her plan for Seth, the piece of paper open on the table. She had her favourite music on as she ate and pondered, still wondering if it was the right thing to do. Or if he'd think she had gone insane.

"He wouldn't be far wrong," she thought. "But I have to do something. Time's too short to waste."

Looking through her list, and given that it was still only early April, she realised that she was going to have to source some of the flowers from the local florist, if she could get them at all. It added another question mark to her already wavering resolve, but she decided to try anyway.

She didn't have time the following day as she and Rose were deep into the book. She left late, just as Seth was coming in to see Rose.

"Hi," he said.

"Hi yourself. How are you?"

In answer, he grabbed her into a big hug, lifting her off her feet.

"Better now, thanks." He smiled as he let her go and it almost reached his eyes. Almost. "Do you have to go? You could stay and eat if you like. Auntie won't mind, she always makes enough to feed an army."

"I'd love to but I'm meeting Tallie in, ooh, thirty minutes. As you can tell, I'm horribly late. Sorry. But thanks for asking."

"OK." He kept his grin in place but his face fell slightly. "Have fun."

"You too. We'll be at the Hare later and I think Nikki and Howie are coming up, if you want to join us."

His face brightened again. "I might just do that. Thanks."

"Maybe see you later then." She got into her car and waved as she drove away.

Wednesday saw Serena with her resolve hardened to send Seth a message. With flowers. He had joined them at the Hare in the late evening, but had been quiet and a little withdrawn. He'd walked home with her, despite her protestations, hugging her hard and long again before almost reluctantly letting her go and heading off back the way he had come. She understood that he found it hard to talk but she knew that just allowing it all to pour out was a relief, at least for a little while. She just didn't know how to get him to let go. Words weren't enough. She was putting her hope in petals.

She left Rose's a bit early and scurried into town to the flower shop, where miraculously they had all but one of the things that weren't growing at the cottage. Then she hurried home and laid them out on the kitchen table. Having cut the remaining elements from the garden, she retrieved an empty jam jar from the cupboard and began to trim the flowers to the right lengths, placing them one by one into the jar, roses, freesias, geraniums, lavender and sage, until she was happy with the arrangement, binding the stalks together with a long strand of ivy. She took Tia's piece of driftwood from her bedroom and tied it onto one of the strands of ivy trailing down the front of the jar, knowing that he was as much adrift as she was. Having written a little card with the flower code so that he would understand what she was trying to say, she tucked it in amongst the blooms. It said:

This is my take on the language of flowers. Hope it reminds you what you are worth and what you deserve.

Scarlet geranium – comfort
Lavender – serenity
Yellow rose – happiness
Pink rose – friendship
Sage – protection
Freesia – trust
Ivy – bonds of friendship

Serena checked her watch. It was after closing time and she was fairly sure that he wasn't going out that evening. The whole of the walk down to his flat she was debating what to do, whether to ring the bell and hand it to him face to face or whether to just leave it on the step by his front door so he would find it later or in the morning. She still wasn't sure if she was doing the right thing, but having come so far she was determined to go through with it. In the end, after standing uncertainly in his porch for several minutes, she opted for leaving it by the step and just ringing the bell so that he would come down and discover it, making herself scarce before he appeared. What she hadn't bargained for was running slap bang into him as she left.

"Hey," he said. "It's good to see you. Were you knocking? I just went to get some milk."

Serena felt herself blush. "I um... it wasn't anything urgent. I'd better go." She tried to slip past him but he caught her arm, looking concerned.

"Are you OK? You look stressed." He pulled her gently towards his door. "You've got time for a coffee, haven't you? Tell me what's bugging you."

"Nothing, honestly," Serena said. "I just thought I'd...'

"Come on, come up for a minute and... hey, what's that?" He let go of her momentarily to bend down and pick up the jar, recognising her writing on the card. She was backing away but he reached out and stopped her. "Is this why you're all jumpy? Did you leave this for me? Why are you trying to escape?"

"Oh, because it's daft and now I feel really stupid," Serena muttered, her face scorching with embarrassment.

"Don't be so silly." He tugged her gently but insistently back into the porch and blocked her exit. "At least let me look before you run away." She hid her face with her hands as he wrested the card from its place and read through it. There was a long silence.

"Oh no," she thought. "It was the wrong thing after all."

But then she felt him move closer to her, felt his arms enclose her as he rested his cheek against her hair.

"Serena, thank you," he whispered. "You just blow me away."

After a while, he released her. "You're not going to run away now, are you?" he asked. "Come up, at least for a bit. I might even be able to rustle up some food if you can stay."

"You don't have to," she said.

"No, but I'd like to. Please."

She smiled then and nodded. "OK. Thanks."

After they had eaten, Serena insisted on washing up. She hadn't asked directly about Jessica but the openings were there and eventually he took one.

"After everything I said to you about her, why did I let myself get involved again? Why didn't I just say no? Tell her to get lost."

"Not so easy to do in the heat of the moment." Serena was sympathetic. "Hindsight's a great thing."

"Yeah, but it's not like I didn't already have hindsight. I don't understand how I can be so damn useless." Seth was castigating himself. "I always prided myself on being quite a strong person. Apparently I'm not though. I just let her ride roughshod over me. Again. You'd think I'd be able to say no but my will is weaker than I care to admit. Hopeless.'"

"You're not useless, don't be so daft," Serena said crossly. "Or hopeless. And you are a strong person. But you use all your strength holding other people up. You don't leave enough for yourself."

Seth looked at her, mystified. "I don't do anything."

Serena rolled her eyes in mock exasperation. "Oh, for goodness sake, Seth, seriously?" But he was still staring at her, genuinely puzzled. She shook her head, incredulous.

"I can't believe you don't see it. Do I really need to explain what you do for so many people?"

"I don't do anything," he repeated.

"Why do you think Gaia and Tallie and Nikki come to you for hugs? Because you hug with your heart not just your arms. Why are you the first one your Aunt phones when she has a problem? And before you say she's family, why are you the first one that at least three of her friends phone when they've got problems too? Because they know you'll always help. Why did Tallie come to you when her Gran was taken ill, and not Gaia or Ethan or me? Because we all know that you're calm and you'll know what to do and that you'll do anything to help anyone. What did you do when you found me crying my eyes out? You hugged me and looked after me and told me it would get better. And you helped me believe it."

Seth shrugged but Serena was in full swing. "You're strong for all of us, Seth. You hold us up when we need it and you're always there for everyone, friend or not. You give out all the time. You never let anyone down, not even when they hurt you. That's why you can't say no to Jessica. You don't want to let her down, leave her needing something you could give. It's not weakness, it's selfless. But she exploits that and she leaves you with no resources for yourself."

"You're sweet, Serena. You're always so kind. But I don't do anything that most other people wouldn't do. Except act like a fool."

"Aargh, Seth!" Serena was exasperated. "What do I have to do to make you see yourself like I see you? Like we all see you? I don't know whether to hug you or shake you or... wallop you with a soggy sponge."

He couldn't help himself, he started laughing then, holding up his hands in surrender. "OK, OK, I'm not a complete fool. I'm an OK person most of the time. And I'll take a hug over a soggy sponge any time."

"You're much more than an OK person," Serena grumbled. "OK is nowhere near enough of a word for you."

"But it's a start," he said. "Can I have that hug now?"

"You're only just out of soggy sponge territory. You'll have to find a better adjective for yourself." She stood there with her hands on her hips. "Try again."

"Oh, I don't know. Reasonable? Not all bad?" She was shaking her head despairingly. "Kind? Helpful? I don't know."

She stared him straight in the eye. "You say kind and helpful like it's a question. You're the kindest, most generous, most helpful, open hearted and unselfish person I've ever met. You're amazing. I don't know why you can't see it."

He looked baffled. "But..."

"You are. And unless you say it I am going to..."

"Serena, you're crazy. I'm not... Whoa." She had turned to the sink and run the dishcloth under the tap. She gave it a gentle wringing. "You're not serious?"

"Oh, but I am." She was laughing now as she advanced on him with the wet cloth. "Your choice. I'm waiting." She had it raised to shoulder height now, holding it away from her as it dripped on the floor.

"OK, OK." He capitulated at the last moment. "I'm kind. I'm helpful.'

"And?" She swung the cloth slowly, aiming it at his head. "And?"

He sighed. "I'm amazing?"

"Is that a question?" She drew her arm back.

"No, no, OK. I'm amazing, I am, really. Please, put down your weapon!"

He still didn't look sure but she took pity on him and threw the cloth back over into the sink.

"Yes, you are."

"So? Have I earned that hug now?"

"Only if you'll promise me that you'll tell yourself that every day." She raised an eyebrow at the look he gave her. "Yes, really."

He hesitated. "Oh. Alright then. If it'll make you happy."

"No. I want it to make you happy." The look he gave her then nearly melted her heart. He opened his arms slightly and she stepped into them and hugged him close.

"Did you know," she said, looking up at him, "that the first time I ever went to the Old Hare was the weekend after I moved in? Sarah came down and we met some of her friends there. And I saw you and Ethan and Gaia and Tallie and the rest. You all seemed so comfortable with each other. Of course I didn't know you then and I sat there feeling a bit lost and a lot overwhelmed, watching you dishing out hugs left, right and centre with a massive smile on your face, and I was so envious. I was this close," she indicated a centimetre with her thumb and forefinger, "to coming over and asking you for a hug myself. But I was too scared."

He squeezed her gently, smiling. "And now?"

She rested her head against him momentarily as she squeezed him back. "Still terrified. As you can clearly tell."

Chapter 11

Three weeks later Seth was sitting in Gaia and Ethan's kitchen, talking about Serena.

"She's been so good to me since Jessica left. She seems to know what I need even before I do. And Rose adores her."

"I think Rose isn't the only one," Ethan grinned, slapping Seth on the back.

"Ooh, Seth, I do believe you're blushing," Gaia giggled, bringing dinner over to the table.

Seth glared at them both mock-crossly. "Desist. Immediately."

"No. It's too much fun," Gaia said, dishing food onto plates and passing them round. "Anyway I think it's great you're getting closer, getting together. You like her, she likes you, you're both lovely... job done."

"Gaia, we're not 'getting together'. We're just friends."

"Exceptionally good friends from what I've seen," Gaia broke in.

"Maybe, but she's just got divorced and I, well, I don't know where I'm at, so I don't think either of us is planning on getting involved."

"Yet," Ethan said. Seth raised an eyebrow at him. "What? I'm psychic. I can't help it."

"What would be so bad?" Gaia asked. "You obviously really like each other, way beyond friendship, and don't even try to deny it Seth, because I know you too well and you're a crap liar anyway. I see the way you look at her. You know that she's nothing like Jessica."

"Yeah, the only similarity is that they're both blonde. And in Jessica's case, even that's fake," Ethan agreed.

"I don't know," Seth muttered. "Like I said, I don't know how I feel. People are confusing. You think you know what's happening and then wham... you didn't know anything at all."

"Jessica gives us females a bad name." Gaia sounded cross. "Most of us aren't like that."

"I didn't mean that," Seth said. "Look at my father. And Serena's ex. Bastards, both of them."

"But you're not," Ethan reminded him. "Most of us aren't like that either. How long are you going to let Jessica hold you back?"

Seth shrugged. He knew that they would counter any excuses he came up with. And he knew that they'd be right. Suddenly, he didn't have the energy.

"So why not ask Serena out? I'd bet my life she'll say yes," persisted Gaia.

Seth stared at her as if she was mad.

"Why would she want to go out with me?"

"Ooh, I don't know, because you're kind and funny and thoughtful and honest. And you don't take advantage and you're a good friend."

"That's her, not me."

Ethan was shaking his head. Gaia laughed. "Seth, that's why you should ask her out. You two are like mirrors of each other but neither of you can see it. Too nice for your own damn good, the pair of you. You'd be really good for each other though."

But Seth wasn't convinced. "Forget it. It'll never happen." "No matter how much I might want it to," he finished silently.

"Oh yes it will," said Ethan. "And you know I'm rarely wrong."

Seth stayed later than he had intended and walked home slowly. When he finally got to bed, sleep was way out of reach. His mind was spinning with the things that Ethan and Gaia had said and the possibilities that those opened up. They had mined into his feelings for Serena, the ones which he had tried to bury because they scared him so much, wrapped in the terror that it would end up like Jessica all over again, even though his heart told him it wouldn't. And he was filled with self disgust when he thought about how he kept letting Jessica back in, even though he really didn't care about her anymore, and how the devil he knew was still easier than the new path that was in front of him. He lay staring into the darkness, trying to make sense of it, any of it, longing for the quiet forgetfulness of sleep.

Eventually he gave up trying to fight and let the thoughts flow. They were mainly about Serena. How it had felt when he had hugged her at

New Year. What he had wanted to do to her ex when he had found her crying in February. The softness of her skin when he had fastened the chain round her neck on her birthday and how he had just wanted to slip his arms round her and hold her there.

For just a few moments, he let himself imagine what it might be like to let her in.

One Saturday night not long after, they gathered at Gaia and Ethan's to eat and afterwards sat around talking and drinking wine. Serena looked round the room at her friends and allowed the happiness to wash over her. Not only had they included her into their circle without hesitation, they had made her feel that she was truly a part of their lives. It meant a lot. In addition to that, Seth appeared to have engineered things so that he was sitting beside her on the sofa, close but not quite touching. His proximity made her heart jump, but she told herself off.

"Don't be stupid," she thought. "That is beyond hope."

Still, it didn't spoil the contentment she felt, especially when Seth found her hand and wove his fingers through hers. She didn't want the evening to end. Ever.

"Do some Tarot, honey," Gaia was saying to Ethan. "If you don't mind."

"I don't mind. It's a good time for it. Nice and mellow. Does anyone want a reading?"

"Yes please," said Tallie.

"Yeah," agreed Seth. "If you're up for it."

"Yeah," Ethan said. He walked over to the cabinet in the corner and retrieved his cards. "Why don't I do a three card spread for each of you."

"Fantastic. If you like," Gaia said enthusiastically.

"OK. Who's first?" He sat cross legged in front of the coffee table.

Tallie leapt up and sat next to him. "Can I?"

Ethan handed her the pack. "Shuffle, cut and pick three. Keep your query in mind while you do. You know the drill."

Tallie smiled and shut her eyes momentarily. Then she shuffled. Serena watched fascinated as Tallie laid out the cards and Ethan studied them, giving a reading of past, present and future. She knew that humans had a wealth of stories and mythology regarding magic, but she hadn't realised that some could genuinely access it. That was what she could feel Ethan doing, and it made the void inside her ache.

"It's looking even better for Gran than I thought," Tallie said happily and skipped back to plonk herself on Rob's lap while Ethan moved on to Gaia. Seth went next, then Rob. Serena's turn came.

"I've never had a reading done before," she said.

"It's easy. Just think of a question while you shuffle," said Gaia, "and the cards will give you some sort of guidance."

Serena settled a little nervously beside Ethan and he handed her the deck. His fingers brushed her hand as he did and she felt a jolt in the part of her where her magic used to be. He felt something too, she could tell, because he looked at her sharply as he withdrew his hand, questions forming in his eyes. She looked down at the cards, worried that he would say something, but he remained silent. She shuffled, cut and selected three, laying them out on the table. She heard Ethan's sudden intake of breath.

"That's interesting," he said. Serena could tell he was working hard to keep his voice neutral. "There's a massive amount of change here. It's indicated at all three stations."

"Well, there has been a lot of change," she said. She was starting to panic although she wasn't entirely sure why. She didn't like the look of the cards she'd picked out, especially the third one, the one that was supposed to represent the future.

"Yeah," Gaia agreed. "With the divorce, that's the past, and then moving here, that's the present, and there's always going to be some change in the future, it's hardly surprising."

"True," Ethan said. "That must be it." He stared at the cards, but every now and then Serena could feel him looking at her. Really looking, as if he was trying to read her as well. He knew something wasn't right.

"What cards?" Gaia asked, moving over to the table. Ethan scooped them up quickly and shuffled them back into the pack.

"Death was one," he said, smiling. "But as we all know, it's not literal death. Often just the death of a set of circumstances and the birth of new ones. That must be it. Right, my turn." He cut the pack and picked his three, distracting Gaia from any more questions. Serena rose to allow her to sit by Ethan, moving to the end of the table and feeling a bit lost. She wished she'd never let Ethan read her cards. She knew there was truth to it and now he had questions about her.

"Hey." Seth caught her hand. "You OK? You look a bit stressed. Don't worry about the cards. Ethan always says they're not set in stone."

She smiled weakly at him, trying to pretend that everything was OK. He could see it wasn't. He tugged her hand until she sat down next to him. "What's up?" he whispered.

She shook her head.

"Did it bring up old stuff?"

She shrugged. There was no way she could explain to him what had happened. He put his arm round her.

"Change isn't always bad, you know," he said. She met his eyes and they spoke volumes.

"Here." Tallie came back in from the kitchen with the wine. "Who needs a refill?"

"Yes please," Seth said, holding out his and Serena's glasses. "Thanks."

After Tallie had topped everyone up Ethan lifted his glass. "A toast," he said. "To the positive power of change." As everyone lifted their glasses and drank, he caught Serena's eyes and smiled at her reassuringly. It made her feel better, but didn't entirely remove the uneasiness that had settled over her.

As they slipped back into easy conversation and laughter Serena began to relax a little again. She hoped that Ethan would just write off her reading as some strange anomaly. He certainly seemed to be past it now, although she did catch him looking at her a few times with an unreadable expression on his face. When she met his eyes the third time he grinned at her and then looked away.

"I'm so excited." It was Tuesday evening and Tallie flung herself down beside Seth on Gaia's big sofa. "A little bird just told me who's playing at the Hare next Saturday." Her eyes twinkled. "Pause for effect."

"You do look more excited than normal," Gaia commented, "which is a worry in itself." She ignored the face Tallie pulled at her. "And as much fun as it would be not to ask you who but just to watch you try not to tell us, I will be kind and gracious and put you out of your misery. Who is it?"

"You're fiendishly mean," Tallie retorted, "but right of course. I'm nearly beside myself. It's Underhill."

Rob was grinning as Gaia, Ethan and Seth's faces lit up. Serena was baffled.

"Really?" Gaia was elated. "Oh, I haven't seen them in way too long."

"Me neither," Seth agreed. "Still the same guys?"

"As far as I know," Tallie confirmed. "Well, Luke, Holly and Bryn for sure. Maybe Jonno, maybe April. Maybe both."

Gaia rubbed her hands together. "That's so great."

Ethan nodded agreement, then noticed Serena's puzzled look.

"They're a band based in Cornwall," he said. "Folky metally fusion."

"Oh, but they're so much more than that," Tallie said pointedly, poking Gaia in the ribs with her elbow. "Aren't they?" She grinned at Serena. "They're the reason these two," she gestured at Gaia and Ethan, "are together."

Rob laughed and Seth was smiling. Gaia explained.

"Tallie and I were at uni together. She was the year above me but we were in the same flat. Luke was in her year, he's the drummer. We were all good friends and Luke's band got booked to play at the Summer Ball. Ethan and Seth came down and, well…" She took Ethan's hand.

"The rest is history," Tallie finished for her. "Oh, I can't wait."

Underhill did not disappoint. Serena had never seen a band quite like them. The energy seemed to crackle off the stage; most of their stuff was quite fast and heavy but the few ballads they played were hauntingly beautiful. The sound of the pipes seemed to reach right into her, touch her soul and the empty place beside it where her magic had once lived. She enjoyed chatting to them afterwards when they came over to catch up with the others. Ethan noticed how Holly, who played the pipes and whistles, seemed to be watching Serena with interest. He moved to stand next to him.

"Picking something up, are you?" he asked quietly.

Holly grinned. "That could be taken in more than one way, but if you're asking about magic, then yes."

"I thought so." Ethan was oddly pleased that he'd been right. After all, he'd picked it up about Holly, so he wasn't sure why he doubted himself. Still… it sounded so far-fetched. Holly wasn't human, he was one of the fey, moving between the realm of magic and the human world as he chose. Despite his psychic gift, Ethan had been truly shocked when he'd realised how close true magic really was. He had never told anyone; Holly had asked him not to.

"I'm not sure what it is," Holly went on, "but there's something wild and mysterious there. I have no doubt you'll find out." He grinned impishly. "Didn't take you long to find out about me, now did it?"

Ethan had concerns about Serena, more so now that Holly had confirmed his suspicions. The Tarot reading he had done for her did not bode well, particularly for a magical being and, if that was what she was, he wanted to help. Deciding that his only option was to talk to her about it, he waited down on the front after work, knowing that she often walked on the beach in the early evening. When she finally appeared, he called to her and she waved as he dropped down onto the sand and made his way over.

"Oh, hey Ethan," she said, as he approached. "How are you?"

He smiled. "Good thanks. You?" She nodded. "Listen, there was something I wanted to talk to you about. Have you got time?" He saw her face change as her guards came up.

"Sure," she said. "Do you want to walk with me?"

They began to stroll along the beach. There was silence initially. Ethan wasn't really sure how to approach what he needed to ask. Eventually he began.

"It was about the Tarot reading I did for you. And what I noticed when I handed you the cards, what I've noticed before around you."

Serena remained quiet. She looked nervous.

"You may think I'm crazy. Most people do, they don't buy the psychic thing, but it is the truth. I've always been able to see things, tap into things that others are completely oblivious to. It's not something I chose, it chose me. And I know there are so many things out there that most people won't accept or believe but are true even so."

"Oh," Serena said.

"Like, for example, other influences on our reality and existence. Spirits, angels, fairies, call them what you want, there are forces beyond our understanding that exist around us. Like how Tarot and fortune telling is usually accurate but being subject to interpretation, can be affected by the reader. Their parameters, expectations, assumptions, beliefs, all that stuff. I'm always aware of that when I'm doing a reading, that's why I say that my interpretation is only one possibility."

"Right," Serena added into the pause. Ethan could sense that she didn't like where the conversation was going, but he continued anyway.

"I think magic is around us all the time. It's our expectation and assumption as humans of what magic is that's the problem. I think it's a lot simpler and more natural than most people think. I'm sure that I feel it sometimes, especially when I'm doing a reading or meditating."

"Ethan, why are you telling me this? I believe you're psychic, that you have an ability beyond most of us. You don't think I'm questioning that, do you?"

"No. No, it's not that. It's just that I think you have an ability too. Or something. There's something about you that resonates with me, I don't know how else to put it. It calls to my ability. I'm far more psychically aware when you're around, it's like you enhance my antenna somehow."

Serena was shaking her head, trying to sound non-committal as she attempted to hide her panic. "I don't think so."

"You sound stressed. You are stressed about what I've said, I can feel it. You don't have to be. But I know there's something different about you, I've known from the time I first met you in Seth's shop. There's a charge off you. And that Friday, what I felt when I gave you the cards and our fingers touched, and then the cards you drew; I've never ever seen that much change and upheaval in a three card before. That's way beyond divorce or moving home or even both together. It's like your existence is a complete transition. And there is magic attached to you somehow, I know there is, even if you don't use it."

"Stop, Ethan, this is ridiculous." Serena was really flustered now, trying and failing to hide it under a stern tone. She stopped walking. So did Ethan.

"I'm sorry Serena. I'm not trying to upset you, really I'm not. I'm actually more worried about you and looking for reasons that you would have pulled those cards. Death, the Hanged Man, the Tower. That's unbelievable. There is something, isn't there? I can see in your face how uncomfortable this is for you, and I know it's not talking about esoteric stuff that bothers you. So what is it? Are you in some sort of danger? Do you have an ability that's putting you at risk? Is there anything I can do to help?"

Serena put her hands to her face, shaking her head. He knew he was close to the truth. Moments later, she pulled herself together and looked at him directly.

"You're barking up the wrong tree. I don't have any ability. Or magic."

"Then what am I picking up on? I know there's something. You are not ordinary. The aura around you is different but in such a subtle way I can't really read why. Where are you from, Serena? And don't say London, or some coastal town. I mean where are your origins? What are you hiding? When you saw the Tower why did you look so devastated when it can be a card of transformation rather than doom? And you knew that by instinct because you'd not had a reading before, had you?"

Serena was shaking her head again. He could see the panic in her eyes. "Please don't ask me. I can't tell you."

"Can't or won't?" His voice was gentle. "Serena, you can trust me. I won't tell anyone if you don't want me to, not Seth, not Gaia, no one. I can keep secrets, hell, I've been doing it virtually all my life. All psychics do. I'm not asking just to be nosey, I am really concerned about you. And sometimes, I don't know, you get this look like you're almost somewhere else and I know that feeling. Except it doesn't look like it's a good feeling for you. Tell me where you're from. What are you truly?"

"Believe me, you don't want to know." Serena took a few steps and sat down on a low rock. After a moment, Ethan followed and sat beside her. They sat staring out at the sea for a while. Serena sighed.

"Please, Serena," he said. "Please let me help you if I can. Tell me what's wrong. And I don't mean the stuff about your divorce. I'm not belittling that because I can't begin to imagine how bad it was, but what's really eating you?"

When Serena's eyes finally met his, he felt almost physically shaken by the emotions they conveyed. He realised that she was letting him see her unguarded, the loneliness, the fear and the exhaustion that she kept hidden all as clear as a summer sky.

"If I tell you, you have to swear not to tell anyone else. And I mean anyone."

He nodded assent. "I swear," he said. "No one will know but you and me."

"You probably won't believe me anyway," Serena sighed. "Oh well, here goes. I'm human now and I don't have any magic, but I didn't start off that way. I came into being out there," she gestured out to the sea, "as one of the mer."

Ethan felt his eyes widen in surprise but Serena continued.

"Only I never really fitted in. The mer are cool and measured and aloof and I was never like that. I wanted company and contact. I used to come and watch the people on the beach and envy their emotions and their affection and love for each other."

"Whoa," he breathed. "You're a mermaid."

Serena shook her head. "Was. Not anymore. I'm human now."

"How is that possible?"

She looked surprised. Probably, he thought, because he hadn't questioned her about the mer part, only the logistics.

"I fell for a human, in a big way. I saw him on the beach, day after day. Steve. And he seemed to sense me too, and then one day he saw me. He had an accident in the water and I dragged him to the shore. I knew I had to be with him so I went to the Sea Witch and she helped me to make the exchange."

"Exchange?"

"My magic for human soul energy. From the vortices of power. The transformation is permanent, no going back but it's governed by certain rules and requirements. When my decree absolut came through, that put me outside one of them. Now, barring a miracle, I'm on limited time."

"Wow," Ethan said. "I wasn't expecting that."

Serena looked at him. "You believe me then?"

"I know you're not lying. I can feel that from you. And that explains why I can sense a force, magic, from you, why my gift is enhanced around you."

"But I don't have magic anymore."

"Yes but you did have it, you were a magical being. There are always traces left and magic calls to magic. That's what I felt when I handed you the cards and I know you felt it as well, I could see it on your face."

"You're taking this very calmly. Most people would be calling for men with sedatives round about now."

"Most people haven't seen or experienced the things that I have."

Silence fell between them again. Serena gave another sigh. Ethan shook himself mentally and went back over what she had said.

"No wonder the cards showed so much change. When you said you were on borrowed time, that you were outside the rules, what did you mean?"

"When there's a transformation it's pretty much always for love. And it can go either way. Humans have become mer and mer humans because of love. It's reflected in your fairy tales and in our history. But certain laws apply. When mer become human, they cannot tell anyone what they were unless asked directly. The one they love can't know, and must love them truly and say it aloud within a year and a day of the transformation. As long as the love lasts, the transformation is permanent. Marriage also makes it permanent. But if the love fails, or a divorce is finalised then it reverts back to having a year and a day to find love or else..." Serena stopped. Ethan had never seen anyone look so sad.

"Or else what?"

"Transformation is negated. The energy returns to the vortex and I cease to be. Return to the sea as foam."

"Oh. Crap."

"Yeah. That's one way of putting it."

They fell back into silence for a while. Eventually Serena spoke again.

"You know, when I came down here to the cottage, I'd kind of got my head round it. Coming to an end that is. I felt so low after all the loss and horridness of the divorce I didn't really care, it almost would have been a relief to get it over with. I came here because this is where I came ashore, this is where my connection between sea and land lies. I wanted to go back to the water here. But that was before I met Seth and he introduced me to you guys. And to Rose. Now I don't want to go back at all."

"There must be some way round it. What if I said I love you, as a friend, would that work?"

Serena smiled wanly. "You're sweet but no. It has to be romantic true love. If I were Gaia I'd be fine."

"Don't I detect something between you and Seth? You don't have to answer that, I know I do. We all do. You're just so right for each other. It's been a long time since I've seen him look as happy as he does when you're around."

"If you say anything to anyone I will kill you, but yes, I really like him. And I think he maybe feels something for me, but..."

"No buts, he definitely likes you. A lot. We've been friends since we were eleven, remember, I know him really well. In fact, it goes way beyond like, I can tell. The way he looks at you speaks volumes. Plus, have you forgotten, I'm psychic. You two are made for each other, I know it. He's just being cautious because of what's gone on with him and with you."

"I think it goes beyond cautious," Serena observed. "We're both scared stiff, but it's easier for me. I don't want to have my heart broken again but I've got limited time if it does happen. It's different for him. That... woman... has messed him around so badly he doesn't know which way is up any more. It's going to take time before he can trust any girl again, let alone anything else. And then there's his family stuff. His father was never really there. His sister and mother moved to another continent. The chances are I'll have to leave when my time's up and that would be worse. I don't know whether I should just go now before we get any closer. He's been hurt badly enough. I don't want to hurt him even more."

"There again, you could be his saving grace. Honestly Serena, he may not be able to vocalise it, but he'd be really hurt now if you left. And if there is a chance for you to be together and be happy don't you both deserve that after what you've been through." Ethan spoke earnestly. He saw tears in her eyes.

"If only. Oh, Ethan, I don't know, I don't know anything anymore. It seems as if everywhere I look there are questions and problems and I don't know which way to turn. It feels like..." she gave a sharp, unhappy laugh, "like I'm drowning. Which, given where I come from, is crazy."

He reached out and put a hand on her shoulder. "Even if you can't tell him that you're... were a mermaid, couldn't I?"

Serena looked at him, horrified. "No. Ethan, you can't tell anybody. You'll be cursed too if you even try. I could only tell you because you asked me directly. If he finds out, or anyone else for that matter, and it's anyway related to something I've said or done, I'm lost. We'll both be foam and there's no way back."

"You've got quite a while yet, haven't you?"

"Five months, give or take."

"Stay, Serena. If what I sense about you two is right, you should stay. And if it helps, I'll do another reading for you, about you and Seth. Then you'll see what I mean."

It took Serena a few moments, then she nodded. "OK. I'll stay. For now."

"Good." Ethan looked relieved. "And I'm not just saying that for Seth's sake. We'd all miss you if you left."

Chapter 12

Tallie skipped into the Old Hare the following Saturday, grabbed Ethan in a big hug and swung him round in a circle.

"Whoa," he said. "Steady. What's going on?"

"You were so right with my cards," Tallie whooped. "They've said that Gran can come home next week."

"Oh, Tallie, that's fantastic," Gaia smiled. Serena jumped up and hugged her friend.

"I'm so pleased," she said.

"So am I," agreed Tallie, her eyes sparkling. "She's going to need some extra help at home for a while and she'll have to go to the hospital for rehab but still. At least she'll be at home. She's been in two months but she says it feels more like two years."

"Impatience runs in your family then?" Seth asked innocently.

"Yeah, like messiness runs in yours," Tallie retorted, poking her tongue out at him. He grinned.

"As far as bad genes go, neither of those are disastrous really," he said.

Rob grunted. "You wouldn't say that if you'd seen her with a bad chocolate craving and an empty cupboard," he said wryly. "Or on hold in a phone queue."

"You're both so mean," pouted Tallie. "I don't know why I put up with either of you."

"Hugs," said Seth.

"A guaranteed supply of chocolate in the cupboard," Rob laughed. "One chocolate emergency was enough."

"Well, I s'pose that kind of redeems you both," she said. "But only a bit so don't get cocky." She sat down next to Serena.

"As if we'd dare," Rob said loudly to Seth.

"Men," Tallie scoffed. Serena couldn't stop laughing. "Oi, you're supposed to back me up here, sister."

"Sorry," Serena choked, trying to bite back her giggles and retrieve a straight face. It was no good and soon they were all helpless with laughter.

"It's a while since I've laughed like that," Seth said to Serena as they walked home.

"Me too," she agreed. "I forgot how good it feels.'"

"Need to try and do it more often."

Despite the raucous happiness of Saturday night, by Monday morning Serena's mood had fallen considerably and the sunshine outside did little to lift her. She left Rose's at five and dropped the car off at home. It was a glorious evening but she still couldn't shake the melancholy that had clung to her all day. The sea drew her hard. She walked down to the shop to give Seth a message from Rose, planning afterwards to wander the beach.

Even though it was almost closing time, the shop was busy and Seth was tied up behind the counter. She replied to his smile with a little wave and then stood by, looking vaguely through the CDs as he finished. Eventually the shop emptied and he came over to lock the door and flip the sign to 'Closed'.

"It's good to see you," he said. He looked at her closely. "You OK?"

She nodded. "Rose asked me to tell you that the plumber's coming on Wednesday. I was going to text you but I decided to go for a walk so I thought I'd pop in instead."

"Thanks. I'm glad you did. Where are you going?"

"Oh, only along the beach. It's so lovely out there."

"Could you put up with some company? Or do you need solitude? I could really do with an airing, I've been stuck in here all day."

"That'd be good," she said, feeling a little flutter in her chest.

"Great. Just give me a moment to sort out a few bits."

"No hurry," she replied.

"Right. Hey, are you sure you're OK?"

She nodded again and he went to finish up.

Shortly after, they left the shop and crossed the road, descending the stone steps onto the beach. It was almost deserted despite the brightness of the evening. The sky was just beginning to change colour as the sun tipped into descent and the sea was calm, sparkles dancing off the surface like fairy lights. There was the gentle, rhythmic rush as the waves broke on the land and slipped back out to the deep.

Serena stopped to look out across the sea. "It's so beautiful," she said.

"It is," he agreed. "Makes me feel really small."

She smiled but her eyes were far away, searching across the water. He waited for a moment, watching her surreptitiously. It confirmed what he had thought before.

"Hey," he said, touching her shoulder. She started violently. "Oh crap, sorry."

"That's OK," she said as they began to walk again. "I was…"

"Miles away," he finished for her. "I could see. You seemed kind of, I don't know, distant earlier as well. Are you sure everything's alright."

She smiled at him. "Yeah. Thanks." It sounded unconvincing, even to her.

There was silence for a few minutes.

"Can I ask you a question?" he ventured.

"You can ask," she said. "I'm not promising to answer though."

"Looking at the sea makes you sad, doesn't it?"

She looked at him sharply. "Why would you think that?"

"Not sure why but I just get that feeling from you. And your eyes go grey when you look at the sea. Why does it? Make you sad?"

She looked away as they continued to walk slowly.

"Perceptive, aren't you? I guess that earns you an answer. Memories, I s'pose. My ex loves the sea, one of the things we had in common. I met him over there by the rocks. And my family, they're close to the sea somewhere but out of reach."

"I'm sorry, I didn't mean to…"

"It's fine Seth, really. You're kind to notice. Although I'm not sure what my eye colour's got to do with it."

"You have chameleon eyes. They're blue when you're happy and I swear I see flecks of green in them when you're cross. But they go grey when you're sad. Not meaning to sound smug, but I know when you're hurting because of your eyes. They're so expressive. You have amazing eyes." He paused. She was too overwhelmed to say anything.

"God, that sounded like the worst cheesy chat up line ever," he continued, "and it wasn't meant to be, well not bad and cheesy anyway because it's the truth, and not really a chat up line either, unless you… I mean I'm not trying to make you… oh, I'm so crap at this." He stopped talking and put his hand to his head.

Serena's pulse accelerated, hope catching in her throat with her breath.

He exhaled slowly. "What I'm trying to say is that I really... I think you're..." He trailed off again. "Dammit, Serena, I want to...'

It was her turn then to gather her courage to speak. She stopped and touched his hand briefly, bringing him to a halt too. He turned toward her but she didn't dare look at him.

"I'm taking a chance here," she said, words tumbling out fast with nervousness, "because you're pretty much my best friend and I may be making the wrong assumption and if I am, I'll be very embarrassed and probably never be able to look you in the face again, but actually, if you were trying, you know, to chat me up, I'd be really pleased." She could feel her cheeks burning as she got to the end of the sentence and stared down at the sand hard enough to bore a hole through rock.

He moved slightly closer to her then. "Would you?" he asked softly. "That's good to know." He reached out to move a stray strand of hair off her face. "So if I asked you if you wanted to go out with me somewhere, maybe today or tomorrow or whenever you're free, what would you say?"

"I'd say yes," she whispered, nerves and relief almost choking her.

He took her hands then and pulled her close to him. "And if I told you that I really like you, that I can't stop thinking about you, would that scare you away?"

She rested her head against his shoulder and it felt so good. "No, because I think about you all the time too."

She felt his arms slide round her to hold her tightly.

"I'm glad," he said and she could hear him smiling.

After a little while they continued to walk, hand in hand now, making their way off the beach and up the cliff path. They sat for a while on the bench, looking out over the water as they talked and then headed back into town to get something to eat. Seth insisted on walking home with her even though she argued that there was no need.

"I want to," he said. "Be with you longer that way."

At her cottage, in the courtyard she fumbled for her key and unlocked the door before turning to him.

"Do you want to come in?"

He was looking at her, eyes intense. "I do, but I'd better not. We've both got to work tomorrow."

She looked down, her face hot. "OK. Thank you so much for this evening. It's been…"

"Amazing," he finished for her. "You're amazing." He moved closer to her, tilting her face up to look at him. His other arm slipped round her, pulling her to him and his lips came down to cover hers.

"Oh," Serena murmured minutes later as she buried her face against his shoulder. She felt him sigh.

"Man, I've wanted to do that for so long," he said softly.

"Really?" Serena sounded unsure.

"Yeah. Since New Year. When all the others were and I was just hugging you, I so wanted to."

"But I thought…"

"I know. Jessica. But after what you'd been through I didn't know if you'd want to be seeing anyone, then, I don't know, just about when I'd got brave enough to ask, you were in bits. That night in February… after that, I didn't want to push you or take advantage. And then I was kinda trying to pluck up the courage again when she waltzed back as she invariably does and I'm just that much of an idiot I let myself get sucked back in. It just seemed… easier."

"Not an idiot, Seth."

"You're kind, but I was. But it did prove one thing to me."

"What?" Serena looked up at him.

"I really don't want to be with her. I want to be with you."

Serena smiled. "I'm glad."

He ran his thumb over her lip. "I think I need to kiss you again now." And he did.

"OK." Ethan sat down next to Serena at her kitchen table. "You ready?"

"As I'll ever be," she replied nervously.

"It's going to be fine. I've got a good feeling about this." Ethan smiled at her reassuringly. He handed her the cards. "Concentrate on what you want to know. Shuffle and then divide the cards into three piles and line them up here, face up."

"Right." Serena took a deep breath and began to shuffle. Seth was foremost in her mind, with her impending demise close behind. "Please, please…" she thought silently. She cut the deck into three and placed them where Ethan had indicated.

"Now," Ethan said, "Bring the top ones just below each pile and the next ones just below. Great. Now we have past, present and future with some qualifying information. So, what do we have?"

Serena crossed her fingers and held her breath. Ethan was studying the cards intensely.

"That's really interesting," he said finally. "Your primary cards are the same as before but in a different order. And your qualifiers, I think there's definitely hope for you yet."

Serena exhaled slowly. "So. Tell me more."

"Well, the Tower is the past rather than the future now and qualified by the Ten of Swords. That makes sense, massive change, new awareness, trauma, despair, sadness. Sums up your initial transformation, your marriage and then the divorce. Then, the present, the Hanged Man, a pause in activity and a change in situation. Qualified by the Page of Rods, who represents someone trustworthy and loyal. Hmm, wonder who that might be."

Serena blushed and batted his arm lightly. "Could be any of you," she said.

"Of course it could," Ethan agreed, his tone falsely sarcastic. "But I'm pretty sure I know who it is, and I'm the psychic, remember."

"Fine," Serena laughingly gave in. "So what's coming. Certain doom, or might I have half a chance?" She kept the smile on her face but her heart was thumping.

"It's definitely not certain doom," Ethan said. "Death is your future card but it's not necessarily literal, can be the end of one phase and the start of something new. Given that it's qualified by the Lovers, I'd say you're in with a chance."

Serena stared at the cards, especially the last two. Her future almost certain but maybe, just maybe there was some glimmer of hope. She remembered back to how she had felt about Steve, how sure she had been when she released her magic to the void and embraced humanity, how, when he had left her in such a cold and calculated way she had felt that same empty ache as when her magic had been pulled from her. And how it had remained that way until she had met Seth and his friends, how they had begun to fill that gaping wound and help her to feel whole again. She didn't want to lose that a second time. And especially now that it seemed Seth really did have strong feelings for her. Death and the Lovers. She didn't know whether to laugh or cry so she ended up doing both.

Ethan handed her a tissue and squeezed her shoulder. "For what it's worth," he said, "I think you're going to be just fine."

As the next few weeks passed the tentative romance between Seth and Serena grew into something much deeper. The understanding that they already had as friends made it easier for them to become closer but they were both cautious about rushing into something new. Neither wanted to risk their friendship and their prior experiences had made them both wary. But there was an undeniable attraction between them and, more importantly, a bond that went far beyond the physical and linked them on a much more profound level. If they thought about it, both of them realised that that had been there from the very early days of knowing each other.

The change in their relationship was obvious to their friends, who were pleased to say the least.

"About blinking time too," Tallie said, poking Seth the first time he kissed Serena in front of them.

"Told you so," was Ethan's retort. Seth grinned and made a rude sign at him.

"I'm so happy," sparkled Gaia, hugging both of them.

Gradually they found they were seeing each other more and more often. Rose was delighted, especially now that Serena often stayed on when Seth was coming up. Serena was concerned that she was taking over the time they usually shared but Rose put her straight right away.

"Good gracious dear, I've been waiting for this since Christmas. Sheila too. I am not going to stand in the way of romance. Besides, I like you being here."

"Yeah, it's kinda become a tradition now, we've been going up there for years on a Saturday night in summer. Since we left school in fact. We take food and sleeping bags, light a fire and then sleep out under the stars," Ethan said.

They were planning their annual overnight camp up on the cliffs.

"It's so much fun," Gaia added. "We just pick a weekend that the weather's s'posed to be good and go. Sometimes it's July, sometimes it's August. This year it's June. You must come with us, you'll love it."

"You must," Tallie reiterated. "Especially if you like stars. And toasted marshmallows."

"You're a nut," Rob said, giving Tallie an affectionate squeeze. She shrugged.

"Can't help it," she said.

Serena laughed. "It sounds great."

They had arranged to meet up on the cliff top around seven thirty. Gaia and Ethan were planning to get there early to light the fire and start cooking. Tallie, Rob and Seth were working all day. Serena had offered to help but the others had it sussed so after working at Rose's in the morning, she had the afternoon to herself. She packed her small rucksack with a sleeping bag, a thick jumper, some wine and the salads she had made. At about half past six she headed down to Seth's.

"Come up," he said, hugging her. "I'm almost there."

He was just putting the last few things in his rucksack. She watched him, thinking again how good looking he was and how unaware he was of that fact. He closed the backpack and shouldered it, looking over at her and smiling.

"Ready?" he said.

They headed out and down the road to the path up to the cliffs.

"I'm so glad you're coming with us," he said.

"So am I.'

At the top of the path the fire was already lively, positioned well away from the cliff edge but at the highest point so that they could still look out over the sea. The sun was bright but just starting to tip into the mellow gold liquidity of evening. As they approached they could see Ethan and Gaia on the far side of the flames, concentrating on something between them.

"Hi guys," Seth said as they got close. Gaia detached herself from what they realised was a small barbecue set up next to a camping stove and flew towards them, grabbing them each in a bear hug.

"I'm glad you're here," she said, eyes sparkling. "I'm so excited, I love this night."

Her enthusiasm was infectious and Serena, laughing, looked around in amazement.

"I thought this was basic camping," she remarked, taking in the pile of big cushions set well away from the fire, the cooking equipment, the plates and cutlery, food and the large bottles of water for washing and drinking. "How did you get all this stuff here? It must have taken ages."

"Well, it's not quite glamping but it'll do," Gaia said. "And actually, when you have a magic chariot," she indicated a pull along trailer, "it's really not that hard."

"I wish you'd let me help," said Serena.

"Ethan and I enjoy it," Gaia replied. "Really, we have fun. I supervise while he has a workout up the hill, and then he gets to exercise his pyromaniac tendencies as his reward." She ducked, laughing, as Ethan threw an empty cardboard box in her direction.

"Well, can I do anything now?" Serena was insistent.

"Yes," Ethan said, coming over with glasses which he handed to her and Seth. "You can relax and drink that. Don't worry so much. You do enough for other people. You can let yourself be looked after for once."

"Good point, well made," Seth agreed, grinning at her pointedly. She laughed and poked her tongue out at them.

"OK, OK," she said. "I give in."

"So what have we missed?" Tallie came bounding up and swung Gaia round in a whirl.

"Nothing except those two picking on me," Serena said, still laughing as Rob appeared.

"Oh well, that's alright then," Tallie giggled. "Something smells good."

They unloaded the things they had brought and put them together while Ethan and Gaia continued to cook on the barbecue. Within the hour they were sitting down to a feast of salads, bread, cheese and sausages followed by strawberries and chocolate mousse. It stayed warm as the sun descended slowly and dipped into the sea. As they sat round the fire talking and laughing, Rob pulled packets of marshmallows, bars of chocolate and skewers out of his backpack. They toasted the marshmallows in the flames, eating them decadently on squares of chocolate.

As the night darkened to an inky blue and the moon silvered the water, Ethan looked at his watch and stood up.

"It's time."

"Oh, goody." Tallie skipped over to her rucksack and started wrestling something out of it. The others were moving to do the same. Serena was mystified.

"Time for what?" she whispered to Seth.

"Midnight stargazing," he said, rummaging and pulling out a sleeping mat from his pack.

"I haven't got one of those," Serena said but he just smiled at her and let his unroll, revealing that two had been rolled up together. He held one out to her. "Oh. Thanks."

They moved away from the fire, slightly closer to the cliff edge and unfurled the mats in a line. Then they lay looking into the bowl of the sky at the glittering array scattered above them. Serena was mesmerised, especially when Ethan and Rob began to point out constellations and tell the stories that were behind them.

"And now for myth creation," Ethan announced.

"Yay. Can I go first?" Gaia asked. "I've seen a really good one."

"Create away," Rob said.

Seth turned his head to whisper to Serena. "We take turns to pick out a new constellation and give it a story. But it is optional. No pressure."

She smiled. "If you can't be inspired out here like this, then where?"

He smiled back, then they both turned back to the sky. As they followed Gaia's silver black ravens seeking eternity across the heavens, Serena felt Seth reach for her hand and hold it tight. Wishing she could freeze time, she wrapped her fingers around his and searched the stars for a story.

After a magical hour they returned to the fire for a last drink before turning in, still sharing stories. Eventually, when Rob couldn't stop yawning and Gaia could feel her eyelids closing, they decided to try and get some sleep. Rob and Tallie took their stuff over to the right of the fire and Gaia and Ethan settled in front of it. Serena could see them unzipping sleeping bags and cuddling in together. That left her and Seth sitting by the fire in silence. She wasn't sure what to do, so she kept gazing into the flames. Hoping he might know.

After a few minutes he let go of her hand and put his arm round her, moving closer to her.

"It's OK to say no, but can I sleep next to you?" he asked her quietly.

She put her head on his shoulder. "I'd like that."

He squeezed her shoulders and then stood up. "Come with me." On a flat area to the left of the fire he set the sleeping mats side by side. Serena went to get a couple of cushions to use as pillows. When she returned Seth had taken off his shoes and was sitting cross legged on the mat fiddling with the zip on his sleeping bag. She dropped a cushion down for each of them and sat down next to him. He looked deep in thought. In fact he could have been meditating were it not for the tell-tale frown line between his eyebrows and the restless movement of his fingers. Bizarrely it helped Serena's nerves, as she thought he might be worrying about the same thing she was. She pulled her own sleeping bag onto her lap and spoke.

"You look like you're channelling a Buddhist monk."

He smiled. "Still searching for inner peace. Do you think we can ever find it?"

"Don't know," Serena said, shrugging. "I'll settle for the peace around us right now. With or without the sound of a zip being tortured."

His hands stilled. "Sorry. I was just…" He looked over in Gaia or Ethan's direction. "I wasn't sure if…" His eyes met hers and she saw what he was afraid to say. Afraid to push either of them too hard. In that moment she came to her decision. She unzipped her sleeping bag fully and opened it out.

"I promise I won't try to jump you, or make you do anything against your will," she said, laying it down. He moved out of her way, watching her silently as she spread it across both mats and evened it out. "Don't worry, I'll behave myself. You can trust me." She could feel her colour rising and looked away as she kicked off her sandals and lay down.

"It's not you I don't trust," he muttered.

She heard him opening his sleeping bag; it fluttered down to cover her and a moment later she felt him lie down beside her. They both stayed there frozen, staring up at the sky, not touching but acutely aware of their closeness. Eventually he moved towards her, reaching over to stroke her hair. She turned her head to look at him, shadowed in the moonlight.

"Hi," he whispered.

"Hi," she whispered back.

He levered himself up on one elbow so he was gazing down at her.

"I'm so glad you're here."

"Me too," was the last thing she said before he kissed her.

Seth awoke before the sun came up, just as the sky was beginning to lighten. For a moment he thought he was still dreaming, but as the last splinters of sleep dropped away he became aware of Serena curled beside him. He tightened his arms around her, bringing her as close as he could, relishing the feel of her against him. She stirred as he moved and her eyelids fluttered open. She smiled sleepily.

"Sorry I woke you," he murmured.

"I'm not," she said. "I'd like to freeze time right now. Just stay here forever in the twilight with you." She shifted slightly to tuck her head onto his shoulder. "Feels so good to be like this.'"

"Feels so good to be with you," he whispered. "Like nothing I've felt before. I don't want anyone or anything else. Only you."

He felt her sigh, felt her hands move over his back. He shifted down so he could look at her.

"Only you," he said as they began to kiss again.

They drifted between kisses and whispers until the sky began to really change colour and then sat close together to watch the sunrise. The others seemed to be stirring as well, coming to with the dawn. When the sky was blue and the sea was shimmering, Gaia got up and put the kettle on the camping stove to make tea. While she and Serena did that, Rob, Tallie and Seth moved the mats over to be either side of Ethan and Gaia. Then they all sat together in a row under the sleeping bags just to keep off the early chill and sipped their tea, looking out across the water.

"Can life get any better than this?" Gaia sighed.

Seth put his arm round Serena. "Nope," he said.

When the sun was higher in the sky and they had eaten some of the leftovers for breakfast, they packed everything away and cleared their campsite. Tallie and Rob said they'd help Ethan and Gaia with the stuff since they were going in the same direction, declining Serena and Seth's offer of help.

"Really, we'll be fine," Ethan said. "Bit of clearing up, then some more sleep, I think. Proper sleep, on a soft surface."

Tallie prodded him. "Wuss."

"Can't help it. Us psychics are just oversensitive."

They walked down the path together and then the four set off up the road, leaving Seth and Serena on the front.

After dropping their stuff in at Seth's they spent the morning on the beach. It was busy but they knew the quieter places where they could sit relatively undisturbed. Then they went back to his flat so that he could have a shower and then on to hers so that she could. It was mid-afternoon and when she came back down he was yawning.

"Keeping you up?" she asked with a smile.

"No, but I didn't get much sleep last night and neither did you," he chided her gently, catching her hand and pulling her in. He yawned again and set her off.

"Oh, for goodness sake. Now look what you've done."

"Sorry. Need sleep." He kissed her. "Just need to curl up somewhere." He kissed her again. "Next to you preferably."

She tightened her arms around him, heart thumping. "Sounds good." She reached up to kiss him and this time he didn't stop, his hand running up and down her spine.

"Where?" he asked eventually. His voice was low. She loosened her grip and led him slightly hesitantly into the living room.

"There's the sofa," she whispered. "Or there's the bed upstairs."

He smiled at her, kissing her again gently. "I'd like to go upstairs," he said quietly, his eyes dark. "But honestly, I'm not sure that we'll get much sleep."

She smiled and they went up the stairs together.

It was much, much later and the light was fading when he slipped from under the covers and got dressed. She sat up, pulling the duvet around her.

"You could stay," she said. "If you wanted."

He came round to her to drop a kiss on her lips. "Tempting, but we do both really need to get some sleep."

"OK." There was something about the look on his face that set alarm bells ringing. She reached for her robe and wrapped it round herself, followed him down the stairs. He pulled her close at the door, kissed her hard.

"I'll see you soon," he said. She nodded and watched him leave, a horrible sinking sensation in the pit of her stomach. She locked up, turned off the lights and went back upstairs. After the happiness of the weekend, she suddenly felt bleak and bereft. As if she had done something wrong. She picked up her phone to text him and sat looking at it for ages, not knowing what to say. Eventually she sent a message.

Hope you are OK. Sleep well.

She sat, waiting, hoping, for what seemed like forever, but nothing came back. She had the most awful feeling that she had lost him. Eventually she put the phone down, curled up into a little ball under her duvet and tried to stop the despair from taking her over completely.

Seth walked home slowly, his mind racing. He had so wanted to be with Serena, had felt so right about it and yet suddenly now he was at sea and full of doubt. Not about her but about himself. He hadn't ever felt like this before, so intensely connected to someone, so desperate to be in her company and so out of his depth. He didn't know if this was what falling in love was like but it felt as though the whole world was shifting. It scared him. He always felt unsteady when Jessica was around but this was different. This was all consuming and though he hated himself for it, he just wanted to run.

On Monday Rose was full of questions about the weekend. Serena kept her tone light and told her all about the Saturday evening and how magical it had been out under the stars. She said very little about Sunday apart from that she and Seth had spent it together. It took a gargantuan effort to hide her feeling of dread, which was growing by the hour in the absence of any text from him. Rose seemed delighted, and continued to look through the documents that Serena had produced, smiling to herself.

Serena stayed later than usual that night, and was so tempted to call in and see him on the way home. She managed to stop herself, thinking that maybe he just needed some space. Tallie had left her a message, inviting her out the following evening so she returned the call and accepted, just needing to chat to a friendly voice. She went to bed late, still having heard nothing and it was all she could do not to pick up the phone and ask him why.

Midway through the following morning she gave in and texted him. By this time she had convinced herself that she had done something wrong but was at a loss as to how to make it right.

Seth I'm sorry. Are you OK? Can we talk?

Sheila came over that afternoon and they carried out some of the final recipe testing, edible ones this time. The chat helped to distract Serena but she couldn't get him out of her head. She was glad to get home and change to go and see Tallie. They went out to eat and for drinks, meeting Ethan and Gaia in the pub. Serena kept hoping that Seth would appear but he didn't, Ethan mentioning something about him working late, stock checking. She couldn't stop the knotting, falling feeling in her stomach each time she thought about him.

Half way home she changed her mind, walking back to the front to look into the shop. It was dark and empty but she could see light emanating from the windows of Seth's flat. She stood by the door for several minutes and then thought better of it, scurrying away with her heart in her mouth. She was half way home when she plucked up the courage to call him, but the call rang out and went to the answering service.

Serena felt cold. She knew Seth always looked at his phone when it rang. The only reason he wouldn't answer was if he didn't want to speak to her.

By the morning, and not really having slept very well, she had managed to convince herself that maybe he had genuinely missed the call and that he would probably phone her back when he realised. But by the time it got to lunchtime she knew that that wasn't going to happen. She was halfway down the stairs on the way to fix some lunch when she heard the phone ring and Rose pick up. It was immediately obvious that it was Seth.

Serena continued down and made her way into the kitchen, half hoping that he might ask to speak to her. That hope was dashed when Rose came through, chatting about what he had said.

"He asked me to tell you he'd see you soon," she said.

"Thanks," Serena replied. "I know he's been really busy this week."

"Have you not seen him then?"

"No." Serena put on the most cheerful voice she could manage. "He's been stock checking. I don't think anyone's seen him."

"You're probably right dear," Rose said, but Serena was aware of her sharp gaze throughout the rest of the day. She focused hard on transferring data onto the computer, avoiding conversation as much as possible, finding it harder and harder to concentrate. That evening she was listless and hurting, her eyes burning drily, yo-yoing between sadness and anger, not understanding what had gone wrong, what she had done to drive him away.

"One last text," she thought. "Then I have to accept that it's over."

"You look tired, dear," Rose said the next morning, looking concerned.

"Not sleeping very well," Serena said, trying to keep her voice light. "It'll pass."

"Is there anything I can do? If you need to take time off, you know it's no problem."

"Honestly, I'm fine." Serena tried to sound convincing, even though she knew Rose was far too astute to be fooled. "I'm better when I'm busy."

She could hardly concentrate though and found it difficult to smile and keep up the pretence of normality. She knew Rose realised that something was going on but didn't push her, although she did ask a few leading questions.

Serena didn't know that Rose was already aware that there was something amiss. She had seen Seth the evening before and even though he hadn't told her anything directly, Rose knew him well enough to pick it up from what he said and avoided saying. When she came upstairs quietly mid-afternoon to see Serena quietly wiping away tears as she worked, she felt she needed to do something. She called Seth and asked him if he could drop in again that evening to help her.

Serena drove home feeling desolate and angry. She had made up her mind to go and speak to him, make him talk to her, so she parked the car and walked down to the front, psyching herself up for a confrontation. But as she reached the corner, she saw him come out of his door and turn to lock it. The sight of him almost made her heart stop, and the fear that he would say what she didn't want to hear froze her to the spot. Before he saw her, she turned and bolted back the way she had come.

She flung herself into the house, locking the doors and pulling the curtains and threw herself onto the sofa, hugging her knees to her chest and staring unseeing at the television which she flicked on for company. She didn't move, as if her stillness could somehow stop time and hold reality at bay.

Hours later Serena came to with a jump. She had dozed off and darkness now covered her, broken eerily by the mindless flickering of the TV. As she came fully awake, she felt the heaviness settle over her again and sat up, sighing, ready to drag herself up to bed. Switching off the box, she stumbled through the all-consuming dark into the kitchen, flicking the light switch. She thought she heard a sound outside, a tapping sound. Stopping to listen confirmed her thought; a soft tapping was coming from the door. She made her way towards it, a little nervous now and glad that she had locked it. She peered through the glass.

Seth stood on the other side, his hand raised to knock again, but when he saw her he hesitated then put his hand flat to the pane. She stood immobile, unable to think or move, watching him looking back at her. He tried the door but obviously it was locked and she saw his lips form her name and the word please, again and again. She should have been able to hear him, even though he kept his voice low, but all she could hear was the blood roaring through her ears. Her hands flew up to cover her mouth and eventually she managed to make herself turn the key to release the lock. As he opened the door, she backed away toward the other side of the room, trying to process the relief that he was there and the pain and anger that his desertion had caused.

He shut the door behind him and moved towards her but she held her hand up, stopping him.

"Serena," he said. He looked haggard.

"Why?" she choked out.

"Please Serena, I…"

"What happened? I need to know, Seth. I thought we… after we…"

"Serena, I'm so sorry. I'm such a damn fool. Please, forgive me."

"What did I do?"

He was shaking his head. "You didn't do anything, nothing. It's all me, all my stupid, stupid fault, and I'm so sorry." He took another step towards her but she backed away again. "Please Serena, I've missed you so much. I'm an idiot, please let me try and explain, please let me hold you."

"I don't understand, I thought you wanted to be with me. And then you just disappeared."

"I did. I do."

"Why then? My heart hurts, Seth. I thought you trusted me. I thought you could tell me stuff. I didn't think you'd just cut me off.'

"I do trust you, I… Serena, I'm a fool. I'm so sorry. I just… it scares me how I feel about you, I don't know how to handle it. I did the wrong thing. You have every right to be angry and to tell me to piss off. But please don't. Tell me how to make it right." He put his hand out towards her. "Please."

"Talk to me." Tears were threatening now, tears of relief more than anything that she hadn't lost him. "Don't run."

He took another tentative step in her direction, bringing him within touching distance, reaching out to her. She hesitated but didn't back away this time, so he moved closer. She stayed still, putting her hands over her face but that was all he needed because his arms enfolded her and he pulled her to him so tightly she could hardly breathe.

"Oh, thank God," he said. "I thought I'd lost you."

They stood there like that for a long time. Serena could feel that Seth was shaking almost as hard as she was, so she wrapped her arms around him too. Neither of them spoke for what seemed like an eternity, but eventually he broke the silence.

"I'm so sorry," he said again, quietly in her ear. "Can you forgive me? Can we try again?"

Serena kept her face against his shoulder. "Seth, you don't need forgiving. But you need to tell me what's going on. I'm not psychic, not Ethan. If you need space that's fine, but just let me know. I can handle that. I can't handle not knowing, thinking I've done something wrong and that I've hurt you or that we're finished and being too afraid to come and see you just in case it makes things worse."

"Damn, is that what you thought?" He tightened his grip on her. "I knew I should text you or call you but every time I picked up the phone I didn't know what to say. I couldn't even explain it to myself. So I didn't. Took the coward's way out and just tried to pretend it would be OK. And it wasn't. I haven't been able to get you out of my head. I wanted to see you so badly, but then…'

"Have you changed your mind about me?" she whispered. "Would you rather just go back to being friends? It's too soon after Jessica, maybe it's just too much…"

"No." He spoke fiercely, moving so that he could see her without letting her go. "No. I want to be with you. I know you're not her. Nothing like her."

"Talk to me next time. I thought we could talk to each other."

"Oh, Serena." He tilted her face up to him. "How I've missed you." He brushed his lips gently against hers in a question that she answered by kissing him back.

"It's late," she said eventually.

"Yeah," he said. "I know." He didn't move and neither did she. There was a long pause. "Would you let me stay here tonight? Please? I'll sleep on the sofa if you want, I just want to be… here."

Her heart was thumping but she tried to stay calm as she looked up at him.

"You can stay Seth. I missed you too. I'm glad you're here. You don't have to sleep on the sofa unless you want to. You know what you can handle so it's up to you."

"I don't want to. I want to prove that you can trust me, that I won't let you down like that again."

Chapter 13

Gaia's birthday fell at the beginning of July and Ethan and Tallie had planned a party. She hadn't been sure at first but Tallie's boundless enthusiasm and Ethan's gentle encouragement had persuaded her.

"You're twenty five, my love," Ethan had said. "Quarter of a century. That deserves a celebration."

They had hired a hall and a DJ. Now that the day was fast approaching, excitement was reaching fever pitch, especially for Tallie. She could barely contain herself and had roped Serena into helping her plan the decorations and the food. On the Friday, the day before, they both took a day off and went shopping, then back to Tallie's to make what they could. They were still busy when Rob came in from work.

"What on earth…" he said as he entered the kitchen to find the place covered in plates, bowls and dishes, and traces of flour, chocolate and edible glitter on every available surface and on them. "On second thoughts, don't tell me. Some questions are best left unanswered."

"Prep, honey." Tallie danced over and gave him a kiss. "Not enough time to do it all tomorrow."

"Have you got much more to do?"

"Actually, quite a bit," Serena said, wielding a wooden spoon. "Oh, crap, Tallie, the muffins, they're not burning are they?"

Tallie dashed over to the oven and opened it. A wave of heat blasted out. "No, they're perfect." She grabbed the oven gloves and lifted them out while Serena made a space on the table. "Good call."

"Tell you what," Rob said, backing out slowly. "I'm going to leave you to it. I'll go down and see Seth and we'll bring back a takeaway in a couple of hours."

"That sounds great," Serena said.

"Coward," Tallie laughed.

"Too right," Rob's voice echoed from the hall. "I'll see you later."

When Rob and Seth appeared, the kitchen had been restored to normality and Tallie and Serena were sipping wine.

"Wow," said Rob, starting to dish out food. "It is a kitchen after all and not some demonic hall of glitter."

"So rude," Tallie retorted.

Seth walked over and kissed Serena's cheek. "Hi."

"Hi yourself."

They talked as they ate.

"We said we'd meet Ethan at the hall at one." Seth was enthusiastic. "Lots of furniture moving et cetera to be done."

"And while you're throwing tables and chairs around, Serena and I will be blowing up balloons and doing other decorative things. Is Gaia coming down?" asked Tallie.

"I think Ethan's banned her until the party starts."

"I hope they're having a nice romantic dinner tonight," Tallie sighed.

"Just like us, huh?" Rob smirked at her. She kicked him under the table. "Oi!"

"Serves you right," said Tallie. "Honestly!"

"I'm sure he'll romance you properly later, Tallie," said Seth, winking.

"Good God, what is this? A conspiracy of testosterone?" Tallie was having trouble keeping her face stern.

"I think it's more sinister than that," Serena added in. "I think they think they're being funny."

"Whad'ya mean 'think'? We're hilarious," Rob stated emphatically.

"Of course you are." Tallie was laughing now. She got up to start clearing the table but Rob stood and picked her up. "Hey, where'd the floor go?"

"Romance starts here," Rob said, swinging her round. Serena laughed.

"OK, that is funny. You two smooch and we'll clear up."

"You should smooch too," Tallie said. Serena got up.

"Yeah, we can clear up later," Rob added.

"It's no bother to... eek." Serena was cut off mid sentence as Seth caught her round the waist and lifted her too. "You nutter, put me down."

"It would be rude not to take notice of our hosts' wishes," Seth grinned, holding her firmly. Rob had set Tallie down with her feet on his and was walking her out of the kitchen and into the living room.

"Too right," he said over his shoulder. "Anyway, you and Tallie need a break from the kitchen, you've been in there all afternoon."

"But…" Serena began but Seth lowered her back to the floor and silenced her with a kiss. "Oh. But I can't leave the place like…" Another kiss stopped her.

"Yes you can," Seth said. "We can do this later before we go. Come on." He steered her out of the kitchen after the others.

Serena got to the hall later than planned the following evening and although it was still early, the place was heaving. Despite the fact that she had been there setting up with Seth, Tallie, Rob and Ethan all afternoon and knew they would already be inside, she still felt more than a little intimidated by the noise and the sheer number of people that she didn't recognise. She slipped in through the main door and stood at the back near the bar, scanning the room to see if she could find anyone she knew. She was glad that she'd worn the long twilight dress; it was pretty but understated. She was more than happy to disappear into the background.

Deciding that that approach was just too much she slipped back out and round to the side door that led to the kitchen and the room where the food was laid out. Tallie was there, just finishing slicing the bread.

"Hi," Serena said. "Sorry I'm late."

"You're not late, you're the one we left hanging around waiting for Mr DJ. I just thought I'd get this sorted now and then we don't have to think about it again. It'll all be done."

"Need a hand?"

"No, that's the last one." Tallie scooped the remaining slices into a basket. "Would you help me take these to the table?"

Serena picked up some filled baskets and took them through. "I love your dress," she said. "Such a pretty colour purple with the black. And that corseting. You've got me hooked on steam punk."

"Thank you. It was a limited edition last summer, I only made three," Tallie said. "All different colours. I love it too. Makes me want to twirl all the time though." She did and the layered skirt flared out from the fitted bodice. "You look gorgeous. I know I'm not the only one who's going to think so." She winked at Serena, who looked down embarrassed. "I'm so glad you and Seth are together. And don't worry later if *she* turns up. He's definitely with you."

"Is she likely to?" Serena's heart gave a sickening lurch.

Tallie smiled at her. "Yes, unfortunately. I thought I'd better warn you. She's down for the weekend, I only heard about an hour ago. I doubt that it's a coincidence, we all still have a lot of mutual friends. I can't imagine that she's just come down by chance."

"Thanks for telling me. Does Seth know?"

"Yeah. I warned him. He didn't look that happy but he said it didn't make any difference. In fact "I'm with Serena now, so I really don't care," was what he actually said."

"Really?" That made her feel better.

"Yes, really. Now come on," said Tallie. "Let's go and party." She saw Serena hesitate. "Are you OK?"

"Just feel a bit overwhelmed by the numbers out there," Serena confessed.

"You won't be on your own, I promise," Tallie said. "There are more people that you know than you think." She paused. "Hang on, did that make sense?"

Serena laughed. "Strangely, yes."

"Right. Come on then." She linked her arm through Serena's. "Let's go knock 'em dead."

They slipped through the door beside the stage into the main hall. The music was loud and the dance floor was busy. Tallie led her round the side to a table where Gaia and Rob were sitting with several people that she didn't recognise. Gaia immediately jumped up and gave Serena a big hug, then began to introduce her to the others that she didn't know.

Serena started to feel even better as she joined in the conversation and was laughing at some story Rob was telling when Ethan and Seth came to join them. Ethan put a glass of wine down in front of Gaia.

"Happy birthday yet again," he said.

"I'll drink to that," said Tallie, raising her glass. "Hey, Serena hasn't got a drink."

"That's OK," Serena said, but Seth was still on his feet.

"I'll get it," he said. "Vodka and orange?"

"Thanks," she said, embarrassed, but he was gone and the conversation turned. Tallie got up and went round to sit on Rob's lap as he returned, leaving him the chair next to Serena.

"Thanks," she said again, as Ethan picked up his glass and toasted

Gaia, accompanied by loud cheering from all sides of the table. The conversation resumed and Seth brought his chair forward a little.

"You're stunning," he said in Serena's ear. She blushed and smiled, shaking her head. "You are."

"Flatterer."

"No, just the truth."

Gradually Serena started to relax and enjoy herself but after a while she noticed that Seth seemed tense and increasingly on edge, distracted by something on the other side of the hall. Looking over she saw Jessica in a bandeau top and figure hugging skirt split to the thigh, laughing loudly and tossing her long blonde hair. She was surrounded by a group of young men and seemed to be flirting with all of them simultaneously. Serena's heart sank. Tallie dragged her back onto the dance floor, but it gave her a chance to comment.

"Jessica's arrived then."

Tallie glanced over and nodded. "Yeah. Not hard to spot, is she? Given her usual low key style and all."

"Seth looks really stressed," Serena said.

"I know. It's the Jessica effect, unfortunately. But he wants to be with you, I know he does. He said so. Don't worry."

"I wish I was that sure," Serena thought miserably. "I don't think he really knows what he wants."

She went and sat next to him again when the song ended, watching his fingers drum restlessly on the table.

"Are you OK?" she asked. He smiled at her tiredly.

"Yeah, thanks," he sighed. "Past come back to haunt us, as I'm sure you've noticed."

"I'm sorry," she said, because there wasn't anything else she could say. "Is it difficult with me here?"

He looked at her, horrified. "No, God no," he said, taking her hand. "I want you here with me. She just makes me feel unsettled. I should be used to it by now."

Serena squeezed his hand, leaning forward to momentarily put her head on his shoulder. They sat quietly for a while, watching the whirl of dancers in front of them and listening to Ethan and Rob chatting. Seth drained his glass.

"I'll get a refill," Serena said. "You probably feel like you need it."

She made her way to the bar at the back of the room, joining the melee around it. Looking back she couldn't help smiling as she saw Ethan and Rob being reluctantly pulled up to dance by Gaia and Tallie. She saw Seth shift back slightly in his chair and noticed with dismay that Jessica was heading towards him. She wondered if she should go back over but then resolutely turned away. It would play out one way or another and there was nothing she could do.

Seth saw Jessica approaching out of the corner of his eye, but chose to ignore her until she dropped into the seat next to him.

"Hey, baby," she said. "I'm back."

"Yes, you are," he replied carefully, turning to look at her.

"Aren't you pleased to see me? Sorry I haven't called. I've been kinda busy." She gave him the innocent face she did so well, wide smile and coy eyes, but he wasn't in the mood for it any more. He looked pointedly over at the group she had just left.

"So I see."

"Aw, you're not jealous are you? It's just a bit of fun. Anyhow I see you've got yourself that piece of arm candy." She looked up the hall to where Serena was standing. "She is pretty."

"She's not arm candy, she's amazing," Seth growled.

"Of course she is." Jessica either failed to pick up or chose to ignore the warning in Seth's voice. "Hey, you want to dance with me?"

"Actually, no," Seth said. "I'm with Serena.'

"Of course you are baby, but come and dance with me. Just one song. Maybe. You know you'll be glad you did."

"Jessica, no," he repeated. "Not this time."

"Oh, come on Seth. Look at me properly and say no. You can't, I know you. I know what you want, and you know it too. One little dance and then maybe later, well, we can see what happens, can't we?"

She rose and bent over towards him, putting her hand proprietorially on his shoulder. He stiffened at her touch, anger and hurt roiling through him in equal measure. Then he stood up, lifting her hand off him and dropping it to her side.

"I said no, Jessica," he repeated icily. "You don't know anything about me or what I want. If you did you wouldn't be here. I'm done with this game of yours. I'm with Serena and I'm going home with her tonight. And from now on. Go and play with your toys over there and leave me alone. I don't want anything more to do with you."

She gawped at him, but he turned and stalked away, relief mixing with emptiness at his core. He had never seen her speechless before. He smiled tightly to himself and headed up the hall to where Serena was still standing, paying for the drinks. He slipped his arm round her waist and felt her start.

"Sorry," he said. "I always seem to make you jump."

She turned to him and smiled, handing him a glass. They moved away from the bar, finding a place that was a bit less crowded.

"Are you OK?" she asked, glancing over in Jessica's direction. "I saw she came over to see you. I wasn't sure but I thought I'd better stay out of the way."

"Why? Did you think I'd go off with her?" He looked perplexed.

"No, it wasn't that," she said. "It's just that it must be really difficult and I know how you feel... felt about her. I don't want to make it any harder for you to deal with."

"You make it easier, actually."

"Oh," she said quietly. "Are you sure? Are you really OK?"

"I'm OK," he said, holding her tighter. "In fact I'm better than OK. I'm with you."

As they went back to their table Seth could see Jessica staring at them, looking Serena up and down with a delicate frown on her face. He decided that the best thing to do was to ignore it, but Serena was aware of it too, continued to be aware of the looks she was getting as the evening progressed. He kept his arm round her; it wasn't much of a shield but it was all he could offer.

After they had embarrassed Gaia with her birthday cake, Ethan came back and sat down looking pleased with himself.

"What have you been up to?" Gaia asked. "I saw you sweet talking the DJ. Who are you trying to embarrass now?"

"As if I'd do something like that," he said innocently.

"Ethan!" Gaia said. "You know I have ways of extracting information. Don't make me use them in public."

"No need, my love, you're just about to find out anyway."

The DJ announced a slowing of proceedings and Ethan winked at Gaia. "Some slushy stuff just for you," he grinned, pulling her to her feet. "Excuse me, I need to smooch with my wife for a bit."

Rob and Tallie followed them as the floor began to fill with couples. Seth hesitated momentarily before taking Serena's hand and tugging her gently to join them, drawing her close. As he stroked her hair she looked up and he had to take her lips in a kiss. When they finally drew apart she smiled at him before she rested her head against his shoulder and he realised just how she made him feel, how he wanted to keep feeling this way. This was what he had tried to find before. This was what had always been missing. As they turned slowly he saw Jessica was watching them. He met her eyes and was glad when she was the first to look away. He tightened his grip on Serena and let himself relax.

Seth was not the only one who noticed that Jessica left early. After the party finished and the last stragglers had gone, the six of them remained to finish clearing up the hall and it was a hot topic of conversation.

"I've never known her leave a party before the end," Ethan said.

"Maybe she's finally had a reality check that actually sank through that steel hide," contemplated Tallie.

"Well, I was glad to see the back of her," said Seth, giving Serena a squeeze.

"You're not the only one," Serena thought, but she just smiled.

"Such a great party, Gaia," Tallie said, hugging her friend as they finally left.

"Yeah, it was great. Thanks, all of you, for all the help and everything else."

They began the walk home together, eventually going their separate ways. Seth and Serena headed towards the sea.

"Stay at mine tonight?" Seth asked, his arm round her waist.

"Are you sure? If you need time after, you know, seeing her, it's OK."

He stopped her. "I meant what I said earlier. I'm with you. And I don't want to be alone, I want us to be together."

Serena was at Seth's one evening the following week, getting ready to go out when his phone rang. She saw a frown cross his face and he looked at her in consternation.

"Sorry, gonna have to answer. It's Jessica," he said, in answer to the question clearly written across her face. "She's been ringing all day and I've ignored it, but…"

"Just keep ignoring…" Serena started to say, but Seth was already connected.

"What do you want, Jessica?"

"Can't I just call to say hi? Why so suspicious?" Jessica's voice was loud enough for Serena to hear and it set her teeth on edge.

"You usually want something, let's be fair," Seth said. He walked over and put his arm round Serena, holding her tight. She accepted the hug but her heart was thumping.

"You know me too well." Jessica's voice took on a wheedling tone. "OK, so here's the deal. I've got a big black tie do on Saturday, industry bash and I can't not go. Have to network, otherwise my boss will be apoplectic. I need a partner and someone's just dumped me in it and told me he can't come. You'll come with me Seth, won't you? I'll make it worth your while."

"I don't think so, Jessica. Not my thing and anyway, I'm with Serena now. There must be someone else you can ask."

"I know, I know you're with that girl, but please don't let me down. I so need to go with *you*, you understand better than anyone."

Serena disentangled herself from Seth's arm, shaking her head in disbelief. Seth tried again.

"I don't think I can, we've got plans for the…"

"You can change them, can't you? I'm sure she'll understand if she's as *lovely* as you say." The emphasis was clear. "Why are you dithering? Is she there? Let me speak to her."

Serena was shaking her head violently as Seth looked at her.

"I don't think that's a very good idea," Seth said. "What is this thing anyway? Where is it? Maybe…" He saw Serena's head snap up as she stared at him intensely. "Maybe we could both come. Serena's got friends in London, she might be able to catch up with them. I need to talk to… Serena, wait."

He dropped the phone, running over to the top of the stairs. She was already at the door.

"Serena, wait, please, it was only an idea. We can talk…"

Her eyes turned him to ice.

"Are you joking? You want me to go back to *London*? To do your *ex* a favour?" She shook her head again. "You do what you want. I'm going."

The door slammed behind her. By the time he got down, out and to the corner, she was nowhere to be seen. He returned to the flat, furious and upset. Jessica was still on the line.

"Well," she said. "Some girlfriend she is. No thought for what you might want."

Seth's anger boiled over. "Actually, Jessica, you've pretty much just summed yourself up. You don't think about anyone or anything but yourself. And I've had enough. I don't want any more to do with you."

"But, baby…" Jessica began. Seth stopped her.

"No. No more. Don't contact me again. I mean it." He heard her sharp intake of breath just before he cut the line. He tried to call Serena but there was no reply. He texted her immediately.

Am sorry. Where are you? We need to talk.

Five minutes later, when he'd had no reply, he sent another one.

Serena flung herself out of the door and took off blindly, running across the High Street and through the warren of little cobbled alleys that held the more offbeat and eclectic shops. She came out into the Memorial Gardens and hurried straight through those as well, out into the residential area where Howie lived. Wandering aimlessly around the streets, her phone pinged messages in regularly. There were six when she finally looked, all from Seth and the phone began to ring as she was reading through. She turned it off and stuck it back in her bag; she couldn't face hearing his voice, how it made her feel. Then she just kept walking, up and down and round the winding lanes at the top of town, desperately trying to make some sense of everything. She lost track of time completely and loneliness hit her like a brick wall as the light faded. Eventually she pulled out her phone and turned it on. There were more messages from Seth and one from Tallie. It made Serena want to cry as she read it.

Are you OK? Do you need to talk? Seth's frantic looking for you but after he told me what happened I can understand you taking off. Please call me when you get this, even if it's just to tell me you're OK.

Serena hesitated then called the number, desperate for a friendly voice. Her hand shook as it rang. Tallie answered quickly.

"Serena?"

"Yeah, it's me."

"Oh, thank God. Are you OK? That's a stupid question, don't answer that. Where are you?"

"Oh, just wandering about trying to stop myself from screaming."

"Tell me where you are. I'm coming to get you."

"Tallie, I'm OK really."

"You couldn't look me in the eye and say that. I want to come and give you a hug at least. Persuade you to come back here for a bit. Please Serena."

"I'm by the stream at the end of Crows Lane."

"OK, why don't you start walking up to us and I'll meet you on the way."

"You don't have to."

"Don't be silly. I'm coming now."

"OK." Serena didn't have the energy to argue. "Thanks. Tallie? He's not there is he? I don't think I can cope with seeing him now."

"No, honey, I don't know where he is. He's been scouring the town trying to find you. I'm going to call and tell him you're alright but that you need some space. Don't worry. It'll be OK. I'll see you in a minute."

Tallie appeared shortly afterwards and hugged Serena wordlessly before linking arms with her as they walked back to the house. Rob had just come in and he hugged her too before making himself scarce so that she and Tallie could talk. They sat at the kitchen table. Serena sipped her tea in silence, suddenly weary and unable to think of anything to say. Tallie sat beside her, a look of concern on her face.

"Sorry," Serena said after a while. "I can't think straight. I don't know what to tell you."

"It's OK," Tallie reassured her. "I know a bit, what Seth told me. Something about Jessica calling, wanting him to go up to London and escort her to some industry shenanigans and how you weren't happy about it. And then when he'd suggested you go too, how you'd been really upset and left."

"That's a fair summary," Serena sighed. She felt her gut twist back into a knot as she looked at Tallie miserably. "I'm so angry. But I'm wondering if I'm just being unreasonable and jealous. I so don't want him to go. And I don't want to go back there. And the fact that he's even considering it..." Her eyes filled up then.

"You're not being unreasonable, no way," Tallie said hotly. "Jeez, if that'd been me, well, I wouldn't have been able to stop myself from taking that phone and telling her what to do with herself. The fact that you didn't... you've got far more self control than I have. And I'm afraid I wasn't very polite when he told me he'd suggested you go too. But believe me, he knows how damn stupid he's been. I didn't have to tell him. Though I did anyway. I was so cross.'"

Tears started to run down Serena's face. "What did you say to him?"

Tallie passed her a tissue. "I said that to consider helping that bitch after everything she's done was beyond my understanding and to even suggest asking you about it was completely out of order. I told him he was an idiot for assuming that it would ever be remotely OK for him to have anything to do with her while he's going out with you, especially after what your ex did to you. And then to suggest you go with him, to London of all places. I really did lose it then. I'm surprised you didn't hear me yelling at him."

"What did you... how did he react?"

"What did I yell? A repetition of how much of an idiot I thought he was and how he was taking advantage of your kind nature, interspersed with quite a lot of swearing and a few choice descriptive words about what I thought of him and his judgement. Rob was more measured as usual, but he still told him how he was way out of line. Like I said, he knows what a fool he's been. He went back out to look for you again then, he's really worried about you. Rob went with him. That was about half an hour before you phoned me. Rob came back when I called to tell them you were OK. He said Seth's desperate to talk to you."

Serena wiped her eyes and shook her head. "I feel like such a bad person."

Tallie threw her arms round her. "That's just stupid. Don't make me shout at you too, one friend in an evening is enough. You don't have a bad bone in your body - you're totally unselfish. But this time you're allowed to put yourself first, and him. She has no right to ask what she has and he was wrong to even consider it. End of story."

"It's only because he's kind," Serena started, but Tallie stopped her.

"Yes he is kind, too kind, but that doesn't mean he shouldn't get his priorities straight. You should be number one and he needs to understand that."

"What do I do, Tallie? I don't want to lose him but she's still got her hooks in him. He wouldn't have even asked her about the damn thing if..."

"You're not going to lose him. Serena, he's crazy about you. Why do you think he's spent his whole evening looking for you? He's worried he's lost you because of what happened earlier, that's what he said to us."

"Really?"

"Yes, really." Tallie smiled at her. "It's going to be OK. You mean far more to him than she ever did, it's obvious to all of us. He'll make the right choice because he wants to be with you and not for any other reason. You can stop worrying. But you are allowed to be cross with him."

Serena smiled back then. Tallie hugged her again. "That's better. Now, it's hot chocolate time." She got up and put the kettle on, getting mugs out of the cupboard.

"I hope Rob doesn't feel banished from his own kitchen," Serena said. Tallie laughed.

"No, but he's very good at knowing when girl time is required. I'll make him a drink too, so he could come and join us if you feel up to it. Otherwise he'll be just as happy in the other room."

"Of course he can come and join us," Serena said. "It's his house for goodness sake."

Serena felt further comforted when Rob reinforced what Tallie had said. It was good to know that a male view on things was similar; it made her feel less unreasonable. The conversation moved on to other things and she felt her mood lifting. The phone rang and Rob disappeared to answer it. He reappeared a few minutes later, a slightly sober look on his face.

"That was Seth," he said, looking at Serena. "He wanted to know how you are, if you're OK, so I said I think you're getting there. He asked if you'd speak to him, if he could see you. I said I'd call him back when you'd had a chance to think about it."

Serena paled. She could feel the panic rising again. Tallie saw and took her hand.

"It'll be alright," she said. "It's up to you. If you're ready you can and if you want somewhere neutral to talk he can come here. But if you don't want to, that's fine too."

"I want to see him, I want to sort it out, but I don't know, I just feel so confused, like whatever I do or say is going to be wrong."

"I think he's the one that needs to worry about that, not you," Rob said. "Serena, you have every right to feel upset and he knows that. So you do what you need to do."

"How is he?"

"He's worried about you and he's furious with himself. But he's OK. He realises that he may have to wait."

"I want to talk to him, I hate feeling like this. Could he really come here? Would he? If it's all going to fall apart I don't want to be at his or mine."

"I think he'd go to Alaska if that's where you said you'd talk to him," Rob said. "Of course he can come here. Are you sure? Shall I call him?"

Serena nodded, biting her lip. She felt suddenly sick with nerves.

"It's not going to fall apart," Tallie said reassuringly as Rob went off to the phone. "He's as scared as you are. More probably. He thinks you're going to tell him to sod off. But you're not, are you?"

Serena shook her head. "No. But if he is going to go to London, I don't know how I'll deal with it."

"He won't go, believe me." Tallie shook her head. "He's got more sense than that."

Rob came back in. "He's on his way. Won't be long."

"We'll just leave you alone in here," Tallie said. "Is that OK? But we're here if you need us. Don't worry about the time or anything. The important thing is that you get this sorted. And you're welcome to stay here tonight if you want to. Just you or both of you, it doesn't matter. Whatever will be fine."

"Thanks," said Serena. Nothing else could get past the lump in her throat but Rob shook his head.

"Just want you two to be OK," he said.

It wasn't long before the doorbell rang. Serena jumped and Rob saw, squeezing her shoulder comfortingly before he went to open the door. Tallie hugged her.

"Don't worry," she said. "He adores you. He doesn't want to lose you. It's going to be OK." She left Serena at the kitchen table.

Seth paused in the hallway by the door and looked nervously at Tallie. Despite her earlier anger she couldn't help giving him a reassuring hug.

"It'll be OK," she said.

"Will it?" He didn't say it, but the anxiety was drilling red hot through his mind. He took a deep breath and entered the kitchen, closing the door behind him. Serena was sitting motionless, staring hard at her cup as she fiddled with the handle. He sat down opposite her.

"I'm sorry," he said immediately, before she had a chance to speak. "I was thoughtless and I never should've suggested what I did. I should have just kept saying no."

She shrugged. "Hindsight huh?" Her voice was tight and carefully controlled.

"I shouldn't have needed it. I should have realised... should have thought."

"Yeah, you should have done. But you didn't." It sounded harsh as she said it but he could see in her demeanour just how hard she was trying to hold herself together. It hurt him badly that he had caused her to feel that way. He sighed.

"I know what an idiot I've been. I didn't need Tallie to tell me. And it should have been you shouting at me. She caught me off guard and I've always been a mug where she's concerned. But…"

"I can't believe you even *thought* that we could both go. When you know that Sarah is away on tour with the band and Lindy is with her. *And* you know London is my worst nightmare and the place I've been avoiding like the plague. What did you think I'd do? Just hang about while you take your ex-girlfriend out for the evening?" Serena's anger boiled over, her voice shaking. She stared at him, her eyes full of storms. It was like a knife in his gut. "How would you feel if that was my ex asking me the same thing?"

He drummed on the table with his fingers, desperately trying to find words that were adequate to tell her how he felt. None came anywhere near.

"God, Serena I know. I can't believe myself either. I've hurt the one person who means more to me than anyone and I don't know how to even begin to put that right. If I could rewind time and change it, I would. But I can't."

"You can tell me what you decided to do about her invitation," Serena shot at him.

"I so wish you didn't have to ask me that. I hoped you would know." He sighed. "I said no. Of course I said no. Then I told her not to contact me again." He took his phone out of his pocket and slid it across to her. "I've blocked her number. You can see."

She took a deep breath and pushed the phone back to him without looking. She remained silent, still biting at her lip. He moved uncomfortably, not sure what to say next, trying desperately to read her expression. Ironically, although he had found it easy to do before, the ability seemed to have deserted him.

"I don't know what to say except I'm sorry," he said. "My judgement was appalling. But I meant what I said to her. You're what matters. I don't want anything to do with her, I want to be with you. I'm just hoping that that bit is still true. That we're together. Because you might be just about to kick my useless butt out the door."

Serena allowed him a small smile at that. He grinned briefly in response, the anxiety quickly returning to his face.

"I deserve a good kicking," he went on. "I've been kicking myself all evening. And if you want to yell at me again and tell me what a damn fool I am, feel free. But I can't bear this feeling that I'm going to lose you. Please tell me we're going to be OK." He almost dreaded her response, chest too tight to even draw breath.

"I think we can be OK," she said slowly. "If you can accept that I don't like her and don't trust her and don't want her around either of us. That's not blackmail or an ultimatum, it's just how I feel. If you're going to feel the need to keep rescuing her, that's going to make it a lot more difficult. You may have blocked her number but that won't stop her, I know it won't. And I'm sorry if I sound selfish, but that's how it is."

He reached out across the table, hand palm up in invitation.

"You're not selfish. I'm kind of glad you feel that way about us, about me. If it was your ex calling you then honestly, I'd want to kill him." He leant forward earnestly. "I really don't want anything to do with her. I don't even like her anymore. It's just... old habits die hard, I guess. It may take a bit of time for me to get my head round everything. Would you be OK with that?"

Finally she put her hand in his. The wave of relief that flooded through him at her touch made his heart jump.

"Yes I'll be OK with that," she said. "But don't ever ask me to come and play third wheel again. Especially in London. You may just find out how much damage a Venus Fly Trap can do."

"I'm sorry," he repeated contritely. "Like I said, I'm an idiot."

"You certainly can be," she replied, standing up. "But since it's you, I'll let you off."

He stood too, moving round the table to hold her tightly.

"Just this once, mind," she added.

Chapter 14

As July gave way to August, Serena had transcribed most of the documents that Rose wanted in the book and they had arranged them into sections and chapters. She and Seth were closer now, the connection between them stronger. Much as she had felt swept away by Steve, it had been nothing like the all-encompassing emotion that she felt for Seth. She had truly fallen in love, helplessly plummeting into unknown depths. But on its own it was not enough to sustain her; her time was ticking away and she needed him to tell her that he felt the same. That he loved her. Much as she felt he cared, she knew he wasn't ready to say that. Hope diminished a little with each passing day.

Eventually her emotions got the better of her. Despite a hot, sunny day at the beach and then Seth insisting on cooking dinner for her, she couldn't shake the dread away. He held her close all evening, sensing that something wasn't right and every time she looked at him her heart ached. Later, lying next to him listening to the slow, even breaths of him sleeping, she just wanted to weep. Eventually, tormented and restless, she went downstairs to make herself a drink and sat at the kitchen table, flicking through a gardening book without really seeing it at all.

She didn't know how much later it was that he came down to find her.

"Hey," he said, sitting next to her. "What're you doing up? It's ridiculous o'clock in the morning." He looked at the book. "Not really the ideal time for gardening."

He grinned and nudged her but she didn't have the energy to reciprocate. She shrugged and flipped the book closed. "Couldn't sleep. Didn't want to disturb you so I came down."

"What's up?" he asked, taking her hand.

"Nothing. I'm fine."

"No you're not. You've been distracted all day and your eyes are greyer than storm clouds. What's hurting you?"

She couldn't speak. She would have choked on the words anyway, even if she could have told him the truth. She shook her head instead. He stood up and pulled her up too, putting his arms round her.

"It's going to be alright. You'll see. It'll all be OK. Now come back to bed."

They went back upstairs and he held her, her head on his chest, stroking her hair.

"Don't worry. Don't be upset. It really will be OK."

"Oh Seth," she said. "I love you."

He said nothing, but she hadn't expected him to. He tightened his arms around her and didn't let go.

In the morning they both got ready for work as usual. Nothing was said. She saw him out and as he moved to kiss her she stopped him.

"I meant it Seth," she said. "I love you. I wanted you to know that."

"Serena," he said, his eyes anguished. "I care about you more than I can tell you, I…"

She put her finger on his lips. "Shh. It's OK. I know you care."

He did kiss her then, slowly, deeply.

"See you tomorrow," she said.

She was in a daze at Rose's. Part of her regretted spilling her feelings out to him, yet she had so desperately wanted him to know, even if he didn't feel the same. But now, if she did have to leave, had it made things worse? Seth knowing how she loved him but her leaving him anyway.

"Is everything alright, dear?" Rose ventured as they ate lunch together in the kitchen. Serena had been aware of her shrewd and watchful eye all morning but had hoped she wouldn't ask anything. "It's just that you seem a little out of sorts today."

"Just tired, thanks," Serena said, hoping forlornly she would leave it there. She didn't.

"Forgive me for saying it but you look anxious rather than tired. Is there anything I can help with? Are things alright with you and Seth?"

Rose could clearly read her as well as the book she was writing. Serena couldn't help herself. Her eyes filled with tears even though she was nodding an affirmative.

"Oh my dear." Rose reached out and took Serena's hand. "I'm sorry. I didn't mean to pry. I just worry about both of you, that's all."

"I'm OK," Serena said, wiping the tears away with the back of her other hand. She took a deep breath. "So stupid."

Rose shook her head. "No dear, you're not. Do you want to tell me what's wrong?"

"Nothing really, it's just... I love him, Rose. I told him so."

"Is that a bad thing?"

"No. Oh, I don't know. He's still so screwed up, I just don't know. And neither does he. I told him but now I'm wondering if it's too much. If I should have just kept quiet."

Rose squeezed her hand. "Those are words that need to be said if it's what you feel. You'll look back with regret one day if you don't. Don't doubt that. For what it's worth, I think he feels the same. I've never seen him look at anyone the way he looks at you."

"Thank you," Serena said. She crushed the dread and fear back into its box and tried to put on a smile.

"It'll be alright, you'll see. He'll come round, in time."

"Yes," Serena thought. "Maybe. But will it be *in* time?"

Seth was out with Ethan and Howie that evening. Gaia came down to eat with Serena and watch a film. By the time she left, Serena was happier. Much as she wanted to text Seth, she decided not to, trying to give him space and knowing that she would see him the following evening. She had a good day at Rose's and left a little early for once, taking a stroll along the beach before she headed home. The water was silky to the horizon and a breathtaking blue. If she allowed her heart to listen hard enough she could almost, almost, hear the songs of her sisters out in the deep. Almost.

She walked home feeling as if she was on a tightrope between her deepest happiness and her greatest sorrow. "How?" she thought. "How can love be such a blessing and such a curse at the same time?"

She showered when she got in and then went into the kitchen to start making dinner for herself and Seth. The kettle had just boiled when a message came in on her phone.

Sorry, can't make it tonight. Need some thinking time.

Serena's heart hit the floor.

Are you OK? Can I do anything?

Yeah, I'm OK. Just need some space. Don't worry. See you soon.

She stood there for long minutes just staring at the words. So cool, so detached, so un-Sethlike. They brought back all the doubt. She thought about sending another one but decided against it.

"Dammit," she said aloud. Putting on her jacket and boots, she grabbed her bag and left the house, unable to face the thought of an evening at home alone just wondering why. As if she didn't know. She headed back down to the beach and sat on the rocks until the darkness fell and she was shivering, not from cold but from the numb emptiness that gripped her.

Her phone pinged. Wrestling it out of her bag, hoping it might be from Seth, she couldn't help a pang of disappointment when she realised it was from Ethan.

Are you OK? Seth's in a foul mood and I thought you were seeing each other tonight.

Serena felt the tears rise again. She was trying to think of how to reply when her phone rang. It was Ethan.

"I know you're not OK," he said, before she had a chance to say anything. "Where are you?"

"Beach," she croaked. "At the rocks."

"Be there in two minutes," he said.

"You don't have to," she said but he had already rung off. She scrambled down from her perch and began to walk slowly back towards the front. She saw Ethan coming down the steps and heading over to her.

"Hey," he said. "What's up? Seth wasn't himself yesterday and after I realised what a bad mood he was in tonight I called in at yours and you weren't there. Did you fight? He wouldn't tell me anything, just shut down completely."

She shook her head numbly. "I don't really know. We didn't fight. I think he's just... oh, I don't know what he is. I don't think he knows how he feels about me and it's difficult."

"Weren't you supposed to go out tonight?"

"Yeah, but he texted me to say he couldn't make it." Serena sighed. "I wondered whether she was back but I didn't like to ask."

Ethan shook his head. "No, no, definitely not. Even if she was, I think he'd tell her where to go this time. He knows it's you he wants to be with. But he turned up at the Feathers about an hour ago and sat there looking like thunder. Hardly said two words to me and Rob and then went home after half an hour. That's when I wandered up to yours, I knew there was something off."

"I'm not sure what's happening. I told him how I felt. I love him. Now he's running. I don't think he knows what he wants.'"

"Serena, he does. He just can't say it. I can feel it. Good grief, we can all *see* it. Don't give up."

"I'm trying but it's hard. I feel like I'm living a lie and on so many levels.'"

"He'll get there, I'm sure of it. He doesn't want to lose you."

"If I have to go Ethan, how am I going to explain?"

Ethan put his arm round her and gave her a squeeze. "It won't come to that. I hope."

Serena barely slept that night. She read until the early hours, trying to block out the pain slicing through her like knives and finally dozed off over her book. She woke repeatedly during the night and just kept reading. She dragged herself up and out to Rose's early, glad to have something to bury herself in. She longed for a text but nothing came and by lunch time she was desperate.

"Why don't you go and see him?" Rose asked, out of the blue. Serena looked at her. "I can see you're distressed. I assume it may have something to do with what we spoke about yesterday. Talk to him Serena. It'll help you both."

"I don't think so," Serena said. "We were supposed to see each other last night but he cancelled at the last minute. I don't think he *wants* to see me."

"I'm sure that's not true," Rose began, but Serena stopped her.

"Please, Rose. He said he needs space. If he wants to see me he knows where I am. I'm not going to crowd him. Please don't say anything to him, will you?"

"Well, if you really insist then I won't, but I want to talk some sense into him." Rose said, squinting over her glasses. Serena was shaking her head. "Alright, I promise. I hope he comes to his senses soon."

"So do I," Serena thought.

That afternoon she gave in and sent him a text.

Do you want to come over tonight? Can we talk?

There was no reply. She went home and paced restlessly round the house, tried to eat, tried to watch TV, put some music on and then turned it off again, read for a while, put the TV back on and then gave up. Somehow she had lost three hours and she still didn't know whether to scream or weep. Yo-yoing between anger and despair, she didn't know what to do. Eventually she decided that she couldn't do nothing any longer and walked down to the front, to his flat, thinking that maybe Rose was right, maybe it would be better if they talked. However when she got there, the whole place was in darkness. She was as sure as she could be that he wasn't there but even so it took her three attempts to pluck up the courage to ring the doorbell. When there was no reply, she wasn't sure whether she was disappointed or relieved.

Later, hiding in the dark under the covers, feeling more alone than she ever had, she knew that the chance of a happy ending was washing rapidly away with the tide.

Serena slept badly. With her heart feeling as if it was hanging in the balance, she was tormented by dark and fragmented dreams. She was back in the deep, fighting dark water and strong currents, trying to get to the shore. The harder she swam the less progress she made. Ahead of her, another was also struggling, pulled down by small ghostly forms. Silver bubbles escaped from him and she knew it was Seth. But as she doubled her efforts, long strands of weed wrapped round her ankles and arms and waist, immobilising her. She kicked helplessly, watching the bubbles slow then cease, watching him sink away from her into the midnight black. The scream echoed through her head…

She woke tangled in the sheets, breathing ragged, the silent cry stuck in her throat. It took long moments to realise that she was safe and Seth wasn't drowning. She could still hear her scream, softening now but raising the hairs on her arms.

Serena threw the sheets off and headed down to the kitchen, deciding that sleep was not within reach. She paced restlessly as the kettle boiled, made herself a drink that she really didn't want and sat at the kitchen table trying to calm her edginess. It didn't work. She was jumping at nothing, couldn't stay sitting, kept wandering over to the door and peering out into the dark. There was nothing there and yet she was aware of a pull, of sound in her head, soft and low, a gentle rhythmic melody. A song from the sea.

She gave up on rest and headed out into the night. As she walked along the beach and the orange streetlight glow faded to nothing behind her, the darkness was almost complete. The tiniest sliver of new moon sliced the sky but the stars seemed distant, out of reach.

"Damn metaphors," Serena muttered to herself. Seth haunted her. She scrambled over the rocks, hearing the sigh of the water. The shadow waves drew on the shadow beach, the tide just turning on its way out. Serena found the long flat rock and stretched out there, trailing her hand in the water, trying to allow the lullaby the sea sang to ease the torment in her head. It seemed familiar, comforting somehow. It reminded her of...

"Tia!" Serena gasped, sitting bolt upright. She could feel her sister nearby, could just make out a ripple in the black water heading straight for her. Moments later, Tia appeared below and pulled herself up onto the rock.

"Tia," Serena breathed. "How did you know I... how are you here?"

Tia said nothing, just opened her arms and they fell into an embrace.

"I've missed you so much," Serena said.

"And I you." Tia finally released her and moved so that she could look at her properly.

"But you're not supposed to be here." Serena's concern was evident. "It's forbidden. I don't want you to be in trouble because of me."

"I couldn't stay away this time. What's happening, Serena? Why are you so sad?"

"I... how do... I'm fine, Tia. Really. What about the others, are they OK, you haven't come to tell me that..."

"No, no, we are all well. But you are not, I can feel it. And it's getting worse. Tell me what has happened to you."

Serena drew her knees to her chest, feeling cold suddenly. She looked into Tia's eyes.

"No one knows I am here," Tia went on. "And I will not tell them. But I feel how much you hurt...'

"How?" Serena interjected.

Tia gazed out to sea.

"When you were leaving I was sad. I watched you give up your magic in the cave, saw the potion change to red in the cauldron as well as the vial. I couldn't help myself; I drank a drop just after the transformation finished. I didn't want to lose you completely." She turned and looked at her sister. "It allowed me to stay connected, to feel some of what you feel. The happiness, the excitement, the heady falling in love."

Serena reached out her hand and Tia took it as she continued.

"The pain when something bad happened. And then that seemed to ease, there was something else, but now..." She squeezed Serena's hand tight. "I felt your heart break the first time, but this is worse. What's happening? How do you bear it?"

Tears shimmered in Serena's eyes.

"Father always thought I was the headstrong one," she said. "I don't think he ever saw it in you."

Tia shrugged. "I was never as fearless as you. But I did understand it."

"I'm not fearless anymore," Serena said sadly. "Just broken. And about to be lost."

"Why?"

"Steve doesn't love me anymore. He divorced me."

Tia gasped in horror. "So that's why…"

"My heart broke then, yes. I know he did love me, at first at least. And maybe I was naïve but I always thought love would be enough. So when he took it away… it hurt more than losing my magic – there was nothing to fill the hole. It felt like the end of everything. But then I met some amazing people. A man who has stolen my breath and my soul and made what I felt for Steve feel like a drop instead of a wave. He makes me feel so… he makes me feel." She stopped momentarily. "I love him. And I know he cares for me…"

"That is good though. That shouldn't hurt like this. And if he loves you…"

"That's the thing." Serena sighed. "I don't know. I don't think he knows. And even if he does, he's too afraid of it to say."

"I don't understand."

"He's been hurt. He doesn't want to make another mistake. It's complicated. Human emotions are complicated and so are their relationships."

"But he must know how he feels.'"

Serena shook her head. "That's why I was always so different, I think. Because not everything was clear cut black and white like it was, is, to the rest of you. So many things are clouded for humans, often there isn't just one answer."

"But if he doesn't tell you…" Tears welled in Tia's eyes now.

"Then I return to the sea," Serena finished. "Full circle."

A crystal drop slipped down Tia's face. Serena caught it and held it up in the scant moonlight.

"Tears of the mer," she whispered. "A rare thing." Tears were falling down her cheeks now, and Tia reached out to touch one.

"Water?"

Serena smiled a little. "I think mer and humans are related. I think they came from the sea. They still weep it when they're sad."

Tia held the liquid drop up beside her own. They both glittered slightly.

"Maybe not so different after all," she said.

They sat together in silence for a long time, until the slightest paling of the horizon lifted the sky from the sea.

"I must go," Tia said. "Be strong, little sister. There is hope yet. I will find a way."

Serena's smile was forced. "Tia, you know what the Sea Witch told me. And I accepted the risk. There is only one way."

"I don't believe that," Tia said fiercely. "There is always another way in magic. And I will surely find it."

"Tia, please." The anxiety was clear in Serena's voice. "Don't. Don't put yourself at risk."

"I lost you when you left, but at least I had this connection." Tia's words betrayed a depth of feeling that shocked Serena. "I won't lose you again."

She slipped back into the water. Serena didn't let go of her sister's hand until the moment that Tia was too deep to reach. Then she lay down, her hand over the edge, until the sun lit the sky and the day gave her no option but to face it.

She felt like lead, anger interspersed with resignation and sadness. There was still nothing from him and try as she might, it was harder and harder to resist sending him another text. Rose hadn't spoken to him for a couple of days either, which was unusual. Not getting any reply from his home phone or mobile, she had finally tried calling the shop, only to find that Tom was in and wasn't sure where Seth was. Serena was cross with herself for not hiding it better, because she could see that Rose was worried. She was furious with Seth. Late that night, feeling simultaneously livid and desolate she gave in, almost in spite of herself, and picked up her phone.

If you don't want to see me anymore, fine. Just have the decency to tell me. And please let Rose know you're OK. She's worried about you.

The anger, although awful, was easier to deal with than the sadness.

Serena dragged herself through the following day, trying desperately to be as bright and breezy as she could for Rose's sake. Rose had received a text message from Seth to her land line before Serena got there, apologising and saying he would see her soon. She had tried calling him back but there was no reply. She asked Serena if she had heard anything and Serena shook her head.

"No," she said sadly. "But the message is getting through loud and clear."

"I know it's strange but I'm sure he'll turn up soon and everything will be fine," Rose said comfortingly. "It's most unlike him, but I'm sure there must be a reason."

"Yeah. Me," Serena muttered, but Rose caught it.

"That's not true. He adores you."

"Oh, Rose, maybe, maybe not, but it's fairly clear at the moment that he doesn't want anything to do with me. I have to come to terms with it."

"That's not true dear, I don't believe it for a minute. And I'm cross that he's put you through this."

"I'm sorry I've worried you Rose. I should have kept my big mouth shut. It just hurts. And he's hurting, I know that, and I can't do anything about it. I may be in love with him but he's not over what happened with *her*, I have to accept that."

"He's so happy with you. I don't understand. I know he wants to be with you, he's told me more than once."

Serena's heart lifted momentarily before crashing down again. "Well, perhaps he's thought better of it. His actions are speaking louder than his words."

"Don't give up on him yet." Rose looked really worried. "You're so good for each other."

Tears filled Serena's eyes. "I thought so. Rose, I'm sorry, I didn't mean to upset you. You know how I feel about him, that hasn't changed. I just don't know where he's at."

Rose squeezed her hand. "I hope he's seen sense. I shall be having words in his shell like. Oh, don't worry," she added, seeing Serena's look of horror. "I won't say anything you don't want me to. But I'm entitled to my opinion and he will be hearing it. Gently, of course."

Serena swallowed down the tears. "You know him best," she said. "Now I need to do some work before I disintegrate."

Serena spent a long time on the beach that evening, hoping the sea might soothe her, act as the tears that had now become solidified and stuck in her core. To have been allowed by whatever higher forces were at play to meet someone else for whom she felt so deeply, so powerfully and to feel it being snatched away, to watch it receding like a migrating bird until it vanished over the horizon was more than she could bear. Again she almost found herself wishing that she could disappear into the waves and let it all be over now. She longed to see Tia again. As the sky began to change at about eight o'clock she dragged herself home and curled up in the sitting room, unable to face the thought of food, drink or actually doing anything at all.

At half past nine a text pinged in and much as she hated herself for it, she leapt up to retrieve it. "It won't be him, you know it won't," her inner voiced screamed at her. "Don't know why you even think it might be." She brought it up.

Sorry doesn't cut it. I don't know what to say. Please can I see you?

Her hands were shaking violently as she stared numbly at the words. "He wants to see you," part of her sang. "Yeah, only to tell you it's over," another part scoffed. Minutes ticked by and she was frozen.

You have every right to be furious and never want to see me again but please, just let me talk to you. Please. I've missed you so much.

Her eyes prickled then as relief swiftly followed by anger flooded through her. She sent back a curt response.

When?

Now? I'm outside your house. At the front.

"Oh," she thought. She couldn't string any coherent thoughts together. Desperate as she was to see him, she wasn't sure it was the best thing. She was barely in control of her emotions.

Please Serena. I know it's a big ask.

She sighed. Making her way to the rarely used front door on legs that felt as though they had no bones, she turned the catch and let it swing open. She briefly glimpsed him standing there but turned round and walked away into the kitchen where she stood over by the counter, hugging herself to try and stop the shaking. She glared at the floor, not trusting herself to do anything else. He followed her, stood just inside the kitchen doorway looking over at her. The darkness around his eyes mirrored her own and a brittle silence stretched between them.

"I'm so sorry," he said quietly. "I don't know what else to say."

There were so many things she wanted to yell, to ask, to spit out at him but she couldn't speak. She just stood there, rigid.

"Serena," he said. She could hear the anguish in his voice. "Tell me how to make it right. Tell me I still have a chance with you."

"Didn't think you wanted one," she managed to say, digging her fingernails hard into her shoulders and creating enough pain to stave off the desire to weep. Or to throw herself into his arms.

He sighed heavily. "I can understand that. I've been a selfish bastard, I know. I broke my promise to you and I've hurt you again, and I'll understand if you tell me to get out and never come back. It's probably what I deserve. But please don't. I want to be with you. I'm an idiot to have even questioned it."

She was too choked to say anything. Even if she could have thought of the right words, the pain was lodged so firmly in her throat, nothing could get past it. She shifted slightly, moving her hand to fiddle with the two charms on the chain round her neck. The silence hurt. She focused desperately on the starfish and the bottle, helpless and at sea, aware of him fidgeting restlessly on the other side of the room and knowing that he felt as unsure as she did. More so, probably. But she didn't know what to say.

"Serena." His voice was closer now, gentle. "Look at me."

She stopped worrying the charms, wrapping her arms back round herself. Then she dragged her gaze up from the floor, forcing herself to meet his eyes. The pain reflected there made her flinch.

"Oh damn, Serena. Your eyes." She heard his voice crack. "I'm so, so sorry."

"Don't," she said. "Don't talk now. Just…"

He reached out to her then and she instinctively moved forward, just the slightest bit but he took her hands and when she didn't pull away, stepped nearer until he was close enough to hold her. He didn't though. He just released one of her hands and started to stroke her hair, such a tender touch and so much what she had missed and craved that she felt herself beginning to break apart. She moved slightly to rest her forehead against his chest and felt his hand cup the back of her head while his other arm slipped around her. She put her hands on his arms, and they stood for the longest time like that, each afraid to move and break the fragile thread holding them together.

Eventually he shifted slightly, moving so that his mouth was by her ear.

"We need to talk," he said. "I owe you some explanation at least, even if it does mean you throw me out."

She pulled away from him, even though it hurt her to do so. "Fine," she whispered. "Talk."

He looked as though she had slapped him, which made her feel even worse. But she couldn't get anything else out.

"I don't know where to start. I want... you know how much I care about you, how much I want to be with you. It feels so different with you, so much more than I've felt before, with anyone. Sometimes it just gets too much and then I don't know what I'm feeling. I don't deal with that very well."

"You're not joking." Serena bit back the snappy retort. She could see how hard he was trying so she remained silent. He paced across the kitchen.

"I know it's not easy for you either. After what he did to you, it must be really hard to trust anyone, and that just makes it worse, how I've been. You're so honest and open about how you feel, despite everything and it makes me feel ashamed that I can't be like that. But I can't. You were right last time when you said that I run. And I'm so sorry. It just overwhelmed me completely when you said what you said. I've got so used to protecting myself that I withdraw. Just in case something I want to hear gets pulled away again."

"I'm not her," Serena said bitterly.

"I know that. I know." He stopped and shook his head, then turned back to her. "I shouldn't have done that to you. I should have talked to you, like I promised. I'm a fool and you deserve so much better. I don't know what to say except I'm sorry. Again. I'm asking you to give me another chance. To try harder, to prove you can trust me. I want to make this work. If you still do. If you still feel the same." He moved towards her.

"I still love you," Serena said, her voice shaky. "I wouldn't say it if I didn't mean it and that hasn't changed. But I don't know whether this is right for either of us. Especially you. I know it's hard for you to trust anyone, I understand why, but I'm not sure I can cope with you leaving like that again, and I can't help but think you might if you feel..." She stopped. It was hard to explain.

It stopped him in his tracks. "I won't."

Serena sighed, trying to stay in control of herself. "I know you mean that now Seth, but you meant it last time too."

His hand raked restlessly through his hair. "So what are you saying?

You love me but it's over? You want me to leave?"

Serena twisted her hands together, shaking her head. Tears escaped at the thought of him going. "No, that's not what I want. It's the last thing I want. But I don't know if I'm good for you, so soon after Jessica. You haven't had any time to get over her. And it feels like..." she hunted for the right words, "it feels like you're doing what she did. Not on purpose, but it hurts, Seth. You know how it feels."

The realisation slammed into him with the force of a tsunami. He shook his head, sucking in a breath against the unbearable tightness of his chest. It took him long moments to regain his voice.

"You're right. I can't believe I could do that to you. After everything... I'm so sorry. But I don't need any time. I want to be with you. Only you. You're the best. I never meant to hurt you. I'll try harder. I'll be honest. To myself as well as to you."

"Seth, I just... I'm confused and worried and I'm scared that I'm going to end up being worse for you than she was." Serena put her hands over her face as the enormity of her predicament and its implications for him hit her once more. "Oh crap."

"You couldn't be anything but good for me," he said. He moved closer to her. "I'm the one that hurt you, remember. What happens next is your call, but know that I want to be with you. So much." He reached out to put his hand gently on her shoulder. "Please Serena. Tell me what you want me to do."

She took a deep, shuddering breath and moved her hands so she could meet his eyes. "Oh hell. I don't know if it's the right thing for either of us but I don't want you to go." It was a desperate whisper. "Please stay. Even if it's only for now. I don't think I could survive it if you left."

Chapter 15

Seth kept her close for the next few days but despite his attention Serena couldn't help feeling that there was a distance between them that hadn't been there before. August was bleeding out and she was torn between hope and the need to make an exit plan. Tallie commandeered her one evening as she got home from work.

"I need to talk to you," she said.

Serena's heart sank but she kept her tone light as she opened the door. "Sounds like I'm in trouble."

"Don't be daft," Tallie scoffed as she followed her into the kitchen. "But I'm worried about you."

"I'm fine," Serena lied as she put the kettle on.

"I knew you'd say that." Tallie emptied the bag she'd brought. "Here's dinner, by the way. No cook. Got some plates? Thanks. Yes, I knew you'd tell me you're fine but I'm not going to believe it until you look me in the eye and say it."

"Tallie…"

"I mean it, Serena." Tallie's voice was gentle. "And if you're not fine, maybe I can help."

Serena spun round to look at her friend, planning to tough it out, but the concern in Tallie's eyes broke her resolution.

"Oh honey, what's wrong? Is Seth still messing you around? I'll have him if he is."

"No, no, it's not like that." Serena sat down at the table. "It's just… there's stuff that's in the way and I don't know how to shift it."

"Like what?"

"He doesn't trust me. Even though I've tried to… aargh." Serena slammed her hand on the table in frustration. "Tried to give him space, tried to show him I won't mess around, mess him around, tried to I..." She stopped abruptly.

"Tried to love him," Tallie finished for her. Serena met her gaze. "I know."

"It's not enough."

"Of course it is. Don't say that." Tallie sat down opposite. Serena was shaking her head.

"It's not. He won't let me, doesn't trust me. Deep down he thinks I'll be like her and nothing I do seems to change that. Every time we get closer, he runs for the hills, and I'm not sure if I can take it much longer."

"He comes back though and then you're stronger together."

Serena sighed. "There's no guarantee that he'll always come back. And I'm getting to the point where I don't know if I'm strong enough to cope if he doesn't. I promised myself when I came here that I wasn't going to let that happen again. If he can't trust me and I...'

"It's not you he doesn't trust, you know that," Tallie interjected hotly. "It's himself. He adores you, it's so obvious. He's never been so head over heels in love with anyone, he just can't admit it."

Serena felt tears jab the back of her eyes. She so wanted to believe her friend. But even if it was true, if Seth couldn't say it, it would make no difference anyway. She shook her head again.

"I don't know. I feel like I'm putting him under pressure that he doesn't need. He needs time to get himself together and I... well, I just need time to..." Her words faded. Tallie was staring at her, horror growing on her face.

"What are you saying, Serena?" she asked quietly. "Because it sounds like you're thinking about leaving."

Serena tried desperately to bite back her sadness but a salt drop escaped anyway. She brushed it away angrily. "I don't know what to do," she said. "But my lease is up at the beginning of October and I'd decided before I came here that I'd only stay a year. Unless... well anyway, I just think it'll be better for us both, for him if I go. Then he won't feel so conflicted all the time, and neither will I."

Because I won't feel anything, she thought.

Tallie was shaking her head vehemently. "No, no, no, you can't leave, you mustn't. You belong here with us. With him. You know you do. Serena, please don't even think about it."

More tears followed the first. "Tallie, I can't... I don't know what to do. That's the only option I can see."

Tallie came round and embraced her tightly. "There'll be another way. We'll find another way. We have to. Damn. Does he know? What you're thinking."

"No. Not yet. I need to tell him but I don't know how. It feels like blackmail but it's not. God." Serena sucked in a breath. "Why does it all have to be so damn hard?"

"Shall I talk to him?"

"No!" Serena was adamant. "Please don't say anything Tallie. I need to do it."

Serena steeled herself to speak to Seth the following evening. She had been going through it again and again through the day and her stomach was in knots by the time she got to Seth's, not helped any when she realised that Gaia and Ethan were there.

"Hi," Gaia said. "Hope you don't mind us gate crashing your evening, but one of the guys Ethan works with is doing an acoustic set at the Feathers and we hoped you guys would come."

"Of course." Serena smiled over her distress. "Sounds great."

"Yay." Gaia rubbed her hands together. "Let's go then."

Serena caught Ethan's eye; he was looking at her intently. She turned and headed quickly down the stairs.

"You don't mind, do you?" Seth asked her quietly, looping an arm round her waist as they walked down the road. "I should've texted you but I got sidetracked and..."

"It's fine, really." Serena kept her voice light. "It'll be fun."

She could feel Ethan watching her through the evening and when Seth and Gaia were at the bar he took the opportunity to speak.

"Sorry," he said. "I tried to talk Gaia out of inviting you guys but obviously I failed miserably."

"It's all right."

"It's not though, is it? I can feel it's not. You needed to just be with Seth tonight. Is everything OK?"

She shrugged. "On the surface but... Ethan, I have to tell him I'm leaving. I can't wait any longer. He has to know."

"Oh, Serena. I'm so sorry. And that was what you were going to do tonight?"

She nodded sadly. "At least tell him that I'm thinking about it. So it won't be a shock when...'

"You still might not have to. He still might...'

"He might but I don't think so. I have to... oh, they're coming back." Serena felt Ethan squeeze her hand as they both painted their smiles back on.

"So," Seth said outside later, after they had said goodbye to the others. "Which way? Yours or mine?"

Serena looked at him blankly, her head so full she felt she would explode. He pulled her against him and held her. "What's up?" he asked. "You've been distracted all evening."

Serena sighed against his shoulder. She hugged him briefly then loosened her grip and moved away. He looked at her, concerned. "What's wrong?"

"Can we walk?" she said. "I need to talk to you."

"That doesn't sound good," His voice was anxious and he took her hand as they walked down onto the beach. "Tell me."

"My lease runs out next month," she said. "I have to decide what to do."

"Oh." She thought she detected relief in his voice which only made her feel worse. "Sarah'll renew it, won't she? You're going to stay, aren't you?"

"I want to," she said. "But there are things I need to think about before I make that decision."

He looked hurt. He stopped, tugging her round to face him.

"You know how much I want you to stay, how much I care about you," he said.

"I know. And you know that I love you." He looked down at the floor as she continued. "It's OK, you don't have to say anything. You don't know how you feel, I understand. But when I came here last September I was only going to stay a year. I told you that if my world shifted again it would be on my terms but you... you're shifting my world and I'm not sure that that's really what you want. That I'm really what you want." She held up her hand to stop his denial. "I don't think you're over everything enough to know and I'm just clouding the picture. I don't want to find out that I'm just rebound girl. I'm in over my head already and I'm afraid to get any deeper. I'm sorry. I don't want to get broken again."

"I wouldn't do that to you. I couldn't," he said.

"Oh Seth, you wouldn't hurt anyone on purpose, I know that. Just like I don't want to hurt you. But I see how much you're struggling with what's between us, how it makes you withdraw, even though you don't want to, and I find it really hard to cope with when you do. That's why I have to think about it carefully."

"What am I doing wrong?"

"Nothing, you're not doing anything wrong. It's just, sometimes you're distant, almost unreachable, it feels like you wish I wasn't around. I know you find it difficult to trust me and I know why. But it doesn't help when it hurts, so I guess if that means hard decisions for self-protection then that's what I have to do. I know it sounds selfish but there it is."

"But I don't want you to go, I... I really..." Serena's heart was thumping but Seth hesitated. "I really don't want you to go."

Her heart crashed down. "I know. I'm just not sure it's enough. I'm sorry."

He pulled her to him. "*I'm* sorry. That I've made you feel that way. Please stay."

She buried her face in his shoulder, hurting for both of them but unable to tell him why.

"I'm still thinking about it."

Things were tentative between them after that. Seth was keen to be with her all the time he could and yet Serena felt the distance between them more keenly. As if he was keeping her close but at arm's length at the same time. It did nothing to reassure her and yet there was nothing that he did or didn't do that she could have put into words. He hugged her, laughed with her, talked to her and held her at night. But sometimes she caught him watching her, an unreadable expression on his face, as if he had taken himself somewhere that she could never reach.

Hard as it was, she also had to warn Rose that she might be leaving. There was no point trying to hide her reasons either; as far as that was concerned, Rose seemed to be just as psychic as Ethan.

"I so hope it won't come to that, dear," she sighed.

Serena woke suddenly, the call following her from her dreams into consciousness. She could still hear it as the last shards of sleep fell from her eyes, as clear as the moonlight that found its way between the curtains and fell in a sharp line across the floor.

A heart call.

Tia.

Leaving Seth fast asleep, she slipped out of bed and dressed in the bathroom, the urgency of Tia's summoning coursing through her. She scrawled a quick note for Seth in case he woke to find her gone and almost ran through the streets to the beach, desperate to get to her sister.

The moon was high and bright, lighting a path across the unruffled surface of the water. Tia was waiting for her on the rocks by the little hidden cove. Serena flew over to her as fast as she could.

"Are you alright?" she asked. "And the others? Is something wrong?"

"No, no." Tia embraced her. "Nothing is wrong. I have something to tell you. An answer to your problem."

"Oh." Serena settled beside her sister, feeling apprehensive. "Tia, you haven't put yourself in danger, have you? We both know what the Sea Witch said. Going against magic that ancient and powerful…"

"Calm yourself," Tia said. "All is well. But I know that magic can be done and also undone and that truly nothing is permanent in this world. I went to visit the Sea Witch again, to ask if there was any way of reversing the magic. Of allowing you to live."

"Tia, you shouldn't have done that. I made the choice willingly, I knew the risk."

"I couldn't do nothing. You are still my sister even though we live in different worlds now. I asked her whether I could give up my magic to allow you to keep your soul."

"Oh, no, Tia. You didn't do it, did you? Please, you mustn't, you can't give up what you are for…"

"I would have," Tia said fiercely. "To keep you safe, I would have done it… lived out the rest of my time as a halfling… but it would not have saved you."

Serena slumped back, gratitude and relief for her sister mingling with the sadness of her situation.

"Then there is nothing to be done."

"That isn't true," Tia said. "There is a way. I had to plead long and hard and even then she was reticent to tell me. This magic is powerful and used only rarely. Most know nothing of it. It is kept concealed for good reason but… it will work."

Dread flooded through Serena. Magic hidden like that was never good.

"I'm not sure…" she began but Tia cut her off.

"You are right to be concerned," she said. "It is dark magic, blood magic, but it is the only way. It will reverse the process, bring you back to us, return your magic and send your soul back to the vortex."

"Leave the human world?" Serena was shocked at the strength of emotion that the thought raised in her. "I don't think I could do that."

"But you would be alive," Tia answered. "You may have to leave it anyway."

"Yes, but..." Serena could barely articulate the myriad thoughts whirling around her head. "But I won't *know*. Because I'll no longer *be*."

"I don't want you to die." Tia sounded desperate. "Please. We would welcome you back. Please just consider."

Serena sighed, torn. "Tell me then."

Tia nodded. She reached down into the bag she had secured round her waist and drew out a small jewelled dagger. The gems threw off glints of coloured light as the moon illuminated a viciously sharp blade.

"This will undo even the deepest and strongest of magic," she said as she turned it slowly. "But it does require blood."

"Whose blood?" Serena questioned. "Mine?"

Tia held the dagger out to her and she took it tentatively, testing the tip against her finger.

"No. Not yours," Tia told her. "The blood of the one you love. The one who will not profess his love for you. And..." She hesitated, looking her sister straight in the eye, "it must be blood from his heart. His must be broken so yours can be healed."

"No," Serena said but Tia was undeterred.

"His heart blood must fall on your feet. It will begin the transformation back. As his soul leaves, it will enter the vortex and then your magic will return to you."

"No, Tia." Serena's voice was stronger now. "I can't do that. I can't kill Seth. I love him."

"Serena, it's your only chance. I don't understand. He's the reason you are facing the end."

"No, Steve's the reason for that. He's the one who betrayed me, not Seth."

"But this Seth. You love him but he doesn't love you. He could save you but he won't."

"Tia, it's not that simple. He doesn't know what I was, can never know. He's oblivious to my predicament. And I think he does love me.

He's just too afraid to say it."

Tia waved a dismissive hand. "Then he is weak. These human ways – I cannot understand them. Why can't he just tell his truth?"

"Tia, this is why I can't return to you. I love you but I'm not like you. I understand why he can't but I don't think you could, even if I explain it. Seth isn't weak, he's one of the strongest people I know. And a knife isn't required to break his heart; that's already been done by someone else and that's why he can't tell me he loves me. And when I leave, it's just going to hurt him again."

"Maybe he would be better off dead. At least it would give you a chance to live."

"No." Serena shook her head. "Human hearts can recover. They just need time. He'll be fine one day and he'll meet someone else. I won't deprive him of that. I love him. I can't kill him. I won't. I couldn't live with myself knowing I had done that." She offered the dagger back to Tia. "Here. Please take it back."

"No." Tia was weeping now. "I cannot. I will not. I don't want to lose you."

Serena put her arm round her sister. "Please don't cry," she said. "You say you don't understand human emotions but you do, more than you think. Losing someone you care for, this is how they feel, how they would do almost anything to stop it from happening. Except what's really impossible."

"I won't take it back," Tia sobbed.

"It's OK." Serena gave her sister a last squeeze then stood up. "It'll find its own way home. Thank you. For trying. For caring about me despite everything."

She stood up and moved to the edge of the rocks, threw the dagger as far as she could out into the sea. It sparked and shone, wheeling through the air, and left a trail of light as it travelled away beneath the water. Eventually it disappeared. She returned to sit next to Tia.

"Please don't be sad for me, Tia. There's still time. I hope he will be able to say the words. And if he doesn't love me, or can't tell me, then I think I'd rather not be around anyway. The sadness is suffocating my heart."

"I can feel it," Tia sniffed. "Some of what you feel at least. I wish I was as brave as you."

Serena grinned. "Father would say I was foolhardy, not brave."

Tia smiled a little at that, her face quickly becoming serious again. "I will be here when... if..."

Serena squeezed her hand. "Thank you. You don't have to but thank you."

The sky was just beginning to lighten as the sisters said goodbye. Not with words but through their hearts. Serena watched Tia swim away and lay down on the rock once more, drifting off into a restless slumber as her tears joined her sister's in the sea.

That was where Seth found her, just as the sun was painting the sky with orange and gold. He had woken to discover her gone and, worried despite the reassuring tone of the note she had left, had immediately set out to find her.

"Hey," he said gently, climbing up beside her. He stroked hair off her face. "What happened? Have you been here all night?"

Her eyes fluttered open. She sat up quickly, confused.

"Seth. What are you doing here?"

"I woke up and you weren't there. I saw your note. I could ask you the same. How long have you been out here?"

"I don't know. Couldn't sleep so I came down. And then..." The memories were coalescing now, vivid and strong. "Must've dropped off. Had some strange dreams."

He moved closer to her, put his arm round her. "Bad dreams? You've been crying." He ran his finger down her face. "Want to talk?"

Her heart was heavy as she shook her head. "Can't really remember," she lied. How could she tell him? He drew her towards him and she shifted willingly.

"You're shivering," he said as his arms closed round her. "Come home."

"Not sure where that is," Serena whispered. He said nothing, just helped her up and led her back to his flat.

The last day of September fell on a Tuesday and Serena knew that she had no choice left. Her time ran out on Sunday night and there was nothing she could do. When she told Rose that she would be leaving at the weekend she could hardly get the words out. Rose was upset but understanding.

"I wish I could make him see sense, dear," she said sadly. "And I wish you would reconsider. I understand that you feel you need to go but I don't think you really want to, do you?"

Serena looked at her miserably and shook her head. "But I can't stay either. Not while he's so confused. It's just impossible."

"He does love you," Rose said. "I'm sure of it."

"Oh, Rose. I'd love to believe you but I don't know. He doesn't know. We're just going to hurt each other if we keep on like this. I don't want that for either of us. Not again."

"So, you're really leaving then," Seth said. They were supposed to be going out to eat and she had come down to his flat a little early. "Aunt Rose said you told her this morning."

"Yeah, of course I told her, I couldn't just go, could I? I thought you knew me better than that."

"I still don't know why you have to leave. I thought you were happy here. You've got friends, you like Auntie, we're together aren't we? You know you're who I want to be with."

"I know that, but I told you, I need control over my world and I'm losing it with you. If I stay and fall any deeper and then you decide you don't want to be with me I don't think I can deal with that. Not again. I want more than you can give and that's not fair on either of us."

"I care about you. I don't want you to go. Doesn't that mean anything?"

"Oh, Seth," Serena said. "Of course it does. I know you care. And you know that I love you. I never thought I'd love someone again after what happened and then I met you. But you don't feel the same about me and you need time to... well, whatever, I don't know that you'll be able to if I'm around."

"That's ridiculous and you know it. If you love me you wouldn't leave. You know how I feel, I know you do. And you're right, I probably do need time but that shouldn't be enough to make you run away."

Serena shook her head. "Sometimes things don't make sense. Sometimes there is no rhyme nor reason, things just are. I can't tell you any more Seth, I'm sorry. And I'm not running away from you. I don't really want to go but I have no choice. Maybe it's me I'm running from. Because I have to."

"Who says you have to? You." Seth sounded angry but really he felt desperate.

"Please. Don't."

"God, this is impossible," Seth said ferociously. "You don't have to lie to me. If you've changed your mind about me, about us, you can tell me. Or anything else for that matter."

"Would it make it easier if I told you I'd changed my mind?"

"No." He wasn't quite shouting but it wasn't far off. He took a breath and lowered his voice. "No, because I know you and it wouldn't be the truth anyway, would it?"

Serena bit her lip. That was one of the things that had always made her different from the rest of the mer. She had never been able to hide her feelings.

"No. No, it wouldn't. Seth, look, I'm sorry but I can't tell you anything else. I need more than you can give and I need to protect my heart. I love you. How easy do you think it is for me to leave? But it's not fair on either of us if I stay."

"Still just sounds like an excuse to me. There's something else, something you're not telling me. I want to know."

"You do know."

"No." He looked at her but it felt as if he looked right into her. "What is the truth, Serena? Don't you think I at least deserve that?"

The pain in his eyes nearly broke her into pieces. There were only two emotions she could feel at that moment, the agony of loss and the anger of injustice. Tears would not help so she went with anger.

"Fine." She slammed her hand on the table and stood up. "My truth isn't good enough for you then. Well try this one. I walked out of a fairy tale but I'm cursed and Prince Charming is emotionally constipated so tomorrow I'm toast."

"That's not funny," he snapped back.

"It wasn't meant to be."

A heavy silence stretched between them, neither looking at the other. Eventually Serena sighed.

"I'm sorry Seth. I didn't want it to be like this. I think I'd better go home. Maybe, I don't know, maybe we should just leave things now."

He remained silent. Gathering up the last remnants of courage and control, Serena walked round the table and gently laid a kiss on the top of his head.

"I love you. I'm so sorry."

He stayed rigidly still and silent. She moved away, picked up her bag and let herself quietly out of the flat. She managed to walk half the way home before the tears started and after that, they just wouldn't stop.

"What's up?" Ethan asked later. "Although I have a suspicion that I know what you're going to say."

"We had a fight." Seth stared glumly into his beer. "She's determined that she's leaving."

"Oh." Ethan wasn't sure how best to approach what had to be said. "Has she told you why?"

"She has but I don't understand it really," Seth sighed. "Some crap about having to stick to the decision she made when she came here. Protecting herself and her heart, all that stuff."

"Well, I guess you can appreciate that," Ethan said. "Her marriage didn't exactly end happily ever after. Being left for someone else; you of all people know what that's like."

"Of course I do, but she knows I'd never do what he did to her. I thought she trusted me more than that."

"I don't think it's a question of trust, Seth. Maybe it's more a question of how you feel about her."

"She knows how much I care about her. She knows I want to be with her, not Jessica. Or anyone else."

"Are you sure?"

"I told her that. I told her when she said..." Seth stopped suddenly and took a mouthful of his drink.

"Said what?"

"She said she loves me."

"Oh," Ethan said again. "And what did you say?"

Seth met his friend's look, eyes full of anguish. "What I told you. I couldn't say it back, I wanted to but I couldn't. I thought she'd know."

"Know what? That you love her? Do you?"

"I think so but how *do* you know? I thought I loved Jessica but that wasn't love. I don't know what that was. And this, this is so different, it feels... perfect, but I just don't know whether it's love or not. Maybe it's too perfect." Seth shook his head. "I feel like I don't know anything anymore."

"Jeez, Seth, Jessica really did a number on you, didn't she?"

"Yeah, OK, you were right all along, is that what you want me to say?"

"No, of course it's not, but she's screwed you up so you can't even tell how you feel. I've seen you and Serena together, *I* can see how you feel about each other and that's nothing to do with being psychic, believe me. It worries me if you don't know what that is. Or are you just in denial?"

"God knows," Seth muttered. "I don't. How can three words be so difficult?"

Ethan shrugged.

"How did you know?" Seth continued. "That Gaia was the one for you?"

"I was talking to a client about change and I suddenly realised that I couldn't imagine a life without her in it. The thought that one day she might not be there... I couldn't stand it. I went straight out and bought a ring. I had to let her know how much I love her and how I wanted to be with her always, even if she didn't want to get married. I asked her that evening and you know the rest. I would not be complete without her. And I tell her I love her every single day. I know she knows, but I think sometimes people need to hear it."

"I'm just afraid that if I get it wrong I'll hurt both of us."

"Is that going to be any worse than what you're feeling now? Or how she's feeling? Any worse than watching her walk away and wondering what might have been? She won't ask you for more than you can give, she's not that sort of person, but maybe she needs to hear how you feel. Without having to ask. Life isn't a fairy tale but if you take a chance you might get a happy ending."

"What's with all the fairy tale stuff? Happy ending, happily ever after. Even she said something about being cursed."

"Oh." Ethan was shocked. "Like what?"

"Oh, she was yelling at me. Because I wouldn't accept what she said, I kept pushing her for her reasons for going. So she just lost it and shouted something about fairy tales and curses and being toast. I yelled back. And then," Seth sighed, "there was the most awful silence. She said she was sorry and she left. And being the idiot that I am, I didn't even try to stop her."

"Have you called her? Texted her?"

"I don't want to make things worse. If I call her I'll probably just say the wrong thing. I did text but she hasn't replied. I'm so worried that she'll just go and I'll never see her again."

"I don't think she'll just go. She wouldn't let Rose down like that, she's got another few days up there, hasn't she?"

Seth nodded. "She said she's actually leaving on Sunday morning."

"Then you've got a few days to get your head straight, haven't you?"

"Why is it so difficult?"

"It's not really. I reckon if you feel it, you should say it. Those three little words have a magic all their own and some things need to be said."

"What if she won't talk to me?"

"Don't be stupid. Why don't you call her or go up to her house?"

"I don't think so," Seth said. "Neither of us are dealing with it very well." Ethan stared at him hard. "I don't know how to even begin."

"I think it's worth…" Ethan began, but Seth was shaking his head. "Not now. Maybe tomorrow."

"It's your life. Don't screw it up."

"Yeah, yeah, I know, you're right. Doesn't it piss you off, being right so much?"

"Somehow, it never loses its charm."

Seth finished his beer. "Right, I'm going home to fail miserably at sleeping. Thanks for your company, man. I appreciate it."

"Any time," Ethan said. He watched his friend trudge dejectedly along the road and turn the corner towards the flat. He gave it a few minutes then drained his glass and headed in the other direction, up towards Serena's, texting her as he went.

Chapter 16

Serena dragged herself off the sofa and into the kitchen after she received Ethan's text. She sat at the table hugging herself and desperately trying to stop crying before he got there. It was fruitless. He knocked and she beckoned him in.

"Oh, Serena, I don't even have to ask how you're doing, do I?"

She shook her head. Tears were still coursing down her face. He came straight over and put an arm round her.

"Can't stop," she managed to get out. "We…'

"I know," he said softly. "I know you had a fight. I've been with Seth all evening. He's doing about as well as you are, just not quite so soggy."

It was more of a sob than a laugh that came out of her then. "I don't know how to bear it. It feels like the sadness is going to kill me anyway, before I even get to Sunday night."

"There's still time," Ethan said. "I've told him that he should just tell you how he feels, but it's…" He shrugged.

Serena shook her head. She drew away from Ethan, desperately dabbing at her eyes. He sat down next to her.

"You're so kind Ethan. You've been so good to me, you and Gaia and Tallie and Rob. And Seth. But he's a mess and he's just not ready to say the magic words."

"He feels it though. You know he does. And he knows it, even if he's too afraid to admit it."

"I hope he does, I thought he… but even if he does, it's not enough. He has to say it."

"That's so stupid."

"Yeah, well, I don't make the damn rules, I'm just cursed by them."

The tears were pouring again. "God, I'll have dissolved by the morning at this rate."

Ethan stayed for a while, talking things over and trying to persuade her to contact Seth. She was reluctant; despite the fact that he had texted her and that his conversation with Ethan made it obvious that he regretted what had happened as much as she did, she felt too emotional to be able to talk to him. Eventually, when her tears had stopped and she was calmer, Ethan rose to go home.

"Thanks, Ethan. For everything. For trying so hard."

"It's OK. I just want it to work out, for both of you. Please Serena, just promise me one thing."

"What?"

"If… if you do end up leaving, promise me that you won't go without saying goodbye. To all of us, but especially to Seth. You two need to say goodbye properly."

She gazed at him, eyes aching. "OK," she said finally. "I promise."

"So what are you going to do?" Gaia asked. "Have you found somewhere to stay?"

It was Thursday night and they were at Tallie's having a last girls' get together. Serena shifted uncomfortably in her seat, trying to find an explanation that would satisfy the others without pinning herself to the wall. "No. Nowhere permanent. I don't really know where I want to go. I thought I might just travel around for a bit, see where things take me."

"I hope they bring you back here," Tallie said hotly. "I can't bear the thought that you're leaving. And when you would stay if he'd just… Grr! I need to bang your heads together."

"Tallie, don't," Gaia intervened. "It's hard enough for both of them." She gestured at Serena. Tallie was immediately remorseful.

"I'm sorry." She hugged Serena hard. "I just so don't want you to go."

"Thank you," Serena whispered.

"You will let us know where you are though?" Tallie went on. "Tell us about your exploits. If you have to go away then at least let us live vicariously through you. I'd make a great armchair adventurer. I know. I'll turn you into a new graphic novel."

"Hey, that sounds great," Gaia said. "Serena's infamous adventuring."

"She might want to be in disguise, though. Shall I stick with Serena or do you want to pick a name? Actually, maybe I'll turn you into a steampunk pirate. How about we call you Serenity? You can ride one of those big, mean looking black and silver motor trikes and..."

Serena breathed a sigh of relief as the conversation turned. She hated lying.

"I'm worried about you," Rose said as Seth put the last of the dishes away. "I need to talk to you, but you may not want to hear what I have to say."

He sighed. He had a fairly good idea what was coming. Not for the first time, he regretted taking up his aunt's invitation. But he hadn't been able to face another evening alone with his thoughts and the gaping void where Serena should have been. And he couldn't face the others either.

"I'm fine, Auntie."

"No, you're not," Rose said. Her voice was firm but kind. "You won't get away with trying to fob me off again. I know you. I can see how unhappy you are. And I can also see how desperately sad she is. I don't understand why you won't talk to each other."

"Everything's been said." He sat down opposite and looked at her. "She's leaving and she won't change her mind. It won't make any difference what I say."

"How do you know that? You can't know."

"I do. She doesn't trust me and that's my fault. I've been such a stupid..." Seth nearly swore but stopped himself, "...idiot and let her down. I thought she knew how I felt but obviously not."

"How do you feel?"

Seth sighed again and shifted restlessly in his chair. "I don't know. I can't put it into words."

Rose took a sip of her tea and put the cup down slowly. "Seth," she said. "If you don't know how you feel, how is she supposed to?"

Seth shook his head. "Crap. I don't know." He looked at his Aunt miserably. "Don't know much, do I?"

"She loves you. You know that. The question is, do you feel the same?"

"Love. I don't know, Auntie. Love is something that makes people crazy. People do hateful things to each other and call it love. Look at my father. And..." He stopped. Jessica hung silently in the air between them.

"Yes. They call it love but it isn't. Look at Ethan and Gaia. Think of your Great Uncle and me. And your grandparents. And your sister. That's love."

"How do you know though? That it's right. That what you feel is really what you think it is?"

"You feel it." Rose reached over and took Seth's hand. "You stop thinking about it and worrying about it and you just feel it."

Seth took a deep breath and let it out slowly. "I know I miss her. All the time. I don't want to think that I'll never see her again. It feels like she's taking part of me that I'll never get back. I don't know if I can bear it but…"

"Talk to her Seth."

"There's no point. I told you, everything's been said."

"Not everything." Rose looked at him sternly but there was love in her eyes. "She's been betrayed just like you have. Maybe it's not you she doesn't trust but herself. Her feelings, her instincts, just like you. Tell her how you feel Seth. Three words, one syllable each. You feel it, I know you do. Trust yourself. Don't let the past hold you back."

Seth enfolded her in a hug. "I'll try."

She squeezed him back. "Good. Now let's go and watch the news."

"Actually, could I have a look at something on your computer?"

"Help yourself dear."

Seth took himself off to the study and fired up the desk top. Then he sat down and started to look through the files that Serena had so meticulously put together.

Serena worked late on Friday and all day Saturday, partly to tie up loose ends and finish the manuscript for Rose and partly because the thought of being in her own company a moment longer than she had to was unbearable. Sheila came in on the Saturday afternoon and the two ladies made such a fuss of her that she couldn't help weeping.

Sheila embraced her. "I do wish you'd stay," she said sincerely.

"If you change your mind and come back, you'll always be welcome, dear," Rose said, hugging her hard and wiping away tears herself. "I was hoping he'd come to his senses sooner rather than later, but I understand why you feel you have to go. But please keep in touch. Let me know where you are so when the book's printed I can send it to you."

"Oh Rose, thank you so much for everything," Serena whispered. "You have no idea how much difference you've made. I have to go now otherwise I'm just going to fall to bits. But thank you."

"I hope we'll see you again," Rose said sadly, as Serena closed the front door.

Serena cried all the way home and although the thought of being alone was bad enough, she was dreading going out even more. But her friends had been insistent about getting together to say goodbye, even whilst trying to persuade her to stay. They had been so good to her she didn't want to let them down. The only way she could remotely ease the pain was to tell herself that shortly after this time the following day she would no longer be feeling anything. It was cold comfort.

She had a shower and got dressed, then trudged down to the pub. They had decided to forego the Old Hare in favour of the Feathers because it was quieter and they could talk. The others were already there waiting for her, all except Seth who was conspicuous by his absence. They chatted and laughed and bought her drinks and asked her more questions about her plans, to which she gave hazy answers while trying to keep some semblance of a smile in place. She could feel Ethan's empathy pouring around her and hardly dared look at him, knowing the kindness in his face would probably break her.

At about ten Seth came in and Gaia moved from her seat next to Serena to let him sit beside her. They both sat stiffly, trying not to touch, not looking at each other. After Seth had finished his drink, he excused himself.

"Take care," he said to Serena. "Be happy."

"You too," she said, biting back tears as she watched him leave. The others were quiet for a moment.

"Do you want me to go after him?" Ethan asked. Serena shook her head.

"No. One more drink and then they'll be kicking us out."

"I wish you would stay," Tallie said. "I'm going to miss you so much. You will let us know where you are, keep in touch. Then when Seth finally gets his act together you can come back."

Serena sighed under her smile. "If only," she thought.

When they left the pub, Gaia asked if she wanted to come back to theirs but she demurred. They all hugged her and told her they'd miss her and she did shed tears then. So did Tallie and Gaia. They set off home eventually but Ethan hung back.

"You going to go and see him?"

"I don't know." She shook her head. "I don't want to hurt him any more than I have already but I can't bear to leave it like this. There isn't anything I can say to hurt him less."

"Go see him Serena. You need to say goodbye properly if that's how it has to be, and you didn't do that earlier. Go talk to him."

She looked at him with such misery that he had to hug her. "Go. See him. And if you need us then call." He let her go and she gave him a look of gratitude.

"Thanks Ethan, for everything. Bye." Her voice cracked.

"You know what, I'm not going to say goodbye. I'm going to say I hope I see you soon." He gave her another quick hug. "Now go."

After a while of hovering uncertainly, she went to see Seth. It was late. She hadn't intended to, had steeled herself to stay away, but after what Ethan had said she couldn't stop herself. He opened the door, smiling uncertainly when he saw her. He looked tired, his eyes dark.

"Hey," he said.

"Hi."

"Come up?"

She nodded and followed him up the stairs into the living room. He had her favourite music playing; it nearly undid her.

"I'll put the kettle on," he said, heading for the kitchen.

"No, I…" She choked on the words. "I just came to say goodbye. I… we couldn't really earlier. And if you're busy in the morning I won't see you."

He stopped, turning towards her. "You're really going then?" There was such sadness in his face it almost overwhelmed her.

"I have to," she said quietly, looking at the floor. "Time's up."

"I still don't understand," he said. "I know what you said but you could renew your lease. You like it here. You've got friends here, a job. And I can try harder."

"Seth, you can't. I know how hard you're trying and it's not fair."

"Is there anything I can do? You would tell me, wouldn't you?"

She shook her head. She so wished she could tell him but she couldn't. "It's too complicated to explain any better than I already have."

"I can try and listen better. I shouldn't have lost my temper the other day. Isn't what we have worth saving?"

"Yes," she said. "And that just makes it harder. I'm sorry." Tears welled up and spilled over but she made herself look at him. "So sorry."

He was across to her in seconds, arms around her. "Don't," he said. "Please don't." He could feel the stabbing behind his own eyes but he fought it back. "I don't want you to go and it kills me to see you cry."

He brought one hand up to cup her face, the sea falling from her eyes like rain. He began to kiss her tears away gently, murmuring softly as he held her close, trying to calm her. And then his lips found hers and they were kissing desperately, clinging to each other like a drowning man clings to the rocks.

Eventually he tore his mouth away from hers to bury his face against her neck. She had hold of fistfuls of his T-shirt, her grip so tight her knuckles were white. Her breathing was ragged from crying.

"It hurts," she said, and he heard his own heart scream.

He straightened up and pulled her head against his shoulder, taking a deep, shuddering breath and stroking her, trying to soothe her.

"Shh, shh, he whispered over and over. "It'll be alright. Shh. We'll find a way."

She let him hold her, couldn't bear to tear herself away even though she could feel the cracks spreading through her heart, wanting the last moments of humanity and kindness, her last moments with him, to be the memory that lingered before she was lost.

As their breathing calmed and her tears eased, she loosened her grip, knowing that she had to say goodbye. She looked up at him, horrified to see tears on his face too. She began to well up again.

"I should go," she said hoarsely.

He shook his head. "No." He slid one hand down to clasp hers and brought it up to hold it against his chest. "Please. Don't go. Stay with me tonight. Tomorrow is tomorrow but please. Be with me tonight." He kissed her fingers one by one. "I don't want to think about the morning. I need you. I need you so much." He pressed his forehead to hers.

Her eyes were wet and she couldn't help herself. She moved up and kissed him again, her love reaching out to him. And this time his mouth didn't let hers go as he guided them slowly into his bedroom and onto the bed. With each caress, each piece of skin on skin, each kiss, each touch, she felt her edges blurring into his until they melted into each other completely.

"Please don't leave," he said. "I love you. I can't lose you."

"Oh Seth," she said as his words crashed like waves through her heart. Her eyes filled up again. "You've no idea just how much that means.'"

"It means I love you. I'm so sorry I didn't tell you before."

"Shh. It doesn't matter. It's just, hearing that, knowing it changes everything. I know it sounds stupid but it does. I could stay. If you really feel that way. If you want me to."

"I do. I want you to more than anything," he said, hope dawning in his eyes. "I don't think I can keep breathing without you."

"Then I'll stay."

His arms tightened around her. "I really do love you," he told her.

"I love you too."

Epilogue

Early in the morning Seth awoke to see Serena peeking through the curtains. For a moment his heart plunged, before starting to lift as he remembered what she'd said. What *he'd* said. He propped himself up on his elbow to look at her. She must have heard him move because she turned toward him, letting the curtain fall back into place.

"Looks like it'll be a beautiful day," she said.

"That depends," Seth said uncertainly. "Are you really going to stay?" He opened his arms to her.

She crossed the room and got back into bed beside him. He enfolded her quickly. "Yes, I really am." She was staring at something behind him on the bedside table. "They're pretty. You don't usually have flowers in here."

"Before you start worrying who they're from, I should tell you they're for you." He released her and levered himself into a sitting position, reaching the vase down. He held it as she sat up. "I've been reading the manuscript of Auntie's book. All that work you've done. I didn't know if we'd be able to talk so I was going to bring this to your house this morning and leave it for you. And wait, hoping when you saw it you would know what I wanted to tell you. So then I really could tell you. Stupid, huh?" He handed it to her.

Serena looked down. Pansies surrounded four red roses with a red tulip in the centre. Think of me surrounding true love with a declaration of love in the middle.

"Oh," she sighed softly. "That's not stupid. It's amazing."

"Not as amazing as you."

"What's this?" She pulled a card from the flowers, then reached over to put the vase back on the bedside table.

"Oh." He sighed. "That's... well it's what I would've written for you if I was any good with words. Which I'm not. I had to borrow it from Avenged Sevenfold. But it's the truth."

Serena flipped the card open and began to read the lyrics laid out in Seth's rounded handwriting. It wasn't long before her eyes were filling again. She looked at him, a lump in her throat. "I..."

"Shh. It's OK, I know." He pulled her towards him, held her tightly. "I love you too. And I will tell you that every day from now until forever. I promise."

Out in the depths of the ocean, beneath water gilded rose gold by the early sun, Tia danced. The Sea Witch gave a sigh of relief as she felt the song of those three words spiral through her heart and into the vortex. The call of the void quietened as she settled back in her chair and relaxed. Serena had found a miracle and she was happy.

About The Author

Izzy Robertson grew up in Slough. She read and wrote voraciously as a child but tended toward science at school. She trained as a physiotherapist and worked in the NHS for about 15 years, treating patients with musculo-skeletal problems and chronic pain. In 2006 she and her family escaped from the urban jungle of the south east to the deep, dark wilds of Dorset. She now works freelance as a complementary therapist, writer and editor, and is proud to be a trustee of The Word Forest Organisation, which plants trees and supports local communities and schools in a deforested area of Kenya.

When not busy with the above, she enjoys time with her husband and two sons, chats to her chickens and dabbles in crafting, usually involving sparkly beads and glitter, to honour her inner magpie. She is most effectively fuelled by tea and music.

Izzy's stories reflect her love of the unusual and magical and are aimed at young adults, whatever their age. "Maybe I never grew up," she says. "I love the thought that anything's possible. Magic is around us all the time. It's not complicated, it's the occurrence of the unexpected. We just have to open our eyes and look." More at **IzzyRobertsonAuthor.co.uk**

About The Word Forest Organisation

The Word Forest Organisation is an NGO started by Magic Oxygen founders, Tracey and Simon West. Its primary function is planting trees and raising environmental awareness in the Coastal Province of Kenya which is helping to improve the health of our planet and all its inhabitants.

Trees planted in this tropical region are incredibly efficient at drawing down and locking in CO_2 and other pollutants and keeping the planet a little cooler. Their forests are also helping to reduce the devastating effects of climate change, encouraging the normal rains to fall and relieving the problems from Kenya's ongoing drought.

Visit **WordForest.org** to donate, or buy the ideal gift of trees for a loved one to celebrate a birthday, anniversary, or perhaps even to commemorate a life.

#legacygift

About The Publishers

Magic Oxygen Limited is a little green publishing house based in Lyme Regis, Dorset. It was founded in 2011 by Tracey and Simon West, who share an enormous passion for organic seasonal food, simple green living and advocating sustainable behaviours in local and global environments; they also share a common love of the written word. They've published titles from some remarkable authors, including Bridport Prize winning Chris Hill and the much loved children's writer, Sue Hampton.

See **MagicOxygen.co.uk/shop** and remember, all of their titles can be ordered from your favourite High Street bookshops and online too. They urge you to visit nearby independent retailers to place your orders. When you spend money with them, you'll help keep it in your local community.

Lightning Source UK Ltd.
Milton Keynes UK
UKOW01f2203030917
308474UK00003B/65/P